"Don't [...] I get my pants on."

"Oh. I'm sorry. I didn't think—"

"I see that, Carolina. What are you doing here?" She heard the whisper of cloth sliding over skin. "Maybe I shouldn't bother with the pants. Is that why you came?"

"I just decided to come," she whispered.

"You could have killed yourself out there in the dark. Do you see this?" She turned and saw his shadowy figure behind a glint of steel. "I might have cut your throat before I knew who you were."

"And I might have been dead these past four days anyway, for all the emptiness I felt."

"Don't test me, Carolina. Not during the night."

"I didn't come to test you. I came to *tell* you. I have never considered doing anything like this before, but something—" She rushed on. "Jacob, the thought of you will not go away. I am consumed with the need to be near you, and I can't—"

"If I were to hold you now . . ."

"I would walk with you anywhere, Jacob."

Dear Reader:

You are about to become part of an exciting new venture from Harlequin—*historical romances*.

Each month you'll find two new historical romances written by bestselling authors as well as some talented and award-winning newcomers.

Whether you're looking for an adventure, suspense, intrigue or simply the fulfilling passions of day-to-day living, you'll find it in these compelling, sensual love stories. From the American West to the courts of kings, Harlequin's historical romances make the past come alive.

We hope you enjoy our books, and we need your input to assure that they're the best they can possibly be. Please send your comments and suggestions to me at the address below.

Karen Solem
Editorial Director
Harlequin Historical Romances
P.O. Box 7372
Grand Central Station
New York, N.Y. 10017

Private Treaty

Kathleen Eagle

Harlequin Books

TORONTO • NEW YORK • LONDON
AMSTERDAM • PARIS • SYDNEY • HAMBURG
STOCKHOLM • ATHENS • TOKYO • MILAN

Harlequin Historical first edition July 1988

ISBN 0-373-28602-3

KATHLEEN EAGLE

is a transplant from Massachusetts to her favorite regional setting, the Dakota prairie. As educator, wife, mother and writer, she believes that a woman's place is wherever she's needed—and anywhere she needs to be.

*For my father,
Sidney Pierson,
in celebration of his life*

Chapter One

Carbon-colored clouds stacked up high in the sky. Carolina Hammond opened the cabin door and stepped outside to watch the brewing of her first prairie storm. Above the jagged horizon, slashed by buttes and rolling hills, the sky took on an eerie, yellow-gray glow. Carolina folded her arms and walked tentatively toward the riverbank, keeping her eyes on the sky. The wind picked up suddenly, lifting her skirt and twisting it around her like a corkscrew. Wisps of hair escaped from the tight knot at the back of her head and blew across her face. She brushed them aside, intent on watching the angry summer sky.

As she approached the river, Carolina noticed the way the small stand of cottonwoods swayed in unison until the wind changed tempo and their dance became wilder, nearly bough breaking. When the rain came, it offered no warning drops. It gushed from the sky in a sudden torrent. Carolina turned toward the cabin, but the wind's shocking punch left her staggering like a wounded animal.

She heard pounding hoofbeats and felt the rush of the horse's body at her back at nearly the same instant. The horseman's identity became part of the blur of motion. Carolina lifted her hands instinctively to protect her face. An arm hooked her around the middle and jerked her off her feet, knocking the air from her lungs. Suspended at the waist, she bounced like a sack of meal over the horseman's thigh. Through tearing eyes she watched the animal's churning forelegs as she fought desperately to catch her breath.

"Hang on to me or I might drop you!"

Carolina tried to turn toward the voice, but the man's grip was too tight. She reached back and grabbed his shoulder; it was an awkward position, but it was all she could manage. Now he had both arms around her, and she felt as though she were slipping. The horse careened down a steep slope into a ravine, and Carolina closed her eyes. Lord help me, she thought. This man isn't holding the reins.

The horse skidded down the embankment as the rider snapped up the reins to stop him. Carolina was unceremoniously dropped to the ground. She made an effort to pick herself up as the horse skittered to one side, but she was snatched roughly to her feet and dragged into the hollow of a rocky outcropping. It sounded as though she were about to be hit by a roaring locomotive, and she sank to her knees, curling her body into a tight ball. The man's body wedged her against the rock, and the howling wind blocked everything else out of her mind.

The prairie around her shuddered from the wind's assault. Carolina sucked her whole being into the deepest hidden recesses of her brain, as if she could protect her life by rolling it up in her tightly folded body to hide it from nature's madness. Nothing existed but the thunderous wind in her ears and her terror of its power.

"If I should die before I wake, I pray Thee, Lord, my soul to take...if I should die...if I should die...I pray Thee, Lord..." The words bobbed up and down in her mind like flotsam on the flow of her fear.

* * *

"It's all right now. The worst is over."

The voice echoed at the distant end of a long tunnel as Carolina's senses began to return, one by one. The violence was gone, and she was rocking, gently rocking.

"It's all right, ma'am," the voice repeated. "It's gone."

Carolina raised her head timidly, opened her eyes and looked straight up at the iron-colored clouds that swirled above her head. Finally she looked for the source of the voice.

Jacob Black Hawk sat back on his heels, startled by the wild-eyed, ghost-white face he saw emerging from tightly clasped arms and legs. Her hair was drenched and plastered to her head, and the blue eyes seemed ready to pop out of her face. There was no color in her lips. She was like a frightened doe, head perched high on a long, sleek neck, ears alert for another threat.

"I'll take you back. You will need to start a fire in your stove if your cabin is still standing. You tremble with fear now, but soon you'll tremble with cold. Come." He leaned forward on one knee and cupped a hand beneath her elbow, but she stared at him and didn't move. He decided to give her a few moments to recover her senses.

"The wind still roars in your ears," he offered with a slight smile. "I hear it, too." Then he recalled the precarious ride that had brought them to this spot. "Are you hurt?"

Carolina blinked. She'd been staring, and the man was saying something to her. "Hurt? I . . . no, I don't think so." She straightened her back slowly, relaxing her limbs a bit at a time. Her body trembled uncontrollably. She tried to stand, but she couldn't seem to communicate her intentions to her extremities, and she wondered whether they were even connected to her any longer. She fell back to the ground and landed squarely on her bottom.

"I'm sorry," she whispered. "I seem to have lost my sense of balance." Even her voice wasn't all there. Her shaking was an embarrassment, and she knew the only way to regain her dignity was to speak sensibly. "I've never seen a thunderstorm like that before," she explained.

Jacob leaned forward over the forearm he'd rested on his thigh as he knelt beside her. "Thunderstorm? You didn't see the funnel cloud?" She shook her head. "I thought you were a crazy woman when I saw you standing out in the open like that."

She brushed her hair back from her face and stared at the man who had snatched her from the jaws of the thing called a funnel cloud, which she wished she had actually seen. She had heard of these prairie storms, and she cursed her cowardice for preventing her from taking a peek.

The man was familiar to her, but she had not been introduced to him in the short time since she'd arrived in central North Dakota. She'd met few people, actually, and none of them were Indians. She thought that strange, since this land was part of the Standing Rock Indian Reservation.

He suffered her scrutiny—ignored it, in fact—as she watched him remove a leather pouch from deep inside his wet buckskin shirt. The pouch was suspended from a thong, and from it emerged tobacco and paper. He rolled a cigarette as he quietly assured her that he didn't mind waiting a few minutes before taking her back to the cabin. Carolina's attention was drawn to his brown hand, which struck a match on its own thumbnail. Her eyes followed the match to his face, and his face stunned her.

She wasn't sure whether it was the rich brown hue of his skin or the handsomeness of his features that struck her first. His face, with its high cheekbones and a strong, angular jaw, could have been chiseled from the very rock they'd used as shelter. Wet black hair hung in braids over his shoulders, and a narrow strip of buckskin was tied around his forehead. He drew on the cigarette and glanced up at her with dark, inscrutable eyes the shape of almonds as he turned his face slightly to avoid blowing smoke at her. His eyes held hers in frank mutual appraisal.

"What have you decided?" he asked finally.

"About what?" The spell had been broken, and Carolina resumed her shivering.

"About how you should react to being carried off by an Indian." There was no smile, and the tone of his voice was emotionless.

"I'm grateful to you, of course, Mr.—"

He stood up, taking another drag on his cigarette. Carolina uncurled herself slowly, following his lead as she tried awkwardly to straighten her wet clothes. Her eyes sought his as another trail of smoke was expelled. She felt as though she were being tested.

"It's Black Hawk," he said.

"I know you work for Charles MacAllistair. You tame horses, don't you? Is it…Jacob?" She was grateful to find that the cogs and wheels in her brain were beginning to turn again.

"Yes. Jacob is my given name, as they say."

"I guess I work for Charles MacAllistair, too. He's the president of the school board." She tried to smile as she extended her hand. "I'm Carolina Hammond, the new teacher. At least, I shall be a teacher when the school is built. May I call you Jacob?"

"Why not Mr. Black Hawk? It has a nice ring to it, wouldn't you say, Miss Hammond?"

"Yes, it does." It was clearly a rebuff, but when she added, "Mr. Black Hawk," he took her hand. He applied no pressure as he enveloped it in the warmth of his. When she reluctantly withdrew her hand, her teeth began to chatter, and she folded her arms tightly under her bosom. "I thank you for what you did. This has been a terrifying experience. I guess I was unprepared."

"I'll get my horse. Can you ride astride?"

"Better than I ride hanging over the side."

That brought a smile back to his face. He took a last puff on his cigarette before grinding it out beneath his boot heel.

The stout, stocking-footed sorrel was grazing close by, the reins trailing. The horse picked up his head but stood calmly as Jacob gathered the reins at the top of his neck. With fluid grace, Jacob levered himself up and swung his left leg over the horse's back. He trotted the sorrel to Carolina's side, then reached down to her. "Pull yourself up along my arm. Use my foot as a stirrup."

She hoisted herself up as he instructed, but she found herself clutching him again. She wasn't sure she could manage to swing her leg over the horse's rump from this angle. The helpless look on her face and the timid glance she offered made him chuckle. "Try to swing your leg up behind me. I'll pull you up."

Again Carolina followed instructions, and he caught her leg behind him with his opposite arm. She tugged frantically at her skirt while he pulled her up behind him. Jacob dug his heels into the horse's sides, and Carolina slipped to the right as the horse stepped out. Jacob reached back to steady her.

"Hold on to me, Miss Hammond, or you may find yourself on the ground again."

She wound her arms around his waist, grateful for the security. "You don't use a saddle?" she asked for want of a better comment.

"Not today. I don't think I would have been able to pick you up at a dead run if I had. I did have a blanket, but it must have blown away."

There was no more talk until they reached the top of a hill overlooking the cabin and the river. As the horse picked its way down the hill, Carolina breathed a sigh of relief that the cabin had not been demolished. The only reason she'd been given a home of her own was that it was already there. Had it been destroyed, she would have had to board with the MacAllistairs. She scanned the scene below and noticed the little stand of cottonwoods. Half a dozen trees had been uprooted. They leaned at various angles like so many onion plants, roots ripped from the clay bank. She had been standing right there!

"You should have plenty of firewood next winter, Miss Hammond," Jacob noted calmly. He signaled his horse for a quicker pace down the hill.

He reined to a stop near the cabin door and held Carolina's arm while she slid off the animal's rump and down its flank. She landed on her knees. Jacob dropped to her side.

"I'm sorry, Mr. Black Hawk. I don't know what's wrong with me. I can't seem to collect myself." Her voice had become unsteady once again.

He bent to help her, lifting her by her arms. Once she was on her feet, he allowed her weight to settle against him while she steadied herself. Tears came to her eyes without warning and rolled down her cheeks. She covered her face with her hands and gave up her shuddering body to wracking sobs. She felt as though she were watching someone else's shameful display, for she had no control over her own useless tears. Attempting to muffle the sobs by covering her mouth with her hand, she continued to gasp for breath between pathetic groans. She leaned heavily against this pillar of a man who patiently offered his support.

Jacob put his arm around her shoulders and moved her through the cabin door. He caught her when she stumbled, even though he was uncomfortable with the proximity of this white woman's body to his. Closing the door behind him, he gave his eyes time to adjust to the dim light. He located a rocking chair near the big iron cookstove and deposited the hysterical woman there.

"Try to get hold of yourself, Miss Hammond. If anyone comes along and hears you, he's liable to think I've hurt you. He'll shoot first and ask you about the details later."

He wasn't sure what the appropriate gesture might be, but he put his hand on her shoulder and gave her a reassuring squeeze as an experiment. Her quivering shoulders transmitted a message of helplessness through his hand and triggered his sympathy. "You're cold. Spring rain seeps into the bones. I'll get the stove going. Is there wood?"

All of her conscious efforts were focused on bringing this outburst under control, and she could not answer. Jacob found the wood box and built a fire in the stove. Then he struck another match and lit the lamp that sat on a small table near the stove. It was out of respect that he ignored her struggle. Such tears were an embarrassment, even to a woman.

He made a point of surveying the one-room cabin. In addition to the stove and the rocker, there were a little table with four straight-backed chairs, a sideboard and cupboards, a spool bed in one corner, with a large trunk at its foot, some shelves, mostly filled with books, and a few other odds and ends. Two braided rugs softened the plank floor, and blue-and-white curtains dressed the small windows on either side of the door. The cabin had a comfortable feeling about it, Jacob decided, and he relaxed his guard.

He turned to Carolina. "You must take off those wet clothes, Miss Hammond. The house will be warm in a few minutes. I'll be going now."

Carolina took a slow deep breath as she wiped her eyes with her wet skirt. "I hate this," she mumbled. "It makes me feel like a child. I saw the trees, and I saw myself stand-ing there, and I... You must think me a fool, Mr. Black Hawk."

"I think you're cold." He paused, watching her attempts to dry her face. "It's the cold of death, which has just passed close by." She lifted her head, and he saw a circle of white around the blue in her eyes. "It's also the cold of being wet to the skin. You need to change your clothes." He started toward the door.

She should have taken exception to the mention he freely made of her skin, but even the most basic convention seemed unimportant at the moment. Carolina, who valued privacy and her own independence above all else, wanted nothing more than she wanted human company just then.

"Mr. Black Hawk, I would be grateful if you would stay a little while. I don't want to be alone. I feel as though I left half my wits out there by those rocks." Carolina closed her eyes, rested her head back against the chair and suffered another tear to slip quietly down her cheek.

Jacob wondered at the fact that her tears moved him. His contact with most other human beings was impersonal. Living in two worlds, he was a man in his mother's house and an Indian elsewhere—at Fort Yates, where the Indian agency was; at the ranch where he was employed; in the white communities that were springing up everywhere. But this woman was willing to call him *Mr.* Black Hawk, and she had asked for a favor, rather than ordered a service.

"Do you have any coffee, Miss Hammond? That might help both of us."

Carolina rose from her chair and made her way to the cupboard. "No, but I do have tea," she offered hopefully. "If you wouldn't mind taking a few moments to get some water from the well, I would change my clothes and brew a pot. It is getting a bit warmer in here, don't you think?" She fluttered about the sideboard, assembling the tin of tea, the kettle and the cups and saucers, which clattered in her hands.

Jacob took the bucket she handed him and left the cabin. His horse remained ground-tied by the doorway. Picking up the reins, he led the sorrel away from the nearby vegetable garden and its succulent new shoots. A low, uneven wire fence, held up by a variety of sticks leaning this way and that, surrounded the little patch. She must have done that herself, he thought.

He thought, too, of his mother's little patches of planted ground. She listened to the missionaries and tried to follow their suggestions, hoping to supplement the family's rations. Some disaster usually befell her efforts—raccoons or horses or drought—but she always tried, and sometimes she was rewarded with a little produce. We are not farmers, he reminded himself as he picketed his horse on a grassy knoll several yards from the house. Then he took the bucket to the well.

The dark clouds were rolling overhead, pushed by a cold northeasterly wind. It felt like more rain. There had been much rain this spring, which was good for the grass, good for the horses. Good for his mother's garden, he admitted, and with a wry smile he included Carolina's. These women adapted.

Even so, the prairie was ruled by the sky, and the wind, the clouds and the occasional tornado were reminders of that. At least that was something the white man had found no way to change. He commanded the wind to turn his windmills, and the wind obliged at its convenience, but when the white man needed a lesson, the wind unleashed its fury and battered the contraptions to the ground. Jacob was still smiling at the thought as he hoisted the bucket off the edge of the well and headed for the house.

* * *

"Yes, please come in. I'm dressed, Mr. Black Hawk."
Carolina slipped a shawl around her shoulders and drew it
close, but the chill was deep within her. She brightened when
Jacob came through the door.

Jacob avoided direct eye contact with the woman. He set
the bucket on the sideboard and moved to the stove. The
cast-iron door creaked on its hinges when he opened it to
stoke the fire.

"You should go back to the house for tonight, Miss
Hammond. I don't see a horse around here. Didn't they give
you one?"

"Charles said he'd have a small corral built here for me
and leave a horse for my use, but he hasn't done so yet. I
think they're still hoping that I will decide to move down to
the house."

Jacob stripped off his buckskin shirt, which was uncom-
fortably soggy. He felt chilled, too, and wanted to dry out
before facing the cold spring wind again.

"But it's so good to have a place of my own," she went
on. "I have employment, and I'm earning the right to stay
here—at least, I will be once school starts." Carolina
glanced up as she set the kettle on the stove. Her first reaction to his near-nakedness was a slight frown, but she banished that quickly as she brought one of the ladder-back
chairs near the stove.

"I certainly don't mind your removing your shirt, Mr.
Black Hawk. Under the circumstances, it's the sensible thing
to do." She took the shirt from his hands and looked away
quickly when he allowed one corner of his mouth to turn up
in amusement. She draped the shirt over the back of the
chair and found more words to keep her going. "I'll have tea
ready soon. Please bring another chair over here by the stove
and warm yourself."

Jacob laughed softly. "I'm not yet so civilized that I feel inclined to ask a woman's permission to take off a wet shirt." He did, however, move the chair.

The man was being sensible, Carolina reminded herself, and good sense should not startle the nerves. She hated to see a grown woman flutter simply because there was a man about, but she was doing just that. She arranged her china teapot, cups, saucers and strainer, then realigned the teapot in the row. She was aware that he was watching her as he stood beside the chair, and she summoned the nerve to appraise him in return.

He was taller than she was, but not especially tall for a man. She saw now that he wore two leather pouches around his neck. The thongs passed over the well-defined muscles of his bronze chest, forming the lines of a V, echoing the shape of his long torso. The pouches dangled in front of his flat abdomen. His denim pants, cinched by a wide leather belt with a brass buckle, rode low on his slim hips. Carolina glanced from the buckle to his face. He smiled at her more easily than she thought was fair, and she turned back to her tea making without comment.

Jacob seated himself as he continued to watch her. Ordinarily he knew what a woman was thinking when she looked at him that way, but he decided to give this one more time before he came to any conclusions about her. She was still shaken, and perhaps he was, too. Why else would he feel such strong empathy for her? Why else would he sit there waiting for her to serve him tea in a little cup with flowers painted on it? By anyone's standards, she was too old to be unmarried and too young to be living alone. For all of that, she was a handsome woman in her own fair-skinned way. Curiosity had always been a weakness of his, and he'd cursed himself many times over the years for his curiosity about white people.

"Why do you choose to stay here when the ranch house would offer you more comfort and safety?" he asked.

"I feel safe here. The prairie is safer than city streets." Her conviction had been challenged by the uprooted trees outside, but memories of Boston were no more pleasant. "I came to North Dakota for the opportunity to be self-sufficient. Charles MacAllistair promised me that when I inquired about the teaching position. I want independence. Perhaps it may be a romantic notion, but I hoped the West would offer a woman the same promise it holds for a man— the opportunity to be one's own person."

Jacob chose not to mention the obvious exceptions to that promise. He watched her sit down in the rocker and pull the shawl tightly about her. Her hair was still wet, but she had taken the pins out and combed it back from her face. It was long and dark, sleek like the wet fur of an otter. She stared at the kettle as though willing it to boil. He studied her profile, noting that she had a high forehead, a long, straight nose, and full lips. He liked the roundness of her eyes and the dark, heavy fringe of lashes that framed them. There was innocence and honesty in those blue eyes, he thought. A rarity.

She had a good face for a white woman, now that a little color had returned to it. For her sake he would wish for more. He would have her invite the sun to chase away the sickly look of the white skinned. She was on the thin side, and Jacob thought that white men should feed their women better. Of course, this one had no man. He wondered what made her covet this strange white man's ideal of independence. Among his own people, to be put out of the community was the ultimate censure. To leave it voluntarily was considered madness. But he had come to accept the fact that white people valued other things. This independence was an example.

Carolina saw the question in his eyes. Happily, it was simply a question, not a judgment, not the usual male resolve to put her in her place. She folded her hands in her lap. "I'm not interested in living under anyone else's roof, you see. I brought my own furniture with me. I want to serve tea from the teapot left to me by my mother, and I want to ask people to stay or invite them to leave as I see fit."

"Among my people, the home and its furnishings belong to the woman, not the man," he told her.

"Is she free to live alone if she chooses?"

He shrugged. "It used to be that a woman needed a man to provide meat."

"I don't," she said firmly. "I can provide my own food."

"Do you hunt, Miss Hammond?"

His expression was serious. "No. I garden and can, and I hope to have chickens at some point."

"My mother does some of those things, too. She's getting better at it. Do you allow red meat in your diet?"

"Certainly."

"Do you like venison?"

She gave him a curious look. "Yes, I do."

"I hunt, Miss Hammond. I would be willing to trade." The quick alarm in her eyes made him chuckle. "My mother's garden isn't always productive, and she dries her produce. I've come to enjoy canned food as well."

"Perhaps we will have to do some bargaining, then." She relaxed and permitted herself to smile.

"What kind of a man are you running from?" he asked.

The directness of his question took her off guard, and she answered, "My father. But I'm not running. I didn't seek his approval to come here, simply because he has never approved of me or my actions anyway. He allowed me to attend a woman's college after my mother's death because it meant that I would be out of the way. I had foiled his attempts to arrange suitable marriages, and he wanted me out of his sight."

"Your traditions allow a father to select a husband for his daughter," Jacob observed. "It is his way of providing for her."

"I don't want to be provided with some rich old man who thinks he has the right to come to my parlor and put his hands—" Carolina nearly bit her tongue when she realized what she'd almost said. Her indignation warred with her manners as she took a deep breath and suffered the knowing look in his eyes. Was there sympathy there, too? "I imagine your people permit a man to foist an unwanted husband off on his daughter, also."

Jacob laughed. "Not often. Young men wait in line outside a woman's door to court her. She chooses the one she loves. Her father's permission and the exchange of gifts between families is part of the ceremony."

"That's the way it should be." Carolina nodded, envious at the very idea. "Marriage shouldn't be part of a business deal."

"Why did you choose North Dakota?"

"Because it's a long way from Boston. Some of my friends at school aspired to do missionary work, and there was much discussion of Indian territory out West. I made a number of inquiries and found Charles MacAllistair to be the most tolerant of my idiosyncrasies."

"And does your father know where you are?"

"I wrote to him." Her eyes twinkled with the satisfaction of having the last laugh. "He probably read it and said something like, 'The devil take her, then!' He didn't need me any longer to care for my mother, who'd been ill for years before she died, or my brother, Andrew, who's grown up to be Father's protégé. Most of the men he fancied as prospective sons-in-law didn't want me any more than I wanted them. I refused to be a quiet parlor decoration, and I stood my ground when it came to—''

"When it came to the old men's hands."

He was smiling again, and she had the feeling that he enjoyed her victory. She would have thought Indian men dominated their women the same way white men did, or more so. "Yes," she said. "When it came to that." She stood to remove the kettle from the stove and took it to the sideboard. "Forgive me for going on so. I haven't told anyone around here that much about myself, and I probably just told you more than you wanted to know."

Jacob stood and walked across the room to the window. It was raining hard again, and it had grown dark outside, even though it was midafternoon. When the rain stopped, he would take her down to the house before someone came up to check on this independent newcomer. The Mac-Allistairs had left early to visit Marissa's parents in town, as they often did on Saturdays. The road would be a quagmire if this kept up, and they probably would not return tonight.

The bookshelves caught his eye. Jacob moved closer to examine the titles. As he touched the spines fondly, he murmured, "So you, too, have brought us the Word of God, Miss Hammond."

"Oh, no, I'm not a missionary. I came to offer a lay education to the children here. I will enjoy teaching the Indian children along with those of the ranchers who hired me." She turned from the sideboard, carrying two cups, and noticed his interest in the books. "Our tea is ready."

Returning to the chair, Jacob accepted the steaming cup from hands that trembled slightly, even now. The cup and saucer clattered. In his hand, they seemed absurdly delicate. She seated herself in the rocker.

"Do you enjoy reading, Mr. Black Hawk?"

His eyes narrowed. "Yes, I enjoy reading." He paused to savor the tart taste of the rose hips in the tea. "Did you expect my answer to be that I couldn't read?"

"No. You're an interesting combination of two cultures, Mr. Black Hawk. Your flawless English, your clothes, your job at the ranch. You've been to school, haven't you?"

"Your friends, the missionaries, got hold of me at an early age. I learned the language for my mother. She thought it would help me walk in the new way. I learned to read for myself, because it was like a game and came easily to me. I enjoy books, but there aren't many available to me."

"You're welcome to read anything I have. I've sent for more."

"Have you always lived in Boston, Miss Hammond?" he asked.

"I attended school in western Massachusetts, but my father's house is in Boston." Her mother was not a Bostonian, and Carolina always made the distinction that Boston was her father's place of residence. She often wondered if she, herself, was *from* anywhere.

"I have not been to Boston, but I have been to the East," he said. It was a part of his life that he rarely discussed, and he wondered at the fact that he even mentioned it now.

"Oh, really? What part?"

Her interest seemed genuine. It occurred to Jacob that this woman regarded him simply as another human being. "I was sent to Carlisle Indian School in Pennsylvania. I was there four years."

"I see why you're so well educated, Mr. Black Hawk. You are a college man." She smiled at him as though they were compatriots.

"It was not a school like the one you attended, I'm sure. I was supposed to learn a trade, so that good hard work would take the savage out of me. I spoke your language. I was curious about the white world, and I wanted to learn, but I did not want to learn about carpentry and farming.''

"Was that all they taught there?"

"No," he said quietly. "They taught us shame. They cut off our braids and made us wear their uniforms and their shoes. They told us that, although we could never actually *be* white men, we should try to be like them. But they knew nothing about us. We were from many nations. Our languages and traditions were different. Some of us were ancient enemies. I almost killed a Chippewa over the use of a horse, but because I was considered the better student, it was he who was sent back home." He smiled, remembering. "Sending a man back to his people was their idea of punishment. They wondered why some of the students took their own lives when they were on the verge of becoming civilized. When they said I had reached that goal, I looked in the mirror and wondered who I was."

His voice had trailed away as he spoke. She saw no sign of emotion in his face. "Are you still wondering who you are?"

He turned to her, looking surprised by the question. "I know who I am now." He paused, realizing that she posed no threat to that knowledge. "I have not told anyone around here that much about myself, either. It was probably more than you wanted to know."

"On the contrary, Mr. Black Hawk. I hope to have Indian children in my classroom this fall, and you are the first Indian I have been able to talk to. I'm certain I have much to learn."

"Then you should know first that there are government boarding schools and mission schools for our children. You will seldom find Indian and white children in the same classroom."

Carolina looked puzzled. "I understand that farmers and ranchers have bought land here, but I was under the impression that this was still a reserve for Indians."

"It is."

"If we're to build a rural school, wouldn't there be some Indian families living in the area who might want to send their children here, rather than to board them away from home?"

Jacob sipped at his tea. It was obvious that this woman did indeed have a lot to learn. "Indian children are taken away from their families, Miss Hammond."

"Taken away? Do you mean they have no choice? But you were..."

"I was educated by missionaries who came to live among us, but that was some time ago. Now our villages are deathly quiet during the winter months. The children are put in boarding schools to have their traditional lives scrubbed from their minds."

A chill shimmied through Carolina's shoulders, and she adjusted her shawl. "Could they come to my school if I...if I invited them?"

"I think you would have to discuss that with Mac-Allistair, and he would discuss it with his board. Or you might discuss it with the Indian agent, and he would discuss it with his superiors in Washington. The army might have something to say about it, or the church mission boards." Jacob's expression said that he forgave her for knowing so little because her intentions were refreshingly simple. "Your invitation might get lost somewhere along the line."

"I had the impression that the MacAllistairs were friendly to the Indian people," Carolina insisted.

Jacob studied the bottom of his teacup for a moment. "Marissa MacAllistair's grandmother and my grandmother were sisters. Her mother is half Indian, her father is white. It is not uncommon for a white man to take an Indian woman. MacAllistair is a fair man, but I am the only Indian he employs. I think he would hire more of us if more would work for him, but for most, it isn't possible. We are a people whose way of life is passing, yet we know no other way to live." He realized that he was not speaking to her of these matters with his usual bitter tone. He wasn't blaming her.

"What will you do?" she asked. She was leaning forward in her chair now, and she was wide-eyed with interest. "What will happen to all those people? And to you, Mr. Black Hawk?"

She had asked the question that burned in his soul, and he was not ready to share any of his guesses, certainly not with a white woman.

Instead he returned his empty cup to the sideboard. "I don't know about them," he said lightly, "but if anyone comes up here to check on you and finds me here, *my* future might be doubtful." He turned to offer a meaningful look. "Not only mine, but yours. A lady who entertains an Indian man alone in her house might not be welcome to teach anyone's children. As soon as this rain stops, I'll give my horse a rubdown, and we can both ride him back to the house."

"That will be fine, Mr. Black Hawk," she said as she rose from the rocker. It teetered at her back, nudging her skirt. "Be assured that, should anyone come, we shall explain what happened, and you will receive credit for saving my life rather than criticism for unseemly conduct. Now, will you join me for supper while we wait for the rain to stop?"

"Do you have any red meat?" he wondered aloud with a soft smile.

"I do, in fact. And I baked this morning." She opened a cupboard door to display three golden-brown loaves of bread. "Aren't they tempting?"

They smelled fresh baked. Jacob's eyes brightened, and he nodded.

The stew she prepared warmed them both. Carolina sensed that whatever grudge Jacob Black Hawk bore her race, he was considering setting it aside for her, as he apparently had for Charles MacAllistair. For her part, she had found few men's company as stimulating as Jacob's was. Moreover she was comfortable with him.

"One thing you should know about Indian people," he began as he leaned back in his chair for a final sip of tea, "is that we don't think of ourselves as Indians. Most of us who have been herded onto this useless patch of ground called Standing Rock are of the Lakota. Within the Lakota we have seven council fires, which are bands of people, like large families. I am of the Hunkpapa."

Carolina digested this information. "But you have used the term *Indian* in our conversation."

"You said that you wanted to learn about us." Jacob's eyes grew hard. "When I am among white people, I think in English, and I use their term *Indian* so that they will understand me. They cannot think in Lakota, nor do many of them want to. But if you wish to know about my people, then you should know who they *know* they are, not who the white man *says* they are."

Carolina lowered her eyes and her voice. "You're right, of course. Like anyone in new surroundings, I've come with some preconceived ideas. I've heard your tribe called Sioux. Where did that name come from?"

"It was given to us by our old enemies, the Chippewa. We're not fond of that name, either, but your government chooses to use it."

"It's strange the way we acquire our labels. I'm not really fond of being categorized as a white woman, but I suppose that will be the way you will think of me. I don't mind American or Yankee or New Englander, but if asked about my origins, I would not say, 'I am white.'"

A smile lurked in Jacob's eyes. "I will make a bargain with you. I will not call you *the white woman* if you will not call me *Injun*. Agreed?"

Carolina returned his smile. "I would take that bargain one step further. You've saved my life and shared supper at my table. I should think our friendship could progress to a first-name basis."

"You are still blind to the way things are here."

"How much more must I learn before I may call you Jacob?"

He could not take offense at her innocence, nor could he resist her smile. "Nothing other than discretion, Carolina. I'm called Jacob by the few white people who are friendly to me, and you seem to be one of them."

"And will you teach me more about the Lakota and the Hunkpapa?"

His face sobered. "Visits between us would cause too much talk. I would not be a friend if I caused people to talk about you in that way."

"Maybe it wouldn't be quite so scandalous if you were to wear a shirt next time," she teased.

"True." Jacob folded his arms across his chest and leaned his chair back on two legs. "The Lakota are very conscious of manners. We always dress properly when we take meals as guests. My uncles would have taken me to task for my behavior today."

"But your shirt was wet."

"Excuses are not acceptable. My family tells me that I've been among the whites too long and have forgotten what is proper. I would also be reminded that it is not proper to be alone with an unmarried woman in her house." They looked at each other. The irony made them both laugh. "It's good that you are willing to make up your own mind about me, Carolina. But you should not be so trusting. You must not invite strange men into your home when you are alone."

"I had no choice but to trust you," she reminded him as she pushed her chair back and began gathering dishes. "It's hard to argue with someone when one is suspended alongside his galloping horse."

"But still, you didn't know me."

She looked up and saw that he was concerned. "I know you now, Jacob. You are a considerate man. You can be sure that I've met few men who fit that description, and there are fewer still who would be welcome in my home under these circumstances."

He looked at her curiously, and she felt compelled to admit, "I can think of none offhand."

He handed her his cup and saucer. It had been a long time since he had wondered what it would be like to hold a woman close against his chest and lace his fingers through her hair. When he took this woman back to the ranch, she would be untouchable. She would be aloof, and they would not share this easy conversation between two equal human beings. Too soon she would see how it was here. She would sense the invisible barriers, see him treated with disdain, and she would choose sides. Steeling himself against that inevitability, he pushed the chair back from the table and stood abruptly.

Carolina turned from the sideboard, sensitive to the change in his mood. "Please smoke if you wish to, Jacob," she suggested quietly. "It will take me a moment to clean up, but I should be ready to leave shortly."

Jacob reached for his shirt. It was damp, so he turned it over. "What do you have that I could use as a scraper?"

She offered a long-handled ladle and a handful of clean rags, and Jacob left the house to attend to his horse.

The rain had stopped, and the early-evening sky was brightening. The mud sucked at Jacob's boots, but he strode through it, hoping that the cool air on his bare chest would bring him to his senses. She was just another pale-skinned woman, an immigrant, probably even less sensible than most. He had only followed his God-given male instincts when he'd sheltered her from the storm. But then they had shared food, thoughts and memories, and he had seen her as a true woman. She had stirred a need in him that he had long ago willed silent. Recognizing that need for what it was, he was determined to control it, even though he wanted her friendship. She was different, he told himself as he set about drying his horse's wet hide. She was no longer just another pale-skinned woman.

Jacob rolled himself a cigarette before leaving the sorrel ground-tied at the door and going inside. He kept his eyes from Carolina as he walked over to the chair that served as a drying rack for his shirt. Feeling some regret over the mud he'd tracked across the plank floor, he balanced the cigarette on the edge of the stove and pulled the shirt over his head. She was watching him, and he knew it. He retrieved his cigarette and finally looked up at her as he drew hungrily on the smoke.

She moved like a bird caught in a trap, fluttering to put the dishes away in the overhead cupboards. Whenever he was quiet, she felt the need to talk. "I'm finished here, Jacob. We can leave when you're ready. I know I'm a little unsteady on the back of that horse, but I'll do my best not to topple us both."

"You will ride in front. I'll see that you don't topple us both."

She grabbed the broom and swept up the little clods of dried mud. That done, she brushed her hands together. He finished his cigarette and tossed the butt inside the stove, adding it to the waning fire. Smoke trailed from his lips as he approached her.

"I like you, Carolina. We have become friends in a short time. But at the ranch, when other people are around you, I won't be friendly to you." He found it necessary to touch her in some way. She looked up at his face, clearly accepting the hands he laid lightly upon her shoulders. "It would cause too much speculation," he said quietly. "Just know that I am your friend."

"I like you, too, Jacob. You have yet to call me a *strange bird*, or any of a number of epithets I'm accustomed to hearing. I have no intention of pretending. People may think whatever they choose to think." She was drawn to his eyes because they returned her regard from the innermost part of him. He, too, hated pretense. She felt his hands stir gently before he lifted the edges of her shawl and pulled it snugly around her slight shoulders.

"The air is still cold from the rain," he warned in a hoarse voice. She felt bereft when he lowered his hands and turned from her. "Come," he said, and she followed him as though hypnotized.

Jacob made a stirrup with his hands, into which Carolina placed her foot and her weight, swinging her other leg over the horse's back and pulling herself aboard. An agile vault brought Jacob over the horse's rump, and he settled himself close behind her. Taking the reins, he nudged the horse into a walk as he slipped an arm around her waist and held her lightly against his body. Sensitive to his contours, Carolina assessed the power in his thighs, which controlled the horse and steadied her own legs at the same time. She was securely tucked in the envelope of Jacob's strength.

"What is your horse's name?" she asked.

"Sagi."

"Sagi," she repeated carefully. "What does it mean?"

"It is the color of him, the red brown."

"He seems very reliable. He doesn't wander away when you leave him standing by himself."

"I have trained him to be so." Jacob looked to the west at the streaking expanse of rosy glow in the blue-gray sky. Holding her felt good, and he decided to enjoy the feeling.

While he had been outside, she had braided her hair and twisted it into a knot at the back of her head. Just below her ear she looked soft, like the down beneath the dove's feathers. He detected the tremor of the pulse in her neck. Her breathing seemed too fast, and he lowered his eyes to catch sight of the rise and fall of her chest with each breath. "You are still frightened?" he asked.

"Oh, no." The answer came too quickly. "No, I'm fine."

Jacob smiled to himself. She felt as he did. His flesh was warm and alive where her slight weight rested against him. He tightened his arm around her body, his fingers stirring almost imperceptibly at her waist. She drew a deeper breath and shivered as she expelled it slowly. Yes, he knew she felt as he did, but she probably did not even recognize the feeling. Even as he berated himself for desiring a white woman, he turned his face toward her hair and inhaled the fresh rainwater smell of it.

The tingling surges of warmth inside Carolina's body confused her. The muscles in the horse's shoulders and across his back caressed her intimately as she sat astride. The animal's moist body heat penetrated her clothing. Even more unsettling, she felt a little breathless with every movement of Jacob's body against hers. None of it was unpleasant.

Jacob heard the thudding hoofbeats of approaching horses before the sorrel topped the rise. He recognized the ranch foreman, Jim Bates, and two of the hands, Tanner and Culley. Bates saw them first and gave the word to the others, and all three spurred their mounts uphill.

"Miss Hammond!" Bates hailed as he hauled on his reins. "We come to see if you're okay. We was fussing around over the damage the wind done down to the calving barn, and Culley here recollected you being alone up there at the old cabin. Figured we'd better look in on you."

"The house wasn't touched, but the cottonwoods by the river were ripped from the ground." Carolina smiled and made an effort to look as though she were completely at ease riding double with Jacob. "Fortunately Mr. Black Hawk saw that I was in a precarious situation and helped me take shelter."

"How did you happen to be up there, Black Hawk?"

Culley had clearly overstepped his bounds with the question. Carolina felt the tension in Jacob's body, and it reflected her own anger. The ferret-faced little cowboy peered past her, hoping to get a rise out of Jacob, but Jim Bates claimed the boss's right to settle the issue.

"I sent him up there." Bates cast Culley a cold glare. "One of the studs got out last night."

Jacob steadied the prancing Sagi and offered an explanation for his boss alone. "I was looking for cover when I saw this woman standing out in the open. I spotted the funnel cloud at the same time."

"Mr. Black Hawk's quick thinking and expert horsemanship saved my life," Carolina added. Following Jacob's example, she pointedly ignored Culley as she spoke.

"He found shelter for us among some rocks, and then that wind—I've never seen the like of it!"

Culley squinted at the pair and persisted. "We didn't see no twister."

Carolina dismissed the comment without sparing him a glance. "You missed quite a sight, Mr. Culley." She, too, had missed the sight, but not the sound, not the driving force of the wind and not the fear. She would share none of that with a man like Culley, however. "Did the MacAllistairs return safely, Mr. Bates?"

"Not yet. I expect they might not come back till tomorrow. Road's pretty muddy now."

"I'm going to stay at the house tonight, anyway," she told him. "I'm still a bit shaken." Bates nodded as Culley leaned over and mumbled something near his ear.

Bates straightened, looking uncomfortable. "Miss Hammond, would you care to ride with me? You might be better off with a . . . a saddle."

"Thank you, Mr. Bates, but Mr. Black Hawk has offered to take me to the ranch, and I'm anxious to be on our way. The storm left such a chill in the air." Carolina turned her head as far around as she could and caught a glimpse of Jacob's stoic expression. "You don't mind, do you, Jacob?"

"No, ma'am." He nudged the sorrel with his heel, informing Bates as he passed, "I'll track that stud down in the morning."

Sagi took the slope at a smooth trot, leaving the three riders behind to discuss this turn of events. The big sorrel carried his added burden easily, putting a comfortable distance between Jacob and the cowboys by the time the trio turned to follow.

"It doesn't sit well with Culley to see you sitting on the same horse with me," Jacob remarked.

"Mr. Culley would do well to mind his own business." The very sight of the man put Carolina in a huff. Since the time she'd arrived, he'd been appearing around every corner. "That man's ears prick and his nose twitches at the very thought of hearing something that doesn't concern him. He's always there when I have luggage, or furniture to move. Doesn't he have a job to do?"

"I try to stay away from Culley. His job doesn't concern me."

"Yours seems to concern him," she observed with disgust. "With those popping little eyes and those buckteeth, he reminds me of a nosy little chipmunk."

Jacob chuckled softly. "Bates keeps Culley and me apart, because all hell can break loose if we get too close. But I can only damage the popping eyes and the buckteeth. You could destroy the man's pride with that tongue of yours."

"I've had some practice." She squared her shoulders and took her satisfaction. "Such puffery deserves its reproach, and I have no trouble delivering it to those in need."

"Staying away from Culley is the best way to deal with him," Jacob advised, then warned her, "He may think he has something to say to you about this, since he and I don't get along."

They crested the last hill. The ranch lay on the flat ground below. The ride had been too short, Carolina thought. "Don't worry about Mr. Culley on my account, Jacob." Jacob tightened his arm around her waist. She touched the back of his hand. "I'll have no trouble convincing him to twitch his nose elsewhere."

"He might have trouble listening. Tell me—" That would be foolish, he told himself. Leave the whites to their own forms of justice. "Tell MacAllistair if Culley bothers you."

The sorrel stopped in front of the ranch house's stately veranda. Jacob hesitated to pull his arm away, and Carolina dreaded the moment when he would. She would have to go into the house, and he would retire to the bunkhouse. She wanted to ask him to sit with her here on the veranda. They would talk as they had at the cabin, and she would serve the coffee he'd craved earlier. She thought she felt the subtle stirring of his fingers at her waist, but his hand was gone before she had time to savor the small gesture.

Using his hands to propel himself backward, Jacob slid over the horse's rump, dropped to the ground and moved quickly to Carolina's right side. He reached for her. "The Lakota mount on this side. The horse is used to it. Come."

Carolina swung her leg over the horse's neck and leaned down to put her hands on Jacob's shoulders. He lifted her off the horse, but neither released the other as they stood close, searching each other's eyes for signs of promise.

"I'm grateful for your help, Jacob."

"Among my people, a good deed brings honor to the giver, and gratitude is not necessary."

She wanted to lose herself in his dark eyes. "I hope we'll be able to talk again," she said tightly. "Soon."

Jacob smiled, but at the sound of approaching horses, he withdrew his hands from her waist. Carolina turned from him reluctantly and disappeared into the house.

Chapter Two

Carolina closed the door and glanced about the parlor, corner to corner, ceiling to floor. The big mantle clock stared back from the shadows. It was after eight, and the house was empty. The floor creaked beneath her feet as she hurried to the front window. Through the lacy curtains she watched Jacob wheel the sorrel and trot him toward the corrals. The other three riders were headed in the same direction. They wouldn't be far away, she told herself. She would light a lamp, set a fire in the kitchen stove and take an allover bath. Marissa had a real cast-iron tub, and her kitchen boasted an indoor pump. With the house all to herself, Carolina would soak in a warm bath and plan to assume Marissa's duties until she returned.

The MacAllistairs had one child, and in addition to carrying out her motherly duties, Marissa did all of the cooking for the hands, who would be here early in the morning for breakfast. As she filled the large kettles to heat water for her bath, Carolina imagined the men seated on benches at the long kitchen table. One thing she'd learned about North Dakota men was that it was unthinkable for them to turn their hands to anything in the kitchen. Even though they knew Marissa was gone, she could see them planting their elbows on the red-and-white oilcloth and waiting for food to appear. She filled the two speckled blue coffeepots while she had the pump running.

Checking the pantry, she found plenty of slab bacon and potatoes. A few months ago she wouldn't have known where to begin in making breakfast for eight ranch hands. She wouldn't have known that it took at least ten pounds of potatoes, three or four pounds of bacon, two dozen eggs and as many baking powder biscuits to keep them going until dinner time. The midday meal was as hearty as breakfast, and supper in the evening would be lighter.

Carolina prepared her bath with boiling water from the stove and cool water from the pump. She climbed into the tub, washed her hair with scented soap and soaked her body until the water grew too cold to enjoy. She'd borrowed a clean shirtwaist dress from Marissa. The dress would be short on Carolina, but at least it was free of horse hair.

By the time she began hauling bucketfuls of bath water out to Marissa's flower beds, it was pitch-dark. She listened to the night sounds, the frogs and crickets and the distant howling of a coyote, and she knew that this was one night when she would wish for more company than theirs. The creaking spring pulled the screen door shut behind her as Carolina returned to the kitchen to get a start on breakfast.

She challenged herself to peel the red-skinned potato she held in one long, continuous spiral as she thought of Jacob. She hoped he would be at the breakfast table with the others. She wanted to show him that she was not always as helpless as he'd seen her that day. With the life she'd chosen for herself, she couldn't afford to be helpless. She remembered the portraits that hung in the halls of the college she'd attended. The strong faces belonged to independent women who had been bold enough to assert that women should be educated. They'd told young women to strike out on their own, use their knowledge, take it to the far reaches of the earth, and Carolina had taken that ideal to heart.

Her father's boorish friends had scoffed at her. She'd known few young men, and she'd rejected the attentions of the older well-situated men her father had brought to the house. Men were a nuisance. Why, then, was it so important that she make a good impression on Jacob Black Hawk? A less suitable attraction could hardly be imagined. Yet the attraction was there. Carolina had read poetry that hinted at the excitement she'd felt when he'd stood close to her today. The feelings were improper, but she was her own person now, and the feelings were hers. She liked them. They were honest. So, too, was Jacob Black Hawk.

She set the pot of cold water and sliced potatoes aside and returned to Marissa's wardrobe for a nightgown. Outside the window, an owl hooted in the night. Carolina set the lamp on the dressing table in the guest room, but she couldn't bring herself to turn the wick down. The house was too quiet. A distant wind filled her head. Dropping the nightgown on the bed, she carried the lamp to the parlor, set it on the table near the front window and slipped out the door.

The veranda felt friendlier than the big empty house. A breeze fluttered the leaves on the cottonwood trees, and a bullfrog sang to his mate. The MacAllistairs' big yellow dog squirmed out from under the steps and came to her, wagging his whole body.

"Hello, dog," she whispered, grateful for his company. With the light in the window, she could tell herself that there was someone inside, and she'd just stepped outside to enjoy the night air.

"Hello, Carolina."

The quiet voice startled her, but the dog was not alarmed. He watched the dark figure walk up the steps to the veranda. The man leaned down to pat the dog's head.

"You said you hoped we could visit again soon. Is this soon enough?" He raised his hand to his mouth, and the ash at the end of his cigarette glowed against his face.

"Oh, Jacob. I couldn't see you in the dark."

"Did I frighten you?"

"I didn't hear you coming, I guess, because my ears are still ringing. The house is terribly quiet." She gestured toward the wooden bench behind her. "Will you sit and talk a while?"

His tread was soundless when he stepped close to her, ignoring the offer of a seat. He leaned against a pillar and peered at her face through the darkness. "We'll talk quietly. Culley has already had his comments to make."

"Did you have a disagreement with Mr. Culley since we returned?" Carolina whispered.

"Culley disagreed with my actions. I had no words to waste on him." He paused. "You've been in the kitchen for a long time."

"Were you watching the house?"

"If Culley had acted on his boast and presented himself at the door, I would have been there, too."

She raised her brow. "Then the two of you might have caught me bathing, and I would have used the broom on both your heads." He laughed softly, and she continued, "I don't want you to have trouble with Mr. Culley on my account, Jacob. He probably won't bother me again."

"I have not been thinking of Culley." Jacob drew slowly on his cigarette and blew the smoke into the night. "I've been thinking of you."

"What have you been thinking?"

"That I enjoyed being with you today."

"I enjoyed being with you, too," Carolina whispered. "You're not like most of the men I've known."

"No, I'm not. We both know the difference."

"There are many differences beyond the obvious," she told him.

"But the obvious is what makes the difference. I've been thinking that you are not like other white women."

"You agreed not to call me that."

"So I did." Jacob shifted his weight. "But that was before I found myself imagining that you were bathing. I imagined the softness of your skin, rather than the color of it."

Her breath seemed to skitter over her ribs as she drew it into her lungs. "I'm not sure you should imagine, either."

"You invited me not to think of you as white, Carolina. When Culley talked about coming up to the house, I tried reminding myself that you are as white as he." He shook his head. "It didn't matter anymore."

"I have nothing in common with Mr. Culley, but I have a great deal in common with you, I think. The differences in our backgrounds will make our friendship more interesting."

"Maybe." He turned to look out at the yard and up at the stars as he continued to smoke. "Most white people don't even see us as human, Carolina. What happened to the tribes in Massachusetts? Where have they gone? When the white men were defeated in your War Between the States, their homes were returned, their arms, their stock. What happened to ours?"

"I cannot answer for history, Jacob. I cannot answer for my race. Our friendship has nothing to do with that." She stepped closer. "Our friendship has to do with a man who saved my life today, a man who was kind to me. We ate together, and we talked about many things. There was no need for pretense between us."

He looked back at her. "When I stop thinking of you as a white woman, I think of you as *woman*. And I am a man."

"I know that," she said softly.

"Can you accept the thought of your womanliness instead of your whiteness in my head?"

"I have been thinking of you, too," she found voice to confess.

"While you bathed?"

She lowered her eyes and nodded once. "And while I dressed. And while I peeled potatoes."

Jacob drew on his cigarette, then crushed it under his moccasined foot as he blew the smoke from his mouth. Lifting his weight from the pillar, he took a step closer to her. She did not back away.

"You smell like flowers," he told her as he brushed her softly waving hair back from her temple with the light touch of his thumb. "I like your hair loose like this." He laced his fingers through it as he had dreamed of doing earlier in the day. It felt cool and damp between his fingers. He caressed her shoulder with his other hand, testing her for a reaction. She looked up at him, her eyes wide, and he felt her uneven breathing.

"All afternoon I have wanted this." He steadied the back of her head in his palm and lowered his mouth to hers. His full lips teased the corner of her mouth, and he discovered that her lips were dry. She was untutored in this custom. He plied her patiently with slow, moist kisses, gently seeking her response. Her breath was warm against his cheek.

Carolina wondered whether the frog she'd felt in her throat a moment ago had slid into her stomach. Her hands, usually the coldest part of her body, were perspiring. Worse, she didn't know where to put them. She lifted them and found Jacob's waist to be a handy spot.

Taking this as a signal of her acceptance, Jacob raised his head and whispered, "This is a custom of the white man that I have come to enjoy." He touched his lips to hers again.

"Strangely enough," she whispered breathlessly, "it is one with which I have little experience."

Jacob leaned back to look into Carolina's eyes. He moved both hands to her shoulders, caressing her as though soothing a nervous filly. "Little? Or none."

"None." The answer was little more than mouthed.

"I am going to hold you, Carolina, and take your mouth with mine." He drew her to him first, watching her as he enfolded her in his arms. She was wary, but she put her arms around him and spread her fingers over his back. His lips parted as they claimed hers, and this time he let her know his hunger as he probed her mouth with his tongue. He coaxed her, and she let her response to him rise from deep within her. Shyly she returned his kiss.

Jacob drew his mouth away. "Now you have a little experience," he whispered. "How do you feel about this custom?"

"It leaves me speechless," she managed. Beneath his soft cotton shirt she felt the hard, corded muscles in his back, and that left her breathless.

"Then don't look for words. Show me how you feel." He kissed her again, harder this time, demanding more response from her as he caressed her back and pulled her slight frame against his body. The hot moisture of his mouth mingled with hers.

Carolina's mind spun away. She tingled wherever Jacob touched her, and she wanted to draw him inside herself with this kiss. She clung to the back of his shirt, feeling as desperate as she had when he'd swept her off the ground and carried her away. She was slipping now as she'd felt herself slipping then, but then she had been cold and desperate. Now she was hot and desperate, and the slipping was a smooth and delicious feeling. She opened her mouth to enjoy it more.

She'd given herself over to instinct now, and Jacob thought that if he didn't slow down, he would be lost, too. Self-control was his forte, but this woman felt good in his arms. She tasted good, and he was hungry for her. Her breast heaved against him as her heart beat inches away from his. In his mind he saw flesh melt and blood mingle, and he knew this had already gone too far. He lifted his head and held her tight against him. Her head dropped to his shoulder.

Carolina closed her eyes and let the feeling of him permeate her being. His braided hair lay against her forehead, but the fact that it was a braid was unimportant. It was Jacob's hair, and it felt good against her skin. He smelled of buckskin, horses and lye soap. Perhaps her behavior was wanton, but she could no more pull away than she could will her heart to stop pounding. She was where she wanted to be.

"Jacob," she whispered under his chin, "I feel almost as helpless as I did after the storm passed."

Jacob rubbed her back. "When a man is holding you as I am, it is not a good time to declare your helplessness. You will recover quickly now and find the strength to slap my face in ladylike fashion."

"Slap you? I think not. Then you might never kiss me again."

He slid his hands to her shoulders and drew back to look at her. The languid, trusting look in her eyes made him smile. "You surprise me, teacher. I come to you late at night, a savage Lakota in moccasins and braids, and you let me give you your first kiss. Why aren't you running away, or screaming for help?"

He knew why, of course. In the moonlight his eyes danced with that knowledge as she returned his smile and tossed her hair back from her shoulders. "You must be out of practice, Mr. Black Hawk. You're not very frightening. In fact, although I find your embrace captivating, I think you took great pains to avoid frightening me." She hesitated. "My own behavior *is* a bit frightening. I had assumed it wasn't possible...that is, I was always told that ladies don't feel..."

Jacob chuckled. "And I was told that white women are as cold as fish, but that is no more true than that 'ladies don't feel.'"

"How can you be certain?"

"I have more than a little experience." Her glance questioned him, but he ignored it as he tucked her under his arm and gestured toward the steps. "Let's walk together," he suggested. "I want to be with you, but not here."

She followed as he led her away from the house, the bunkhouse, the barn, the buildings of the white man. She had no thought of danger, even though he seemed to be anxious to have her truly alone. A grove of cottonwoods and willows lined the bank of a small creek, and she followed willingly as Jacob made his way in silence through the trees.

It wasn't a leisurely stroll. He wanted to get away from the house and the trappings of her world. He wanted her on his own territory. He noted her surprising lack of questions. She followed him, trusting him, now that he'd seen to her safety once, not to endanger her in any way. She was innocent; he knew that. But he had shown her his desire, and she had responded. She chose to be with him now.

The trees thinned to a small clearing on the creek bank, a place of thick grass and a few Juneberry bushes. Jacob slowed his pace as he neared the clearing and turned to let her catch up. Her breathing was heavy.

"I thought we were going for a *walk*, Jacob." Carolina laughed a little nervously. "Perhaps I should have brought my shawl."

"You are cold?" His voice sounded harsh.

"No, not really. Not with all this exercise."

The innocence in those blue eyes irritated him. She was as trusting as a faithful dog. He wasn't sure he deserved that trust—didn't think he even wanted to deserve it. What he wanted was to be alone with this woman.

"I should have brought a courting robe," he told her. It was an honest statement, and he offered an honestly suggestive smile. The smile she returned was simply honest. Absurdly innocent. He put his arm around her shoulders and drew her to his side. "But I didn't. I'll shield you from the cold, little one. The wind has dried the grass, and the air has stilled."

"Why are we here, Jacob?"

At last, the question. He walked slowly with her now, heading for the Juneberry bushes. "Why did you come with me?"

"You suggested we go for a walk."

"When you rode the same horse with me this evening, there was no alternative. You had no horse. Still, they questioned my right to touch you."

"I think Mr. Bates was merely offering—"

"I can't sit with you on your veranda in the daylight, and I should know better than to sneak around with you at night."

"I didn't feel that we were sneaking, Jacob. I'm certainly too old to need a chaperone."

Jacob tipped his head back and laughed. "But you just kissed a man for the first time, Carolina."

"It isn't that others haven't tried," she said quickly. "I simply turned them away." She smiled up at him, and her eyes sparkled in the moonlight. "So you see, a chaperone is unnecessary."

"A shotgun might be necessary if they catch me kissing you." He turned up the corner of his mouth in half a smile. "I brought you here because this is where we are free."

"Free? Are you going to take liberties with me, Jacob?"

He touched a strand of her hair. "Have I yet?"

"No," she said quietly.

"I will take nothing unless you give it freely. In the days of my father's youth, I might have taken you. I might have swept you up as I did today and taken you to my village, and you would have been mine. But those days are gone, and I can't have you that way." He plucked a handful of berries with his free hand. He knew they weren't ripe yet, but he held one to her lips, and she took it in her mouth. She pinched her eyes shut when the burst of tart juice filled her mouth. He chuckled, and she held out her hand for more.

"Is that the way you would want me?" she asked. "You said your own women were permitted to choose."

"You are one of *their* women, not ours." He emptied the berries into her hand and picked a few more. "There was a time when we took horses and women from our enemies if we had a shortage—or if we saw a pretty one we liked."

"A pretty horse, or a pretty woman?"

He lifted a shoulder. "Either."

Carolina followed him to a grassy spot. He sat cross-legged, and she sat near him. She liked the puckery tartness of the berries, but it was difficult to be discreet with the pits.

"Why aren't you married, Jacob?"

"Did I say that I was not?"

She looked at him incredulously. "No, you didn't, but since you . . . Are you?"

"No, I have no woman." He laughed softly. "I have no place to keep one."

"Were you ever betrothed?"

The Juneberries had banished the stale taste of smoke from his mouth. He stretched out on the grass, planted his elbow and propped his head on his hand. "The women in my past have nothing to do with you, Carolina. I have no woman now."

"I'm sorry. I didn't mean to pry." She hastened to change the subject. "These will soon be ripe enough for making jelly. I must remember this spot. You said you like canned goods, Jacob. Does that include jelly? I could—"

"I already know that you can cook."

Carolina frowned. "I was only thinking out loud." She began smoothing her skirt over her thighs, her eyes cast down to the invisible wrinkles in her lap.

Jacob stilled her hand by covering it with his. "Since the white man introduced us to his sugar, we have craved sweet things." He brought her hand to his mouth and lightly bit the knuckle of her thumb. Then he turned her palm to his lips and gently nuzzled it. "Yes, little one. I would like to taste your jelly on my bread."

She shivered and closed her eyes with the thrill of it. He pulled her toward him, bringing her hand around his back. Her eyes flew open, and she stiffened. "Jacob," she whispered, "it cannot be prudent for us to recline together."

"It was not prudent for me to come to the house tonight, nor for you to leave it. But I will not hurt you, Carolina. I will hold you, smell the flowers in your hair and taste the *wipazukan**, the Juneberry, on your lips."

"*Wipazukan,*" she tried. He repeated the word for her, and she tried again, improving her pronunciation and relaxing her shoulders as he lowered them to the ground. She kept her hand where he'd put it, at the small of his back, and smiled up at him when he touched her hair. She wanted to hold him this way.

---

* A glossary of Lakota words and phrases follows the final chapter.

"I seem to lose my senses when you hold me and kiss me," she told him. "What's worse, I don't seem to mind losing them."

"You haven't lost your senses, little one. Do you feel my touch and hear the sound of my voice?"

"I do," she whispered. "You are very pleasing to my senses. What I've lost is the power to be sensible."

"Trust me, Carolina. I will enjoy your lips and no more." He dipped his head to taste the fruitiness of her mouth as he stilled her lips' trembling. She answered by lifting her chin to exchange kisses with him. His braided hair swept across her cheek, and he brushed her hair back from her temple. His fingers were unsteady because he was working so hard to hold them at bay. He traced a line from her temple to her forehead with his thumb, and then strayed along the side of her face to her delicate jaw. His tongue flickered at her lips, and she parted them to allow him access.

He was a gentle explorer. He offered small, pretty kisses, and she found them to be new and exciting. She accepted his gifts and welcomed him. It was too easy, he thought. Her innocence was too lovely, and she valued what he offered her simply because she'd never seen the like of it. He kissed her eyelid and caressed her cheek with his as he nipped at the soft lobe of her ear. Then he pressed his lips to the side of her neck.

"Jacob," she gasped as she pushed her palms along the hard ridges of his back to hook her fingers over his shoulders. "You have my stomach tied up in knots."

"Does it hurt?" he whispered, smiling.

"Oh, no. It feels delicious."

"Then enjoy it. I will make it even better." He kissed her neck again, spicing it this time with the tiny flicker of his tongue.

"Lord help me, Jacob, I don't know what I'll do if you make it any better."

He raised his head, and an affectionate smile warmed the angles of his face. "You will hold me close to you and return my kiss. You fear yourself more than me."

"You have the advantage, Jacob. You know how your body behaves under these circumstances. Mine surprises me at every turn."

"Shh. Trust me, *wiwaśteka*." His lips brushed hers before he claimed her mouth fully. She gripped his shoulders, hoping that with his strength above her and the earth beneath her, she could savor the warmth, the wetness and the wonder of his kiss without floating away. When his fingertips made small circles on the side of her neck, she moaned softly and thought she must be on her way. He traced a path over her high-necked cotton dress, along her collarbone and down, up, down again over the small mound of her breast.

He could count the fragile ribs under his hand as he held her just beneath her breast. Exploring with his lips along the trail his fingers had blazed, he longed to tear the fabric from her body and feel her flesh against his mouth. He hovered over the apex of her breast and knew she held her breath. Like an exhausted child, he sank his face into the valley between her breasts. She moaned again, and he felt her grip tighten on his shoulders as she arched the whole length of her body against him.

Jacob felt some measure of triumph in the knowledge that this woman wanted him. She trusted him and allowed him to bring new life to her body and make her blood sing. He'd promised not to take her beyond this point tonight. He damned himself for it, but he would keep his promise. His need was great, but the power of his promise was greater. Perhaps if she'd had a man before—but to slake his need with a maiden without offering her marriage would bring him shame. It would be good between them here, but not in the world in which they spent their days.

He drew back, bracing himself on the arm that pillowed her head as he brought his breathing under control. Beads of perspiration gave her pale face an opalescent glow in the moonlight. He wanted what she wanted, but he misrepresented his desire with an easy smile. His eyes burned with his need, but they burned in the shadows, while hers were moonlit and rivaled its brightness.

"Beautiful whippoorwill," he whispered, "I must put you back in your nest before the dove's song intrudes to announce the morning."

"And will you take the dove from her nest and stroke her, too?" she asked as she lifted her hand to caress his smooth cheek.

"The hawk hunts at night. Small birds should stay clear of him," he warned.

"Not if they can have him for a friend."

"Mmm." He touched her forehead. "If I continue to stroke you this way, being your friend will not be enough for me. But the hawk cannot mate with a whippoorwill."

"The analogy ceases to function, Jacob. We are two people."

He watched her for a moment. Her breathing was steady, but her eyes were still bright. "Would you have us mate, then?" She closed her eyes and sucked her lower lip between her teeth. "No, you wouldn't," he whispered. "Neither would I."

He helped her to her feet. Her head was spinning. She adjusted her dress as she adjusted to the change in altitude, hoping he would say something else, because she could not counter his last remark. She had no idea what she wanted, but she knew how she felt in the arms of a man who did not judge her. It seemed paradoxical that he could accept the essence of her as no one else had, but he could not accept her heritage.

He read her mind. "You are a good woman." He put his hands on her back, and they started their return journey. "Let no one tell you otherwise."

Carolina smiled. "You're the first man to pay me such a genuine compliment."

"I seem to be the first man in many ways. Have you known only blind men?"

"I have known few men, and those have been convinced to keep their distance. My father says that I have a sharp tongue, and that I do nothing to enhance my plain appearance." She glanced up at him. "You said so, too."

"I said that your tongue could destroy Culley's pride. A man is honored for his humility, not his pride. As for your appearance—" He looked up at the sky. "What could be done to enhance the moon's beauty? Yours is as natural."

"I only speak my mind," she mumbled. "And I haven't the patience to wear frills and play parlor games."

He laughed. "You won't find many here. You should do all right."

"Even with my sharp tongue?"

He raised one thick eyebrow. "That will depend on who you use it against."

When they came to the edge of the yard, Carolina grabbed his hand. "Will you come for breakfast?"

He returned her smile and touched the hair that framed her face. He was not inclined to refuse her anything tonight, although he knew it was foolish. "Yes, I will come."

She surprised him by planting a quick kiss on his lips before she turned and ran into the house.

Chapter Three

Carolina was out of bed before daybreak. Sleep might have come to her during the night at some point; she wasn't sure. Sleep was a trivial matter. Jacob was coming to breakfast, and everything had to be perfect. Of course, the other men would also be there to benefit from her special efforts. She wondered if they would know. She lit the lamp on the dressing table and peered into Marissa's mirror to see whether her face still glowed from the attention he'd paid her hours earlier.

It was the same old face, unfortunately, with the added touch of shadows under the eyes. She washed it, pinched her cheeks and smiled into the mirror this time. Better. She wondered if a little flour might help. Probably not. She didn't want to look like a dumpling. She wanted to be pretty. She wanted Jacob to imagine stealing her when he saw her this morning. She didn't want him to *do* it, but she hoped he would *want* to.

The dress she'd borrowed was grass stained. She would have to take care of that after breakfast, and she would have to borrow another one. They were all so short waisted! She chose a gray skirt and a white blouse with a bit of ruffling. It was an unnecessary frill, she told herself. It enhanced her appearance, another part of her argued back, and perhaps it disguised the fact that Marissa's clothes were too large in the bust and too short for her.

Carolina rebraided her hair in a circlet around the back of her head. Once again she sought the mirror's reflection. Wholesome. She could have been a Scandinavian milkmaid. Why couldn't she be *pretty*? Neat, clean and comfortable had served her well in the past, but now, Lord forgive her, she wanted *pretty*. She looked better in blue, she decided. She had one blue dress in her wardrobe. Perhaps she would add a ruffle to it somewhere.

Carolina was frying potatoes in one huge skillet and eggs in another when the cowboys came in from the bunkhouse. She heard the rumble of low voices and the shuffle of boots on the floor of the mudroom. It was Culley who opened the door. Carolina turned and saw the hats on pegs, several hands slicking back several heads of hair and, finally, Culley's thin-mouthed grin.

"Good morning, Mr. Culley."

"Morning', ma'am. Sure smells like Sunday mornin' in here." Sober-faced cowboys filed into the kitchen as Culley held the door. "Don't know as you've met all the boys yet, Miss Hammond. Course, you know Bill Tanner." The tall, quiet cowboy nodded as he came through the door. "Him and me was with the boss yesterday, out looking for you."

Carolina nodded. "Yes, good morning, Mr. Tanner."

"This here's Joe Angus, Rufus Prine and Ben Davis. And here's Will Ashworth. Clean your boots off, Will."

Will scowled at Culley. A working man washed his hands and face and combed his hair before coming to the table. Will knew the requirements. He wasn't expected to worry about his boots.

"Please have a seat, Mr. Ashworth," Carolina invited.

"Thank you, ma'am." He cast Culley a satisfied glance.

"I hope the coffee is strong enough," Carolina said as she made her way around the table to fill the cups. "I know you men like strong coffee."

The aroma of the coffee battled with the smell of day-old sweat and unwashed socks. Yesterday's storm had apparently precluded the usual Saturday-night bath. Looking down one side of the table, at broad shoulders and plaid shirts, Carolina noted a pattern of sweat stains. On the other side, she noted a pattern of mustaches and freshly oiled hair.

Carolina turned quickly when she heard the screen door swing open. Jim Bates clapped his hat on a peg, and Carolina squelched her disappointment when he glanced through the kitchen door and offered a smile.

"Mornin', Miss Hammond. It's real kind of you to get us breakfast. Thought that job might fall to me this morning."

"I hope I've succeeded in approximating Marissa's wonderful meals, Mr. Bates."

"Long as it's woman-cooked, it's bound to please a cowboy. Ain't that right, boys?" There was a murmur of assent around the table as Bates took his place in the chair at its head. The wrinkles in Bates's face fell into a natural squint and a permanent frown. In his presence, the cowboys were like a troop of soldiers waiting for orders. They paused in the slurping of their coffee until Carolina had filled his cup.

"Thank you, ma'am. Eggs and bacon sure do smell good on a Sunday morning when you know you can take it easy after breakfast. Right, boys?"

Bates was roundly supported by echoes of, "Sure do."

Carolina had just set the platters of steaming potatoes, eggs and bacon on the table when she heard the back door open again. Her heart did a little jig. Don't watch the door, she told herself, and she moved to the stove for the biscuits and the coffeepot.

"Well, looky who's here," Culley intoned in a singsong. "The smell of that good hot coffee gettin' to ya, Black Hawk? You got the best nose on the place, I'll say that much."

Bates cast a quick, hard glance at Culley as he gestured to the empty place to his left on the bench. "Take a seat, Jake. You won't have to eat my cooking this morning after all."

"Yes, ma'am," Culley put in. "You can be sure the smell of your cooking ain't nothing to sneeze at if it brings Black Hawk over to the house on a Sunday mornin'. He usually sleeps in."

Will looked up from his plate. "You're the one usually sleepin' in on Sunday mornin', Culley."

"Usually hung over, especially if it's the end of the month," somebody mumbled, and another added with a chortle, "Ain't we all?"

"I don't think the lady wants to hear about your bad habits, boys." Bates didn't want to hear about them, either. He was a teetotaler, and he hated rounding up his strays once a month.

Culley refused to take any hints. "If there's a guest in the house, Black Hawk usually doesn't show up for meals. He must figger the lady owes him something after he rescued her yesterday."

Carolina bit back an angry retort. She looked at Jacob, who glanced at her over the rim of his cup. His eyes betrayed no emotion. She gave him a warm smile. "I owe Jacob more than breakfast," she said quietly. "If not for him, I might have been carried to the opposite side of the river by that wind. I doubt there's a ferry running on Sunday."

There was polite laughter, followed by a coarse whistle. Culley would not back off.

"Whoo-ee, Black Hawk! The lady claims she owes you. Wish I'da been out looking for that stud yesterday."

Jacob set his cup down slowly. His black eyes had suddenly grown hot, and they bore down on Culley. Bates's intercession came in a low growl. "Your table manners need polishing, Culley. Finish your meal out at the bunkhouse." Culley hesitated, clearly surprised by the foreman's order. "*Now*, Culley. And if there's a man in you, you'll say your apologies to the lady on your way out."

Culley climbed over the bench, mumbling, "Didn't mean nothing by what I said, ma'am. Just joshing Black Hawk, here." He left his half-finished meal on the table and headed for the door. "Thanks for breakfast, ma'am. Real tasty."

Carolina felt the same sympathy she might feel for a child who'd been sent away from the table for a breach of etiquette. Indeed, Culley had behaved like a child.

"Sorry, Miss Hammond," Bates offered. "Culley's good with cattle, but he ain't got much sense with people. Don't know what gets into him sometimes."

"Culley is a fool," Jacob said.

"Let it be, Jake," Bates suggested quietly. "I'll see to it he stays out of your way."

"Gentlemen, please enjoy your meal," Carolina said, injecting what she hoped would be a light note into her voice. "I won't let Mr. Culley's rudeness ruin my day. I was hoping to go for a ride this afternoon."

"Horseback?" Bates asked.

"Yes, if you think you have an animal gentle enough for me. Your tack is a bit different from what I use, but I think I can manage."

"Well, I guess we could arrange something for you, ma'am." Bates drained his cup before he turned to Jacob. "What do you think, Jake? We got a mount out in the barn for Miss Hammond?"

Jacob did not look up from his plate. "Mrs. Mac-Allistair's mare is pretty gentle."

"Jake here's our wrangler," Bates told Carolina. "Never seen a man handle horses better. He'll fix you up with a mount, and I'd be pleased to take you out for a ride, ma'am."

Carolina managed a smile. She knew Jacob wouldn't volunteer to take her for a ride, especially not after Culley's comments. Even so, she was disappointed. For the sake of her independence, she needed to convince these people that she could be trusted with a horse. For that reason alone, she would ride with Jim Bates.

The men discussed horses, fences and yesterday's twister, enjoying a leisurely meal and a second round of coffee. Jacob said little. He finished his meal, bade Carolina good morning and left the house. When the others followed suit, she was left with the kitchen chores. She left a ham baking in a slow oven and set her dough. Then she scrubbed the stain from Marissa's dress and washed her own. After she'd hung the clothes on the line, she laid her apron aside and ventured out to the barn.

She passed a long row of stalls on her way to the door she'd spotted at the far end of the aisle. Dust motes danced in the shafts of sunlight that slipped through the cracks in the walls. Carolina opened the door and peeked inside. A high glass window shed its light on rows of leather bridles hanging from wall pegs. An array of saddles sat on wall-hung saddle racks. Another door stood open at the back of this room. Carolina heard a noise, and she called out, "Is someone here?"

"Looking for Bates?"

Carolina moved to the doorway, following the sound of the familiar voice.

Jacob looked up from the rein he was braiding. She had no damn business coming here to the back of the barn. Nobody did. The workroom was his domain. She smiled at him, and the churning in his gut started all over again.

"You'll probably find Bates out by the corral," Jacob grumbled. "He's anxious as hell to take you for a ride. He's been pacing like an old bull who's just smelled cow." He reached for the cigarette he'd left balanced on the edge of a broken bit and sucked smoke into his lungs. Hoping to smother his anger, he dammed the smoke up for a moment.

Carolina stood quietly in the doorway. Jacob was seated on a stool beside a high workbench. The smoke he exhaled was drawn quickly out the small window above his bench. He watched it dissipate, laid the cigarette aside and went back to his work, pointedly ignoring her.

"I wanted it to be you, Jacob."

He leveled a long burning gaze at her. She wanted what to be him? The bull who'd smelled a cow? It was, he thought disgustedly. Without lifting any more than her sweet voice, she could have every man on the place locking horns, if that was what she wanted.

"I wanted *you* to take me riding."

"Did you expect me to put in a bid at the breakfast table?"

"A bid?"

Her naiveté infuriated him. He looked out the window. "I explained to you why that isn't possible for me. It's good that it was Bates. It could have been Culley."

"Culley was gone by then," she reminded him. "In any event, I would not have agreed to a ride with Mr. Culley. Mr. Bates is a gentleman, and I do intend to learn this Western style of riding. I want my own horse."

"Keep smiling at Bates. He can get you what you want."

Carolina folded her arms closely about her and nearly voiced the first retort that came to her mind. Something about his profile and the tight set of his jaw made her think better of it. Relaxing her arms at her sides again, she spoke evenly. "There was no one around when I entered the barn, Jacob. If we might have a few moments to talk—"

"There is nothing to talk about, Carolina."

"May I come in?"

"No."

She crossed the threshold anyway. The room was filled with equestrian trappings—leather, tools, saddle blankets—but there was also a cot in the corner, neatly blanketed, along with a small potbelly stove, a small table with a lamp and a large wooden box with a hinged lid. Carolina breathed deeply of the leather smell. "Who sleeps here?"

"I do."

She frowned. "Why?"

"Because this is my room. This is where I stay and where I work. You shouldn't be here. You are an unmarried woman." He spoke in his own terms. Then he slanted her a look he hoped she wouldn't like and used her terms. "A *lady* doesn't seek a man out in his room, Miss Hammond."

She wouldn't be intimidated. "I was not seeking you out," she said quietly as she moved about the room. She seemed to be drawn to touch a piece of hide, examine a strip of leather, but then she smiled at him. "It was just a happy coincidence that you were here."

"Hardly a coincidence." Realizing a sudden need for air, he pushed the window open wider.

"You're fortunate to have your own room," she offered lightly. "I'm sure it's far more pleasant than the bunkhouse, with all those men. The smell of leather and hay is nicer than—"

"Than the smell of white men." He chuckled and allowed his shoulders to relax. "Yes, this is a good arrangement for me. I prefer it. I don't like trouble."

"You were correct in your evaluation of Mr. Culley. He's a fool. I'm sure everyone noted the distinction between your behavior and his."

"I'm sure they did." He reached for his cigarette. "When I fight back, I'm hostile, and when I remain silent, it is because I have learned my place." Before placing the cigarette in the corner of his mouth, he glanced her way. "Or because I am a coward. Which do you prefer?"

"I prefer your self-control to Mr. Culley's rudeness."

"And I would prefer to take you riding myself."

He had returned his attention to his work, jerking hard at the rawhide strips. "Ask me," she said softly.

"You don't understand what you're suggesting."

"Then I shall ask you."

"And then you would be the fool." He raised his head and took the cigarette from his mouth. "Would you have them all speak to you as Culley did?"

"They're not all like Mr. Culley."

"They think alike when it comes to this." He leaned forward on the stool. "I am an Indian, Carolina."

"You are Lakota," she corrected, imitating his inflection as she remembered it.

Her words were an embrace. He found it difficult to look away, and even more so to tell her, "There is no place in my life for a woman like you."

"There seemed to be last night," she said tightly.

Jacob took one last, long pull on the cigarette before he stubbed it out. Turning to the window, he let the smoke curl slowly from his mouth, making a point of watching it. He decided he must be a coward, because he knew he couldn't look into those clear blue eyes as he spoke.

"I guess I could put some excitement into your life, Carolina, if that's what you want. We might meet somewhere, or I could go to the cabin. If we're careful, it could be a good arrangement—convenient for me, and you would not be disappointed. I've serviced other white women, much to their satisfaction."

He felt sick when he heard the soft sound of her gasp.

"I don't believe any of this," she said, struggling to keep her voice steady. "Yesterday you were—"

"Yesterday was one day," he told her calmly. "You know nothing about me. If what I have to offer is of no interest to you, try Bates. If you keep looking, Miss Hammond, you can be damn sure you'll find someone to suit your plans."

Jacob listened to the measured sound of her footsteps as she walked the length of the barn. When he heard the barn door swing shut, he clenched his fist and slammed it into the wall.

Carolina had her ride with Jim Bates. After what she thought was an appropriate length of time, she told him that she had dinner in the oven and needed to get back to it. Gallantly offering another lesson any time she wanted it, Bates complimented her on her first efforts. Carolina took pains to avoid the barn and the corrals, but when she heard someone call her name, she whirled in anticipation of an apology. It wasn't his voice, she chided herself immediately. Then she saw Culley duck under the corral rails, and she turned back and kept walking.

"Miss Hammond, I just want to tell you how sorry I am about what I said this morning." He trotted on bowed legs, and his steps sounded like someone trying to run with a limp. "I didn't mean nothing bad," he insisted as he caught up with her. "I know what a fine lady you are."

Carolina walked faster.

"I meant it when I said I wished I'da been there to help you yesterday."

"Thank you for your concern, Mr. Culley."

"I don't want you to take no offense, ma'am, about that Injun. I know you're a real lady. I know that for sure."

"No offense taken, Mr. Culley," Carolina clipped.

"I admire you. I have since the first day you came. So if you ever need any—"

Carolina had reached the steps. She was too impatient with the man to pause even slightly, but her breeding compelled her to say, "Excuse me, Mr. Culley." The screen door shut soundly in his face as she added, "I must see to dinner."

"Yes, ma'am." Her few words left him grinning foolishly as he walked away.

The MacAllistairs returned while Carolina was serving dinner. Nine-year-old Charlie made it known that he was hungry, and he was offered a seat next to every cowboy at the table. It was the only interruption the men would tolerate at mealtime. Any supplies to be hauled in could wait. Part of a cowboy's wage was his food, and no one questioned his right to eat while the food was hot. Charles took a chair at the end of the table opposite Jim Bates and joined in the man-talk.

Pretty little dark-haired, dark-eyed Marissa was older than Carolina, but her enthusiastic manner seemed more youthful. Donning an apron, she busied herself immediately with dinner, praising Carolina's efforts and filling her in on tidbits from town. Carolina's comments were few and far between. Her mind was elsewhere. Though she knew it wouldn't happen, she was listening for Jacob to come through the back door.

He had shamed her, she reminded herself. He had said things that made what they'd shared seem tawdry. It was as though he'd exploded a beautiful myth she'd treasured as fact. She felt foolish, yes, but not because he'd called her a fool. She'd been called a fool many times. She had never let it bother her. Not until Jacob said it. Not until the one man whose words she'd taken to heart had belittled her. She didn't care if she never saw him again.

Yes, she did.

"A tornado!"

Carolina jerked her head around at the word.

"A tornado," Marissa repeated, her eyes wide with amazement. "Jim says you saw a tornado, Carolina."

"Jake saw it coming and got her to shelter just in time." Bates rose from the table, draining the last of the coffee from his cup. "Sounded like we almost lost our teacher before we even got school started." He offered Carolina a warm smile. "Thanks for keeping us fed, ma'am. Sure was a good meal."

Carolina realized that the men had come and gone, and she hadn't said two words to them. "You're quite welcome, Mr. Bates," she called after him as he left the house.

"You must have been terrified," Marissa said. "Good Lord, girl, a tornado! I saw one once, but it was pretty far off. Where were you when it came?"

Carolina began gathering dishes from the table. "I was standing by the river up at the cabin," she said. "I was completely unaware of the danger. Jacob happened to be nearby, happened to see me—"

"You might have been killed!"

Yesterday that thought had taken precedence over all others in Carolina's mind. It had since been replaced.

"How long has Jacob worked here, Marissa?"

"Jacob? He's been with us full-time for about three years." Marissa added hot water to the flake soap she'd sprinkled in the dishpan. "Before that he worked for

Charles off and on whenever Charles could persuade him to come and break horses. That man is wonderful with horses, and Charles prides himself on raising the best around.''

''Has he ever been married?''

Marissa looked up as Carolina delivered a stack of plates to the counter. ''Married? Why would you ask that?''

''He told me about his schooling, but he didn't say very much about his family, and I was wondering.''

''No, he's never been married. I believe there was a girl, a childhood sweetheart. I think he expected to marry her, but when he came back from school, she had gone off with someone else. A white man, I believe.'' Marissa sloshed a hand through the soapy water, churning up suds. ''He's a handsome man, isn't he?''

''Yes, he is. And he seems to be far too intelligent to be satisifed to be a ranch hand all his life.''

Marissa looked up again, surprised. ''Carolina, Jacob is an Indian.''

''I realize that.'' After the day she'd had, Carolina felt like rocking the boat. ''So are you.'' Marissa's silence made Carolina regret her words immediately, but it was too late to retract them. Now it was necessary to air them thoroughly. ''Jacob told me that your grandmothers were sisters.''

''You two seem to have had quite a little visit. I didn't think he would tell anyone that. Not that it's a secret. It's just that some people don't understand.''

''I want to, Marissa.'' The two women looked at each other over the pan of suds. ''Jacob explained that Charles's acceptance of Indians is unusual among the white people around here.''

''A number of white men have taken Indian wives,'' Marissa said stiffly.

''And made happy marriages, I'm sure.'' Carolina touched the smaller woman's shoulder. ''Like yours.''

Marissa squeezed the suds from her hands and tapped them on the edge of the dishpan, shaking off the water. "I have never really lived as an Indian. My grandfather was a French trapper. I sometimes think it would have been better for the Indians if the French had kept this land. The men came to trap or to trade, and they married Indian women and were accepted among their wives' people." Marissa began sliding plates into the water as Carolina handed them to her, one by one. "My father came to the Dakota Territory from Minnesota, opened a store and married my mother. Because her father and her husband are white, people don't think of my mother as Indian."

"Or you?" Carolina asked.

"I am Mrs. Charles MacAllistair." Fierce pride flashed across her face, which then softened as she added, "I'm also Jacob Black Hawk's cousin. I'm glad he told you. Perhaps that means he has a place in his heart for his mixed-blood relations." She smiled wistfully. "In all the time he's been here, we've never discussed our kinship, and I've wanted to."

"If it's not a secret, why is it so hard to acknowledge?"

Drying her hands on her apron, Marissa moved to the table and sat down on the long bench. When Carolina followed suit, Marissa looked up at her. "We live between two worlds here, Carolina. We try to make the best of it, and we make choices. My grandmother chose a white man, and with each generation her daughters have become more white. But there is something inside me...." She paused, then shook her head. "I can't explain it. I grew up minding the store. My mother speaks French, English and very little Lakota. I only know there's something in me that feels as lost as..."

"As what?" Carolina prodded.

Marissa studied her hands as she spread them in her lap. "Those people fought so hard for their freedom," she reflected quietly. "And even when they had nothing left to fight with, they tried to get away from our army. But here they are. They live in little clusters, relatives sticking together because that's what they have left—disease, despair and each other."

"Does Jacob have any family besides his mother?"

Marissa saw the anxiety in Carolina's face. "His parents live in a cabin with one or two younger children, and there is an older brother, I believe. Jacob helps them with his wages. It's his choice to keep to himself here."

"What do the others do? How do they live?"

"The government has parceled out the land, issued farm implements and told them to farm. Some of them try. The government rations keep them from starving."

"Jacob told me of his mother's garden." Carolina smiled, remembering.

"It's unusual for him to talk so freely to anyone, especially a—"

"Especially a white woman?" Carolina nodded. "I know. I gathered that." Her eyes reflected more than gratitude as she recalled, "He saved my life, Marissa."

"It's not an easy life he's chosen for himself. His heart is with his people, but his mind... He has more education than most people here, white or Indian. He's seen more of the world, and he knows his people can't go back. But the young men don't know what to do with themselves."

"We talked about many things," Carolina reflected, thinking past the angry moments. "I like him. He's a considerate man. Mostly."

"Mostly?" Marissa made a face, both frowning and smiling in the role of the exasperated female. "Men! Just don't let yourself like him too much, my friend. He wears a thicker shell than most, too."

"I would be his friend if he would let me."

It was a confession of more, as only another woman would understand. "It would bring heartache if you allowed yourself to feel more, Carolina. It just isn't accepted. Not an Indian *man* and a white *woman*. People see it differently somehow."

"And if I feel more," Carolina said, "how shall I *dis*allow it?"

Marissa covered her friend's hand with her own. "Women are expected to *dis*allow."

"I know. I've made a practice of it." Carolina offered a sad smile. "I'm destined to be an old-maid schoolteacher, Marissa. There's no heartache in that, is there?"

Marissa had no answer. Heartache, too, was something women shared with a clasp of hands and a knowing exchange of softness with their eyes.

The evening shadows drew long fingers across the yard as Carolina stepped outside for a quiet moment with the streaked orange-and-blue sky. Where she'd come from, the trees were dominant, and one had to look up to see the sky. Here the sky was a huge dome of ever-changing color and character, and no tree had the strength to intrude on its dominion.

Carolina heard some activity at the corral. She was drawn to the sound, but the sight of Jacob with a black colt at his side stopped her in her tracks. He spoke softly in his native tongue, and the horse's nostrils quivered, but it stood still while Jacob eased a hackamore over its head.

She watched the muscles work in Jacob's bare back and shoulders as he reached over the horse's head and settled the brow band over the ears. He continued to talk, rubbing the animal's neck, reassuring it with his gentle touch. Carolina could almost feel those hands, that touch against her own skin, and something fluttered inside her. She turned away with regret and retreated to the house.

Jacob felt a kindred regret as he watched her walk away.

It had not been easy to persuade the MacAllistairs to allow her to return to her cabin. She reminded them that six miles was almost within shouting distance, and that separate roofs and separate kitchens made for better friendships between women. She had gone, and it was Wednesday before she heard the sound of wagon wheels once again rumbling over the pair of ruts that served as a road to her door.

Carolina straightened her back and shaded her eyes with her hand. Her heart thudded against her ribs when she saw that Jacob was driving the team, with Marissa sitting beside him on the seat of the lumber wagon. Carolina stepped away from her laundry tub as Jacob pulled up the team, jumped down from the seat and walked around to Marissa's side to help her down.

Marissa offered a gift-bearing smile. "Where would you like your corral, Carolina?"

Carolina noted the load of rails at Marissa's back. "Wherever Mr. Black Hawk suggests." She spoke to Jacob, but she was careful to say, "It's good to see both of you."

"You're looking well, Miss Hammond. I'll put your supplies inside." He hopped back up on the wagon to retrieve a box from under the seat, then followed the women to the cabin.

Jacob set the box near the sideboard and turned to the window. "The corral should be on this side of the well. You should be able to see both the corral and the road from this window. Will that shed by the garden keep your feed dry?"

"I think so." Carolina stood beside him and envisioned the scene.

"I'll check the roof." He glanced at her, his eyes alight. "You won't be offended if I remove my shirt while I work, will you, Miss Hammond?"

"Of course not. You may dress or undress as you please, Mr. Black Hawk."

Jacob stripped off his shirt before he began heaving rails off the wagon. He wondered whether Carolina had hastened to explain his question to Marissa after he'd left the cabin, or had she let it stand as a private joke? It was good to see her, too. She'd been on his mind. It was not unheard of for a woman to live alone on this prairie. Sometimes their men died, or wandered from home. He knew of one white woman who ranched on her own, but that one could have been mistaken for a man.

These were a strange people, these white ones, strange because of their penchant for striking out on their own. Until now it had just been a source of curiosity to him, but here was this woman, who could never be mistaken for a man, and he had helped her, held her in his arms, then hurt her deliberately. Now he was pleased to see her again. Perhaps he was becoming as strange as they were.

Among the supplies Marissa had included a freshly butchered chicken, and Carolina decided to stew it with dumplings for her unexpected guests. Jacob had come to build her corral. It could have been Bates. She remembered Jacob's bitter words and thought, it could have been Culley. But it was Jacob, and her heart sang for the mere fact that he was there.

"I'm just glad this isn't an old soddy."

Marissa's comment brought Carolina's head around as she set a kettle of water on the stove. "You said this was your first homestead."

"It was, and thank God, Charles insisted on a log house, even if there *is* sod on the roof." She began working on the vegetables Carolina had set aside. "I really wish you would reconsider this arrangement. Room and board for the teacher is part of the bargain, and we have plenty of room for you at the house."

"I don't want to be a boarder, Marissa. Charles says the schoolhouse will be built near here, so this will be a good situation for me. I need to have something that feels like my own." She handled her dishes carefully as Marissa looked on, admiring the pattern. "Please understand. I appreciate the trouble you've gone to, to repair the roof and help me transport my belongings out here."

"As far as I'm concerned, the cabin is yours, Carolina, but when winter sets in, I won't hear of your staying out here alone. Besides—" she smiled, bursting with the news she needed to share with another woman "—it's going to be hard for me to keep up with everything this winter. I'm going to have another baby."

"How wonderful!" Carolina exclaimed.

"It's been so long since Charlie—more than nine years. I have to be careful, but this time I know it will be all right."

"How many have you lost?"

"Two since Charlie was born. If I have to spend six months in bed, I'll carry this one through." A handful of carrots fell into the stew as Marissa made her resolution.

"I'll have my own transportation now. I'll help you all I can, and when winter comes . . . we'll see."

"*You'll* see, when winter comes." Marissa smiled knowingly. "I'll have my houseguest after the first good snow."

Carolina had heard stories of terrible midwestern winters, but she thought they were probably greatly exaggerated. Marissa had yet to appreciate the hardiness of a New Englander, at any rate. "Will you finish making our tea, Marissa?" Carolina asked as she set the lid on the kettle. "I was washing out a few things when you came, and I should get them out on the line."

Once outside, she resolved to let Jacob tend to his business while she attended to hers. He dug his post hole without looking up from his work, and he couldn't have noticed the glances she sneaked his way as she hung her clothes out and emptied her wash water on the garden. Tucking a wet pair of bloomers into her apron pocket, she hurried inside to join Marissa for tea. She hung her apron on a peg. A wet circle was already spreading at the pocket.

Marissa had stirred up the dumpling batter. She left the bowl on the sideboard and joined Carolina at the table. The door was left open to admit fresh air, and they could hear the clanging of the post-hole digger each time it was thrust into the ground.

"Was Jacob sent here to build the corral, Marissa, or did he volunteer?"

"Actually, Jacob made a point of telling Charles that you shouldn't be up here without a horse. When Charles said he'd ask Jim who could be spared to put up a corral, Jacob insisted upon doing that himself, since he would be breaking the horse." Marissa looked puzzled. "The logic there escapes me. I don't think Jacob liked the idea of someone else coming up here, do you?"

Carolina looked out the window. "I have no way of reading a man's mind—certainly not *that* man's. I'm just glad he wasn't sent here against his will."

She watched him set the post and tamp it into the ground. Sweat glistened on his chest in the morning sun. A buckskin headband kept the perspiration from rolling into his eyes. He wore a cross-cultural combination of denim pants and moccasins. Above his brass belt buckle, the muscles in his abdomen flexed suggestively while he worked.

"The two of you seem to have made quite an impression on one another in the short time you spent together," Marissa said.

Carolina ignored the comment. She had decided several days ago not to think about the kind of impression she might have made. He had impressed her, and that was more than she could deal with at this point. She had half a notion to deny it altogether. Men did not impress Carolina Hammond. Lord, the way he handled that mallet!

"You're a beautiful woman, Carolina. Most beautiful women know they're beautiful, but I don't think you do."

Carolina glanced at Marissa with disbelief. "Does pregnancy affect the eyesight, Marissa? I'm quite plain. Dowdy, if you want the truth."

"Dowdy?" Marissa gave a girlish laugh. "I don't know whose eyes you've seen yourself through, my friend. The men around here certainly turn their heads when you walk by."

"Only because they don't dare turn their heads when *you* walk by," Carolina countered. "But, considering the shortage of women, if I wanted a man out here, I guess I could have one."

"I think there's one you want. And I think you would get more than a disapproving stare from some people if they saw the look on your face just now."

"What people?" Carolina snapped. "What look on my face? You seem to be jumping headlong to some ridiculous conclusions."

"Carolina, I've heard the men talking about the tension between Jacob and Culley. This morning I saw Culley try to pick a fight with Jacob, and he was loaded for bear. Culley wants your attention, too."

"Culley is a fool," Carolina declared, pleased with herself for echoing Jacob's words. "And you're talking nonsense, Marissa." She pushed her chair away from the table. "He'll need soap and a towel to wash up for dinner."

Carolina watered the team first, using her washtub. She filled the tub again and left it beside the well. Jacob tamped the dirt around a post as he watched her approach him.

"Dinner is ready when you are, Mr. Black Hawk," she offered quietly. "I have the washtub ready for you." He wiped the back of his arm over his forehead, still watching her. She turned to walk away.

"Carolina."

It was the same voice that had soothed the wild colt. She turned and found that a slight smile had softened his eyes.

"You will make a good horsewoman."

"Why do you say that?"

"You thought to water the team." He set aside the post he'd used as a tamper and stripped off his headband. "Now, how about me?"

"I made you a full-course meal, Jacob." He motioned to her, and she followed him to the well.

"I would prefer the river," he said as he knelt beside the tub and began soaping his arms, his chest and his face.

Carolina was mesmerized. The soap slipped over his muscles like soft butter. He would prefer the river to her dinner? "We'll wait for you if you—"

He laughed. "I'd soon hear giggling in the bushes. I don't trust you, Miss Hammond."

"Mr. Black Hawk, really!" It was a relief to hear him laugh, a joy to play along.

"A woman who is shy and proper on her own can get together with another woman and find nerve she never knew she had. I know how it works with you women." He pointed to the bucket. "Pour."

"What?"

"Pour some water over me."

"Oh. Certainly." When she'd drawn a bucketful of water, she found him leaning over the tub. "Pour it over your head and everything?"

"Not everything. I would not want to have my pants hanging by your stove. Not today." He grinned. "Did you think the sight of your underclothes on the clothesline would drive me to do something desperate?"

"Oh, you!" Laughing, she tossed the water over his head and watched it run down his back. He lifted his face to the deluge.

"Ahh, that feels good."

She laid the towel over his shoulders as he wiped his face with his hands. He paid little attention to the towel as he squeezed water from his braids and turned his face to the sun. They walked to the cabin together, joined Marissa and shared a meal as three friends.

Jacob returned alone the following morning. He rode his sorrel and led Marissa's saddled chestnut mare. He assured Carolina that the mare was only on loan, and that he had started a fine mare for her. A woman should ride a mare, he told her, because their temperaments were compatible. Carolina was struck by the fact that everything Jacob said seemed to be virtually inspired. They had lunch together in the cottonwood grove. They laughed and talked freely, but they avoided touching each other.

By late afternoon the corral was finished, and Jacob went to the cabin door. She expected him to come inside, but he did not.

"Please have supper with me, Jacob. I have everything ready."

Her tone was light, and his heart felt like a piece of iron. He could have taken more time, he thought. He could have left some of the work for tomorrow. But he had not. It was done.

"I cannot be here any longer, Carolina."

"Why not?"

He glanced toward the horizon. "It will be nightfall soon. I was sent here to build the corral, and those at the ranch know where I am."

"They know you're entitled to a meal when the work is done," she insisted.

His eyes seemed to darken. "It was good to be near you these two days, but I know *myself* that it's time to leave. I won't have them talking about you."

She looked down at the toes of her black shoes. "*You* talked about me, Jacob. Last weekend." She heard his sigh, but she couldn't look up at him. "Nothing they could say would hurt me as much as it did to hear those suggestions from you. Do you believe what you said about me?"

She needed to see his answer in his eyes. What she saw was his own pain—the pain of his lie, the pain he felt at having hurt the one he sought to protect. Words became superfluous, but he gave them to her anyway.

"No. I know who you are, little one. Your kiss was a rare gift to me."

She smiled, gratified. "And you made up all that nonsense about servicing white women, didn't you?"

"No. That much was true."

Carolina was stunned. If she was not that kind of woman, neither could Jacob be that kind of man.

"At Carlisle we were assigned to apprenticeships away from campus, and I worked for a blacksmith. Young women brought their horses there. I came to know some of them quite well." He paused, knowing that the emotion had gone out of his voice. It was not something he wanted to tell her, but it was something he decided she should know. "They served my needs, and no doubt I was a novelty to them."

She imagined Jacob holding an aristocratic young temptress dressed in a fancy riding habit, while she cooed and clucked to him, marveling over his virility. "Is that why you held me and kissed me? To serve your needs?"

"I kissed you because being near you felt good. It feels good now. But my needs run deeper, and that is why it's time for me to go." He touched her chin with aching tenderness. "This can go no further, Carolina."

"What can go no further?" she asked. She wanted to banish the urgency from her voice, but she could not. "All we've done is enjoy one another's company."

"We've done more," he reminded her. "We know what we would make of this, what this would have to become, and it cannot be."

"Our friendship cannot be?"

"Friendship would not be enough for either of us. We both know that. I spoke honestly when I told you there is no place in my life for a woman like you." He let his hand fall to his side and took a step back from her. "Carolina, there is no place in *your* life for a man like *me*."

"You're wrong, Jacob."

He shook his head once, stepping back again. "You are blind, little one. I must think for both of us in this."

His retreat brought more pain than his insults had. Carolina felt the last of her pride making ready to bolt, and she snatched it back and covered herself with it. "Very well,

Jacob. Thank you for all the work you've done here, and for bringing the horse.''

"I will bring a better one when she is ready. One that will do what you ask at the moment you ask her."

Carolina nodded, because she could not speak. He was edging away as though she threatened him somehow. She turned away, knowing that the tears burning in her eyes were about to betray her, but she listened until the last echo of hoofbeats had faded away.

Chapter Four

During the next four days Caroline went through the motions of her daily activities like a walking corpse. She made her cabin too clean to be inhabited, and her garden flourished without a weed. She washed, sewed, read and washed again, often late into the night when sleep would not come. One night she found herself standing in the corral and talking to the mare, and she knew she must be losing her mind.

She decided she couldn't continue this way. If she loved this man, she would have to tell him so and be done with it. His worries about harassment from people who would no longer matter to her could be damned. Saving her reputation with those people was not worth losing her sanity. If they were not to see each other by his choice, let him tell her that he didn't want her around him. Perhaps then she could hate him and get him out of her mind.

Carolina saddled the mare. It was dark, late—she didn't know the time. No matter. She'd lost touch with time, anyway. The ranch would be asleep. She would ride the six miles and put her heart on the line for the first and last time in her life. With that mission in mind, she discounted the hour and the social proprieties.

There was no barking when she approached the yard. Starlight brightened the night, and Carolina watched the dog lope across the yard toward her. He squeezed under the corral rail and wagged his body in recognition of a friend. She patted his head, scratched him behind one ear, took a deep breath and slipped through the big barn door, leaving the mare tied to a rail. The door gave a rude creak. Darkness overwhelmed her.

Carolina felt her way from stall to stall, moving as quietly as her shoes would allow. The saddle racks were guideposts, and she moved hand over hand from one to the next toward the back room. With her heart in her throat she found the door to his room, opened it slowly and crept over the threshold.

"Jacob?"

The oath he muttered made her freeze. It came from behind her. "Don't turn around," he ordered. "Don't move until I get my pants on."

"Oh. I'm sorry. I didn't think—"

"I see that." His voice moved about her, but she obeyed the order to stand still. "What are you doing here now? What do you want from me, woman?" She heard the whisper of cloth sliding over skin. "Maybe I shouldn't bother with the pants. Is that why you came?"

When she moved toward the window, her heel caught on a floorboard, and she reached quickly to catch herself on the workbench. She'd memorized the room and spent much time imagining him here.

"What do you want, Carolina?"

"I don't know," she whispered. "I just decided to come."

"You weren't at the house today. I would have known."

"Would you?"

His voice edged closer. "How did you get here?"

"I rode the mare."

"You could have killed yourself out there in the dark. I might have killed you myself. Do you see this?" She turned and saw his shadowy figure behind a glint of steel. "I might have cut your throat before I knew who you were."

"And I might have been dead these last four days anyway, for all the emptiness I felt. I had to come."

"Don't test me, Carolina. Not here. Not during the night, when—"

"I didn't come to test you. I came to *tell* you." She gripped the edge of the workbench and tried to steady her voice.

"I don't want to know."

He speared her with his merciless tone, and she wanted to run, but she stood her ground with the support of his workbench. "I've come a long way, Jacob. Let me say what I've come to say."

"Think before you say anything, Carolina. *Think*."

"I've done nothing else for the past four days. I know I'm not much to look at, but I'm strong. Truly. You saw me at my worst, hysterical and completely foolish after the storm. I swear to you, I'm not usually like that."

"The wind frightened me, too," he confessed quietly.

"And I am not a wanton woman." Her breath caught in her throat, but she plunged on. "I have never...known a man. I have never considered doing anything like this before, but something—" She paused, then rushed on. "Jacob, you have touched something deep inside me, and the thought of you will not go away. I am consumed with the need to be near you, and I can't—"

"Carolina, if I touch you..."

The tears were rolling unchecked now as she nodded. "Yes, yes. Oh, God, I have no pride left."

He laid his hands on her shoulders. "Pride does not bring us honor," he said softly.

"Nor does meeting in secret, but I will do that if you want. If you would hold me, I would try to fill those needs you spoke of."

"If I were to hold you now—"

"I would walk with you anywhere, Jacob."

"Carolina, Carolina." He slid his hands down her arms and turned her toward him.

"Let me be near you, at least for tonight. Don't send me away without—"

"Carolina, *wiwašteka*, I haven't the will to send you from me now. I want you, and I've thought of nothing else." He folded his arms around her carefully, as though she were his treasure. "This time I will allow myself to have what I want."

She turned her face to his shoulder and tried to control her tears. Taking slow, deep breaths, she blotted her face on her sleeve. "I'm making myself look even worse with this foolish crying. I'll wash my face, and I won't be so—"

He brushed the hair back from her face and tilted her chin up with his thumb. "You are a pleasure to look at. You should let the sun bring color to your face, but I have seen few women who are as beautiful as you are." He kissed her forehead and touched her cheek with his palm. "Your skin is soft and smooth. Your eyes are bright with honesty and innocence. Your mouth is sweet with kindness." His lips touched hers with a zephyr's kiss. "I don't want to hurt you, Carolina."

She heard both need and dread in his voice. "I didn't intend to force myself on you, but I could not stay away. I don't even know myself anymore." She looked up at him. "I don't know what has happened to me, Jacob, but I will not be tiresome. I won't be a burden to you. I can take care of myself. I only ask to be with you for as long as it suits you."

"Are you asking me to make you my woman? To make your body part of mine?"

She wanted so much more, but she said, "Yes, that's what I want."

"But you are frightened."

"Yes, but not of you. It's frightening not to know. You kiss me and touch me, and I want something else to happen, and it isn't what I thought it was."

He smiled. "What did you think it was?"

"I thought it was a dreadful thing, something to be suffered. But your touch fills me with warmth and life, and I will follow you anywhere to know that feeling again."

"I will bring you great pleasure, little one, but I will bring you pain, as well."

She slid her arms around his back. "I have known pain. One survives that. Teach me pleasure, Jacob, and joy and caring between two people. Those are things I have not known."

He claimed her mouth with a hard, possessive kiss. He had taught her need, and he would not deny her fulfillment. Nor would he deny himself any longer. He took her to his cot, and she nestled in his arms. They delighted in slow, warm kisses. She had come to him, and he celebrated. He had not forgotten her, and she was glad.

It was dark in this corner of the room, but Jacob could see the delicacy of her features. It was incredible, but she was here, and she was his. Her eyes were languid with her longing. In the darkness there were no colors; there was only brightness, which shone for him. He needed to take her away from this place and find a better one, a place that was his.

"We are going for a ride, Carolina," he whispered.

"Now?"

"Where is the mare?"

"In the corral just outside."

"It will be light soon. We will leave now, before anyone awakens." He took her hands and drew her to her feet. "This is not the place for us to be together."

"Shall we go to the cabin?"

"There's a better place for us. I have a camp where I stay when I hunt. We will go there."

He opened the large wooden box that stood near the cot. In the dim light that reached them from the window, Carolina watched him pull a shirt over his head and tie moccasins on his feet. Then he handed her something made of soft buckskin. "Wear these under your dress," he instructed.

"You want me to wear your pants?"

"Those are leggings. You must have blisters already from riding in a saddle like that."

Her face felt hot. "I tried to keep my dress tucked under me, but my legs are a bit chafed." She sat down on the cot and struggled into the leggings, then tied them around her waist. She had to roll them up at the bottom.

He watched her. "White women's clothes make no sense."

She glanced up and caught him smiling. He must have been quite familiar with the intricacies of white women's clothing, she thought. She felt a pang of jealousy.

She followed him to the tack room and held a large rawhide bundle for him while he hoisted a saddle from a rack. He moved silently as he saddled his horse and tied his gear to the saddle. He gave no verbal instructions, and she found that she needed none. He gestured for the bundle, for the opening of the door and the gate, and for her foot as he helped her into the saddle.

The leggings were a godsend. Her legs had not blistered, but she knew they would have on this trek, without protection. She followed Jacob as their horses picked their way

along in the darkness, leaving the MacAllistair ranch behind.

The moon's nightgown of thin white clouds brightened
the sky, along with the myriad stars. The land rolled like
waves at sea. There was no need for talk as they rode. Having come to this decision together, they were now moving
toward its fulfillment together. They had left their differences behind them. Ahead lay a place where they could be
simply a man and a woman who were drawn to each other
by a force as old as humanity.

They were heading southwest. Carolina kept glancing
behind to see the dawn light stretching long pink arms above
the outline of the buttes and hills. She lost the view as they
descended into a draw and caught it again as they rode up
the side of the next hill. She enjoyed the rocking-horse can-
ter along the sidehill and the hip-swaying walk down the
other side as the hills rolled on and on like ripples in a huge
green, yellow and brown quilt.

They reached a small river-bottom area, where the cottonwood and willow grew in abundance. Crossing a grassy
meadow, Jacob watched Carolina's body sway with the
movement of the horse as she rode just ahead of him. The
sun sparked fire-red highlights in her brown hair. She turned
and caught him smiling at her.

"The sun dances in your hair. As soon as we reach camp,
I will bury my face in it and feel the warmth of the sun in my
soul," he told her.

Nestled in a small clearing within a grove of cottonwoods beside the little river stood a tipi. Its hide cover was
stretched over the conical frame formed by poles pointing
arrogantly at the sky. It was covered with colorfully painted
designs, including a stylized black bird that soared over a
herd of stiff-legged horses, which were headed in the direc-

tion of the tipi door. The door itself was a flap of hide, laced closed with thongs and sharpened sticks.

"Jacob, is this yours?" Carolina was as wide-eyed as a child who had just discovered a gingerbread house in the middle of the woods.

"This is my camp, but the lodge is truly my mother's. Men do not own tipis. Only women do. Most of the people use the government canvas to make them now, but my mother has kept this, and she painted it honoring me." He gave a soft chuckle. "She scolds me for not having my own woman to provide a lodge for me."

Jacob dismounted and reached up to Carolina. When her feet touched the ground, he felt the unsteadiness in her legs. He gave her his support. "My mother sometimes chooses to forget that life has changed. The government promises to provide for all our needs," he said ironically. "It is no longer necessary for a woman to devote herself to this kind of work."

"But it's so beautiful!" She took a walk around the structure, pulling him with her by the hand. Because he agreed, and also because no one was looking, he suffered this minor indignity.

"Your mother's pride in her son is quite obvious. This bird must stand for Black Hawk, and the horses... Do you leave it standing all the time?"

"No, only when I come to hunt. I returned to the ranch yesterday to bring your mare back with me so I could work with her here. I have been restless." He cocked an eyebrow and gave her a wry smile. "Woman on my mind."

"I don't want to keep you from your hunting." Was she actually being coy? She smiled, wondering if she could be as attractive as a young sophisticate dressed in a fancy riding habit.

"You won't. You'll keep me from working with your mare." He gave her hand a quick squeeze before he went back to unsaddle the horses. "She was to be a reminder of you."

"Did you find one who looks like me?" she teased, coming to help him.

"Yes. She's beautiful." He slung his saddle to the ground and grinned at her. "A little high-headed, but she likes it when I rub her neck. She settles down when she hears my voice."

"I find the sound of your voice to be rather unsettling."

"You're not a horse."

They shared a laugh while he picketed the horses. "Will Charles mind your leaving without telling him?"

"He doesn't know where I go, but he knows that when I'm gone, I'm usually hunting. I wouldn't work for him if he questioned my time. I am paid to do a job, not to be busy for certain hours." The door flap fell back as he unlaced the thongs and pulled the wooden picks out.

"Your jobs for pay seem strange to us," he explained. He carried a saddle and a scabbarded rifle into the tipi. "We do what needs to be done when the time comes. My family needs meat now, and so I hunt."

Carolina saw that he meant to take everything inside, and she brought him the rawhide bundle and his saddlebags. "I thought the government provided everything for them now."

"Like hell," he grumbled. "They provide us with—" He cut himself off when he looked at her. "I need to provide for them myself, Carolina."

"I can understand that."

He smiled, knowing that she did. "It's hard to work for pay," he continued as he retrieved the other saddle. "Not that the work is hard, but because it isn't our way. If it's a good day to hunt, or a good day to swim in the river, or a good day for a horse race, then that is what we do." He went to her and took her hand. "Today is a good day to spend with a beautiful woman."

A current of excitement surged through her body as Carolina followed Jacob into the tipi. Inside there was a fire pit where at least one fire had already burned. A heavy hide was rolled up with the hair to the inside and stashed under the sloping wall, and there was a neat pile of several trade blankets, white with colored stripes. Carolina noticed another rawhide packet, similar to the one they'd brought, except that it was painted with geometric designs. Next to that was a pair of brightly colored beaded moccasins. They caught Jacob's eye at the same time.

"Ina," he said.

"Ina?"

"My mother. She has been here. She was probably out picking Juneberries."

Carolina picked up the moccasins and admired the fine work more closely. "Does your family live near here?"

"They have a cabin a couple of miles away. The government has allocated this land to me, and my father's land is not far away. My older brother's, too, and several uncles'. They have divided it among us in small pieces and sold what was not allocated to white men like Charles MacAllistair."

He unrolled the curly-haired robe and spread blankets over it. It gave Carolina a strange, terrible, delicious feeling to watch him prepare their bed.

"It's beautiful land, Jacob," she said absently. "Good bottomland. It would make a fine farm."

"Yes, it is good land, but it's foolish to think it can be bought and sold. Years from now, when my bones are part of the earth, someone else will claim to own the same land."

"But you can use it while you're here."

He smoothed the blankets. "Farmers use land," he said. "We are not farmers. We are hunters, and there is not enough game left to feed our people." He rose to his feet. "But there is some for those who still seek it, and you will see that I am a good hunter."

He saw the signs of her nervousness when he came to her. She glanced here, there, anywhere but into his eyes. He took her shoulders in his hands. "In the days of my father's youth," he began softly, "I would have provided more meat than you would have been able to use. I would have given much away to the old ones and the families in need." He stood close and stroked her arms. "I would have brought you to my family, and my mother and her sisters would have taught you to tan the hides and make our clothes and our lodge. My mother's work is still much admired, and yours would have been as fine as hers."

He gathered her against his hard wide chest, and he buried his face in her hair as he had promised to do. She hardly breathed. He whispered close to her ear, "And I would have filled your belly with our babies, *wiwaśteka*."

Her stomach somersaulted, and she wrapped her arms around him, clutching at his doeskin shirt.

"I want you now, Carolina."

She felt panicky. She did not want to be ignorant and clumsy now. "I don't know how, Jacob. I don't know what to do."

"I will not force you, little one. I will not take your maidenhood unless you give it to me."

She gave a jerky little laugh. "My maidenhood. I am twenty-six years old, Jacob. I think it's old maid-hood."

"You are a maiden," he insisted, "and I have no right to take you."

"I am giving you the right. I hope I won't be a disappointment to you."

He kissed the side of her neck. "That isn't possible."

"But I don't even know what lies beyond the need that brought me to you. Whatever it is, I want it to come from you." Her head dropped back, and her hair cascaded into his hands. "Tell me what I must do, Jacob."

"I am going to give you pleasure, *wiwaśteka*. Your body will tell you what to do."

"Will I give you pleasure, too?"

He drew back from her, smiling. "Oh, little one, you will give me much pleasure." Lowering one knee to the sod floor, he took her shoes from her feet. She put a hand on his shoulder to steady herself, and he examined the heel and tapered toe of one shoe. "You should be lame from wearing this."

She laughed nervously. "My feet are accustomed to them."

He whisked his shirt over his head while she turned away and fumbled beneath her skirt to remove the leggings. She turned back to find him watching her, enjoying her struggle. When she scowled, he laughed, pulling her into his arms.

He saw that the scowl soon disappeared, and in its place was expectation.

She heard the abrupt end to laughter and the deep, unsteady breath he drew.

His kiss was possessive, hard and hungry, and she welcomed it, parting her lips, inviting his tongue into the sensitive recess of her mouth. The buttons at the back of her dress came away from their buttonholes quickly. He slipped the bodice off her shoulders, over her arms, and let the dress drop to the ground. Her petticoat followed. When he looked down at her, he laughed, but gently this time. Appreciatively.

"Undressing you is like plucking a goose. Under the feathers there is still the down."

She stood timidly in her camisole and pantaloons, wondering whether she should apologize or try for a sharp retort. None came to mind as he lowered her to the pallet, kissing her again. "It's a good thing," he whispered against her neck. "It forces me to go slowly with you."

With a light touch he massaged her breasts in slow circles while he kissed her. Deep in the pit of her stomach a fire was kindled, and it grew gradually under his care. He touched the ivory lace that bordered her camisole, tested the smooth white satin ribbon between his fingers, gave it a tug and watched the bow come away under his hands. He unlaced the garment and drew it away from her small firm breasts. The catch in her breath caught in his chest, also, and he reassured her with a kiss while he traced ever-smaller concentric circles around her breasts with his fingertips. The center jewel of her breast was hard and round, and he touched it briefly before attending to the other breast. Finally his lips found their way to her nipple. She gasped when he took it in his mouth and played with it with his tongue.

She lifted her shoulders from the pallet, but he held her still and suckled her until she moaned. He pushed the pantaloons over her hips and kissed the crest of her hipbone and the depression near her navel. Then he pulled this last piece of clothing from her. Taking her in his arms again, he kissed her lips, desperate for her now as he touched her hip and caressed her thigh.

Tension quivered deep in her abdomen. Carolina touched his chest tentatively and found it be warm, smooth and damp. She spread her fingers, felt his heart beating beneath her palm and then slid her hand down to his belly. A low groan gave voice to his approval as she reached his belt buckle. Her hand stiffened.

"Can you help me with my belt, Carolina?" he whispered, his lips teasing her earlobe.

She fumbled with the leather strap and pulled it free, but she drew her hand back when she sensed the hard throbbing under the buttons of his pants.

"My body aches to become part of yours, just as yours aches to be taken." He pressed her hand to his belly, and then he began to unbutton his pants. "Don't take your hand from me, Carolina. Don't be afraid of me. A man's body is not beautiful and small like a woman's, but that is as it must be."

Carolina felt a chill when he rolled away from her, and she turned to see his handsome face, intense with desire, as he returned to her and took her in his arms again. He pressed the hard shaft of his manhood against her thigh and saw her eyes widen as she turned her head away. "It's part of me, Carolina. Look at me." She did. His eyes were dark and hot. "It's part of me. The part that belongs inside you."

She nodded quickly. This was good. That part was bound to be... He kissed her again and touched the inside of her thigh—close, too close, not close enough. His finger found her secret self so gently that she wasn't sure—yes, yes it was there, and she wanted it there, because it made her ache so sweetly. She had no idea that her hand was kneading the muscles of his chest, or that she arched her pelvis instinctively to press herself into the palm of his hand.

Carolina wrapped her arms around his back and squirmed as his fingers explored her soft harbor while he sought to nourish himself at her breast. "Jacob," she gasped, her senses reeling. "Jacob, I can't... I'm going to..."

"I know, little one," he whispered. "Let it happen. Let your body show me how it feels." He devoured her mouth, plunging his tongue inside as her body shuddered beneath him. She was as ready for him now as he could make her, and he rose over her, reaching down to spread her thighs. Her eyes were glassy, her lips red and moist, and her skin was mottled with the flush of her desire.

"Now let me show you how my body feels," he whispered as he positioned himself with great care. "Relax, now, *wiwaśteka*, and ease my way inside you."

Slowly, with the gentle rocking-horse motion that came naturally to him, he pushed through the entrance to her most private and protected recess. She cried out and clamped her teeth over her lower lip until the searing sensation faded. She watched Jacob's face, saw him wince at the sound of her pain, saw the pleasure he felt as he slid beyond her maidenhead and found refuge within her body. He closed his eyes and groaned, then opened them and smiled. It was that warm, soft smile that drew her heart's response.

"Am I still hurting you now?"

"No," she said quickly.

"A little?" She nodded. "It isn't fair that I have to hurt you first."

"You made me feel wonderful first."

"I will again. Let me be part of you. Let your body enjoy mine." He moved inside her with a slow rocking rhythm, stoking the fire within her. She wanted to pull him inside her, but her hips were untutored in the rhythm. "Meet me, little one," he whispered. "Lift yourself to receive me. Yes. Hold me, hold me, yes. Don't let me go."

It was the rhythm of life, the rhythm of breathing, the rhythm of the ocean's waves reaching to kiss the warm sand, drawing back, then plunging toward the shore again. He slipped a hand beneath her buttocks and found his way deeper into her body. She rose to meet him, clutching at his back, calling his name.

His voice was hoarse and hot with his promise. "I am going to soar to the sun, and I am going to take you with me, *wiwaśťeka*."

She cried out again, this time in joy, as his body touched some ready spot inside her, and a white light shattered brilliantly in her brain.

They lay quietly in each other's arms for a long time, all thought pushed aside by the feeling of full satisfaction. Jacob braced himself above her and traced her soft contours with a reverent hand. He watched his sun-bronzed hand touch her porcelain body and thought the contrast was beautiful. Carolina snuggled against his chest, holding her arms over her breasts, but he would have none of that. He brought her hand to his mouth and nipped the juncture of her thumb and palm before he placed her hand on his hip.

There was a warm liquid glow in his eyes. "Don't hide from me, *wiwaśťeka*. Now is the time for me to enjoy the beauty of what has just become part of me. You have not looked at me, and yet I know your curiosity."

"I didn't imagine it would be this way, Jacob. I thought that men must get some enjoyment from it, but not women. Not unless they were shameless and—"

"Who told you this?"

She glanced away, hoping this was not a betrayal of her sex. "My mother told me, and my aunt was present. She agreed."

"Then you must pity your mother. Her man was not worthy of her."

"My father did not care for my mother. He left her alone much of the time, and he took his pleasures with other women. She said she was relieved, that she was glad he didn't bother her." She smiled at him and touched his cheek. "I wish my mother could have known someone like you."

He dipped his head to kiss her shoulder as he wondered what her mother would have said if she knew that her daughter had come to know someone like him. At the moment, he didn't care. He only wanted to touch, to admire, to know more. The curve of her waist, the plane of her belly, the soft flesh of her breasts. He touched them all and made her blush.

He smiled. "Would you care to touch, too?" She laid her hand on his chest, and he laughed. "Look down, Carolina. Put the last of your fears at rest."

"I am too ashamed," she whispered.

"Ashamed of what we have had together?"

"No. I feel only joy and wonder over what we just had."

"Are you ashamed of me?" His voice held a tight edge.

"No, never, Jacob." She kissed his shoulder just as he had kissed hers. "I am in awe of you."

"Then how are you shamed?"

"I am ashamed to be so bold, Jacob. What would you think of me?"

Jacob pulled her against his chest and laughed at the perversity of the joke white society had played upon its women. Even in their own beds they made love dressed from ankles to chin, the women constrained to maintain a cold attitude toward the whole process or fall from grace. He had listened to the bravado of many a cowboy after a night on the town with a bold woman. He didn't understand how white men measured their sexual prowess when they left their wives so unsatisfied. He vowed that this woman would learn from him, would know the full potential of her response, and would never be satisfied with less.

"Don't laugh at me, Jacob," she pleaded.

He hugged her close. "It's not my laugh on you, it's *our* laugh on *them*. I would think you wanted to see what pleased you."

"*You* pleased me, Jacob. I'm looking at you."

"I have just made love to you, woman. How can it be bold for you to know with your eyes what you have known deep within your body? Give me your hand." She resisted only slightly as he placed it on his half-aroused member. The look in his eyes reassured her, and she took him fully into her hand. "I know I pleased you. And I have no secrets from you now. Is it so terrible?"

"No. It's part of you, and you're beautiful." She smiled up at him. "My hand is cold, isn't it?"

"Yes, but it makes my blood run hotter."

"Jacob, you're—"

"Caress me, Carolina."

"Changing. I hadn't imagined that a man could—"

"That happens when a man desires a woman."

He was hard and velvety, tough and tender, and he could hide nothing from her. She heard his breath catch deep in his throat when she moved her hand. "What did I do?"

"What I did when I touched you."

"Can it be done again so soon?"

He closed his eyes and grinned. "Let us see how hot I can make your blood run."

He took her a second time, bringing them both to a pinnacle of ecstasy as sweet as the first. Afterward they slept in each other's arms.

Chapter Five

Jacob had left their bed. Carolina heard one of the horses nicker and stamp a hoof, and then she heard Jacob speak softly. She couldn't make out the words, but the deep tone of his voice was comforting. Daylight poured in as the door flap was moved aside, and she smiled when he stepped inside wearing only a breechclout and moccasins. He greeted her with a broad grin.

"It's time you got up and took a bath, little one. I want to eat something before I begin the hunt."

Carolina covered herself with a blanket. "What time is it?" she asked.

"Time for the deer to come down to water," he told her.

"But the hour?"

"Did you bring a clock with you?" She laughed, her throat morning-husky, and shook her head. He continued, "Then there are no hours here."

"I was up all night, and now I've slept the day away, and you're going hunting." As she adjusted the blanket around her, she noticed the red stain. Her face grew warm as she tried to cover it, bunching the blanket and clutching it to her breast as she sat up. He came closer, and she cringed. Staring at his moccasins, she dared not look up. A second blanket swooped down over her shoulders, and then Jacob knelt beside her.

"Does it hurt?" he asked gently.

"What?" Her eyes were riveted to the curve of his shoulder, and she held fast to the sign of her humiliation.

"Where I pierced you, Carolina. Is it still painful?"

She shook her head quickly, but she contradicted herself. "It stings a little." He touched her hand, and she glanced up. "You saw?" she asked.

"I was there when it happened." He smiled almost sadly. "Remember?"

She swallowed hard. "It seems to be my time of... But I don't understand how it could be. It isn't—" He tipped her chin up in his hand, and she closed her eyes. "I'm embarrassed, Jacob. Please give me a few moments."

"You knew I would spill your blood the first time, didn't you?"

Her eyes flew open. "You?"

"How do they prepare you, Carolina? Do you learn nothing from the older women?"

"Nothing of any importance, obviously."

He passed his hand over her cheek and slid his fingers into her hair. "Only one man, *wiwaśteka*, and only one time. It will never happen again. You have honored me."

"That's why it hurt?" It was a shy question. He nodded. "And that won't always happen?" He shook his head slowly as he offered his sympathy through his eyes. "The second time it hardly hurt at all," she reported. "I thought perhaps there would always be some pain before... before the rest of it would come."

"The rest of it?"

She put her arms around his neck, forgetting the soiled blanket and her nakedness. "The wonder of it, Jacob. The beautiful feeling."

He wrapped her in the clean blanket and gave her his new moccasins to wear. They both laughed at the way his moccasins dwarfed her feet. He took the soiled blanket, becoming solemn as he folded it.

"When your woman's flow comes upon you, you must warn me. I cannot sleep with you then."

"Why not?"

"It is believed to destroy a man's power, his medicine."

"Do you believe that?"

"A man believes what he learns from those he trusts, from his family. Our beliefs come from the way we know all things to be, and nothing I have learned from the white man changes these things."

"I want to know, Jacob. I may not fully understand your way of thinking, but I want to know everything."

He laughed. "You cannot know *everything*, little one."

"Because I'm white?"

"Because you are a woman, and there are some things a man doesn't tell a woman."

"But I'm supposed to tell you all about my—"

"One word is enough, and I understand that word in two languages. Now come and let me bathe you."

"Come, come. You always say come."

"And you follow." He stepped outside, and she stood, taking a moment to stew over this. Did they have to follow *all* of his customs and *none* of hers? Should her stubbornness take precedence over her bath?

She pushed past the door flap and found him waiting for her with the usual grin.

"Jacob, some things you do seem disrespectful."

"You would have me say, 'After you'?" He imitated the customary gesture.

"It's a small thing. It wouldn't hurt to compromise."

"This suggestion comes from a woman dressed only in a blanket." She blushed easily, and he enjoyed the sight. "In my world, the man is expected to be first to face whatever is on the other side of a door. Does a white man hold the door open while his woman takes the first bullet?"

"Not intentionally."

The light in his eyes drew laughter from her. He reached for her hand, and she followed him to the water's edge, where he dropped the soiled blanket from his hand. He took off his moccasins, and a quick pull on a string left his body bare. She watched him wade into the water with the power and grace of a panther, and she admired him openly. His back was long and brown, tapering to a low waist and small lean buttocks. He spoke to the water as he splashed it over his chest. When he turned, she glanced away, but not quickly enough.

"Are you coming, woman, or do you intend to watch me bathe?"

She grabbed the stained blanket and took it into the water with her, clutching it in front of her in place of the clean one she had discarded on the bank. He laughed as he untied his braids and tossed the buckskin ties ashore.

"It's worse than I expected," he said. "Even without another woman, you cover yourself while you spy on me."

"I'm not spying!" He tugged on the blanket, and she surrendered it to him. He tossed it ashore in the tight ball she'd made of it. "I didn't mean to stare," she amended.

"But I *do* mean to stare." He nodded once in appreciation. "You're worth all the trouble you've caused me, *wiwašteka.*"

"I beg your pardon," she huffed. But she smiled and reached out to him.

"I never beg," he assured her. "At least, I haven't yet. I might if you become too fond of that word I told you about."

"You mean *no*, which in Lakota is—"

"*Hiya*. That's the one." He turned her toward the sun's low rays, then stood behind her and chanted while he ladled water over her breasts from his cupped hand. The sun was still warm, and the cold water made her tingle. Carolina felt blessed. There was no need to ask him what he was doing.

He produced a chunk of soap in his other hand and began lathering her. His hand slipped easily over her skin, and her muscles relaxed. When her turn came, she moved her hands over him slowly, acquainting herself with every firm contour of his arms and chest. She reached his belly and glanced up at him. His eyes challenged her. Her hand disappeared below the waterline, and she cleansed him.

When he filled his hands with her buttocks and pulled her close, she clasped both arms around his waist and laid her cheek against his soapy shoulder. "Jacob, I am becoming shameless," she whispered.

"That pleases me, Carolina. Shame has no place between us. Is it good when I touch you?"

"Wonderful."

"It is also good when you touch me."

"Oh, Jacob, I do want to please you."

He drew away from her, grinning. "Then wash my back, woman."

They washed each other's hair, got soap in each other's eyes, and splashed each other in the face. Like two otters they played, laughing, dunking, laughing again. When they tired of their play, Jacob pulled her close and kissed her, letting her hips float against his beneath the water.

"Ouch!" Carolina shrieked. "How did you do that?"

Jacob tucked his chin and looked down at her, surprised. "What?"

"Pinch my foot. That hurt."

"I didn't." He pulled her downstream a short way.

"What did, then? *Something* pinched my foot."

"Some little water creature," he guessed. "A snapping turtle has a pretty—"

"Snapping turtle! I think I'm clean enough now," she decided. The mud between her toes seemed less innocent as she sloshed toward the bank. "You didn't say anything about any water creatures," she mumbled.

His laughter followed her. "I'm the meanest creature in the water, and you don't seem to fear me."

Carolina wrapped one blanket under her arms and around her body and stooped to rinse her blood from the other one. Jacob was still grinning when he waded back to the riverbank.

"This is not funny, Jacob. Look! I'm bleeding." He examined the small cut on her instep. "I could probably get hydrophobia from a bite like this," she said, pouting.

"I will bind it for you and take the necessary precautions against hydrophobia." He handed her her moccasins, slipped into his own and swept her up into his arms. "The first is to get the victim off her feet."

His eyes twinkled with his grin as he carried her toward the campsite, but she refused to be charmed. "And the second?"

"I can't tell you the secrets of my medicine." He set her down and draped the wet blanket she carried over a bush. "I will tell you only that it involves taking the head from the infected animal and hanging it around the victim's neck for four days."

"You're not hanging any turtle head around *my* neck, Jacob Black Hawk!"

He managed to look offended. "Have you no respect for my medicine?"

"Not if I have to wear a turtle head. Anyway, you can't get hydrophobia from a turtle."

"You can't?" His feigned amazement dissolved into laughter as he picked her up again and carried her to the tipi. "You can get it from me, though. Be careful, woman." He growled and nuzzled her neck. "You're driving me mad."

Jacob built a fire while Carolina dressed. She set a tin cup of water to boil on one of the fire pit stones.

Jacob sat beside her, producing the big rawhide envelope his mother had left. "Are you hungry?" he asked as he untied the fastenings. "I brought dried meat, but this is something you may like better."

Carolina touched the stiff rawhide, moving her fingers over the painted designs of red, blue and yellow. "What do you call this?"

"It's a *parfleche*, made from buffalo hide. Since there's little hide these days, we are not making them anymore." He unfolded the long ends as she watched. "My mother made this long ago."

"And you carry food in these?"

"These were our pantries," he told her. "My father was a good provider when he was a young man, and I remember my mother's *parfleches* hanging in the lodge, always full. Some were left in caches in the ground when the camp moved, so that there would be food when we returned."

When he folded the sides of the envelope back, she leaned closer to peek inside. The contents looked unappetizing. "What is it?"

"We call this *wasna*, which is dried meat ground together with marrow and tallow. Sometimes berries are added for—" He lowered his chin and inhaled deeply. The smell was full of memories. He nodded. "Buffalo berries."

"It looks rather . . . heavy."

He smiled. "We cannot get through a winter on your white flour and red potatoes. *Wasna* keeps the body warm and the spirits high." He touched the food with appreciative fingers. "The time came for us when game was hard to find, and the soldiers hounded us all summer long. When winter set in, the *parfleches* were empty. The people left them lying along the trails they took to the forts, where hunger drove them to surrender. But my mother kept her *parfleches*, even though they were empty. She told my father he would fill them another time."

"I would like to know your mother," Carolina said. The image of hunger made her aware that she had not eaten, and the food in the *parfleche* was looking better all the time.

"You are much like her, little one. You will bring a man strength by your faith in him."

She looked into his eyes and saw his affection. She heard him speak of something she had within herself to give, something he wanted from her, and she thought it was a beginning. She smiled at him. "Why do you call me 'little one'? I've never thought of myself as a small woman."

Her shoulder disappeared under his hand, and he gave her a little squeeze. "You are like the willow—tall for your kind, but delicate. When I hold you in my arms, I'm afraid I might snap these small bones. Our women have strong bones. Their shoulders are made for hauling wood, and their hips for carrying children."

"I can do those things," she protested.

He laughed. "When I saw you standing in the wind, I thought that you would surely be carried away before I could get to you. Now I know that your stubbornness held you to the ground."

"My stubbornness has carried me far."

"Not without food." He held a pinch of *wasna* to her lips. "If you met my mother now, she would scold you for being too thin."

The stuff smelled both meaty and sweet and tasted the same. Carolina chewed slowly. The rich flavor was not at all unappealing. She nodded. "I could eat this."

"You *will* eat this, woman. This or the *papa*."

"*Papa*?"

"*Papa* is dried meat. We also dry wild turnips and onions and corn."

"Corn? But you keep saying you're not farmers."

His eyes twinkled. "Corn is easily stolen."

"Stealing makes one a thief."

"Getting away with it makes one a Lakota warrior, especially if a man brings a few horses home as well."

"Oh, Jacob." She sighed and shook her head. "They hang people for stealing horses."

"So we've learned."

Carolina was relieved when he said nothing more. When Jacob spoke of *we*, he meant his people, and *they* were hers. At the moment, she was his. She and Jacob were *we* and *they* were the rest of the world. Let it remain that way, she thought. Let them all stay away and leave us in peace.

"I can see why this would be good to store for winter." Carolina helped herself to more, and Jacob ate, too.

"It was always taken on the hunt, which is why my mother left this for me. But I have told her to keep hers for the others and stop troubling herself over me."

"She is like all mothers. She worries about the son who's on his own now. With what you provide, she must have meat to spare."

"A few deer and an occasional antelope," he reflected. "There is no food to spare among my people now that the buffalo are gone. It's hard to provide for winter. They live from day to day.''

They ate quietly, savoring what was precious. Then Jacob brushed his hair with a bristle brush and rebraided it, still damp. Carolina washed her wounded foot, and Jacob bound it for her.

"I will not be gone long," he promised her. "The deer come to the river to water at dusk and at dawn. I should not have to go far. Tomorrow you will learn to prepare hides and make meat."

She touched his cheek and nodded. She was anxious to learn. Even before he was gone, she was anxious for his return.

Jacob brought in a large buck shortly after nightfall. He gutted it and cut the throat for bloodletting before he hoisted it high in the trees to keep it from the coyotes. He removed the offal from camp and left it for the scavengers before he cleaned himself up at the river.

"I wanted to make you a hot meal," Carolina told him as they walked to the tipi with their arms about each other's waist. "But I had nothing to cook the meat in, and I wasn't sure—"

"Tomorrow I will teach you. For tonight there is the *wasna*, which is what we are meant to eat on the hunt. As you see, it served me well."

She had kept the fire pit alive with hot coals, and when she added more fuel, it burst into flame. She turned to him and found that he had already undressed. Wordlessly he undressed her. She knew his feeling for her by the way he touched her—carefully, intimately. Their lovemaking was slow and deliberate, as they sought more ways to please each other. Happily sated, they lay in each other's arms, watching the smoke from the small fire rise through the smoke hole and drift toward the stars.

"Will you tell me about the girl you lost?" Carolina asked. "The one you planned to marry."

"Why does a woman ask about the women a man has known before her?"

"Out of jealousy, I suppose." She turned her head to him. "Not vengeful jealousy, but more a wish to be the only woman ever to have touched him."

"Possessive jealousy?"

"A little, I suppose."

"I will put you alone in a room with my mother," he teased. "And then I will listen through the wall."

"But you won't tell me about your fiancée?"

"Fiancée." The word amused him. "Marissa must have given you this bit of information. What else would you like to know?"

"I can't imagine why she would—"

"Choose someone else over me?" He was quiet for a moment. "I don't know that she did. It happened a long time ago."

"What happened? Marissa said she married another man."

"A soldier took her. I never knew whether she chose to go with him. If she did, I assumed it was because he was white. When he left to go to another fort, he left her, too. She could not live with her shame, and she took her life."

Carolina told herself to ask no more, but there was one more thing. Just one more. "Was she very beautiful, Jacob?"

"Yes, she was beautiful. But he did not marry her."

"I'm sorry," she whispered. "I shouldn't ask so many questions."

"It's part of the past, *wiwašteka*. Ask me about the good memories. Let me tell you of those. The dead are best left alone. I get tired of grieving over what is gone."

"Sometimes we must grieve."

"We must live in the present." He touched the soft skin under her chin. "You are here, and I am here with you. We have this time to be together."

Only this time? she wanted to ask. But she didn't, because she was afraid of the answer. "What does *wiwašteka* mean?" she asked instead.

He traced her jaw with his thumb. "It means that you, too, are very beautiful. I call you *beautiful woman*."

"Do you really think so?"

He smiled. "I have said so many times."

"You make me feel beautiful, Jacob. It's a new feeling for me. I feel warm inside, and safe and happy—completely, incredibly happy." He lifted her chin and stretched his neck to offer her a slow, soft kiss. When he drew back to see this happiness in her face, she smiled and touched the ridges of muscle in his chest. "Are you happy, too, Jacob?"

"You give me much pleasure, little one."

"Tell me more of the good memories. Tell me what it would have been like for us when your father was a young man."

He could promise her nothing for the future, but he could give her a dream of an idyllic time when he could have been master of his own destiny. There was little in this camp to remind him of the new life. Under the hide of his tipi, he could look up at the smoke hole and imagine that nothing had changed. The buffalo still roamed in great herds, and his people were still free to travel up and down the grasslands as they had been since the time of the ancient ones.

"Where would I have found you?" he wondered aloud. "Riding in a covered wagon? Would you have come west looking for children to teach?"

"I think I would have driven my own wagon, loaded with books and slates, looking for a little schoolhouse."

"I would have seen you, and you would have touched my soul just as you did when I saw you standing in the wind. I would have taken you, and you would have been mine."

She turned her face to his shoulder. "You must know that I am yours now."

He kissed her forehead and his chest felt tight when she hugged him closer. "If I could make a home for you now, Carolina, you would be mine."

"It's up to the woman to make the home," she reminded him. "Get me the hides, Jacob. I can make you one of these tipis."

His chuckle came to her ear as a rumbling in his chest. "My mother will love you, and I will have two strong-willed women on my hands."

"Yes, you will," she whispered, and she kissed the middle of his breast.

"A home is family—a man and a woman who belong together, whose union is honored so that the woman can bear him children and the man can provide all they need. If I could make that kind of home for you—"

"If you can't, then there is no one who can," she declared fiercely. "I am yours whenever you want me, Jacob."

"Now is all we have, *wiwašteka*, and I want you now."

They claimed each other in the way they made love. They withheld nothing from each other. No promises were necessary. He became part of her, and she knew the important requirements he'd set down were all there—the man, the woman, and the honor between them. The rest, she decided, would come.

Carolina awakened when the morning chilled her bare backside. She straightened the blanket and wrapped herself in it while she listened to the quiet sounds of morning. The river's swift current swooped over fallen limbs and stationary rocks, gurgling as it passed. The mourning dove cooed softly. Carolina stretched and groaned with satisfaction, then rose lazily from her bed, dressed, washed and waited.

Jacob returned to camp with a pronghorn buck and a whitetail doe, both lashed to an improvised travois. He swung his leg over the horse's neck and leaped to the ground, grinning proudly. His woman was waiting, and he'd brought meat.

"If you have water boiling, we'll have tea." Tucking her under his arm, he handed her a small pouch.

She opened the drawstring and smelled the minty leaves inside. "I have a fire going, Jacob, but what am I to boil water in? I searched for something resembling a kettle among your things, but—"

"A kettle? You mean one of those big, clumsy metal things? Bring my saddlebags."

She ducked into the tipi and returned to find him building a fire outside. He dug in the saddlebags for a rawhide cooking pouch and held it out to her. "Does this resemble a kettle?"

"Not at all."

"But my *parfleche* doesn't resemble a pantry, either, does it?" She shook her head. "Yet you will admit that it serves the purpose." She nodded, smiling now. "Will you admit my horse resembles a horse? And my mouth resembles a mouth?" He hooked her about the waist with a quick arm and reeled her in. "See if this resembles a kiss."

"Mmm." When his mouth came away from hers, she had to agree. "It's very much like all the kisses I've ever experienced."

"Shall we see if I have anything else you might recognize?"

"Perhaps you should show me how it works." Her eyes matched his for mischief. "Your kettle, I mean."

"My kettle, indeed." He growled and nipped at her neck. "I've shown you how everything else works."

"The kettle, then."

"The kettle, then, is a paunch. If the soup is bad, I can always eat the kettle."

He showed her how to suspend the paunch over the fire on four sticks. They had tea and *papa*, and then they passed most of the morning skinning the three carcasses and butchering the meat. Carolina learned to fillet the meat in thin strips. Jacob fashioned drying racks high off the ground, so the meat could be cured in the sun. By midafternoon, the bulk of it was prepared, and some was boiling with wild onions in the paunch. He taught her to use the small fleshing knife to scrape the hides so they could be tanned later. She learned that little would be wasted from his kill.

When Carolina finally pushed herself to her feet, her back ached, her hair felt stringy, and her right hand was blistered. Wiping her forehead with her wrist only left a gritty smear across her skin.

"Jacob, if you tell me there's one more job, you're going to hear language you thought no lady would ever use."

He came to her, smiling. He'd been pleased with his kill, but his pride in her had long since surpassed that. She stood while he unbuttoned her dress. "Bathing you will be my job. If you promise not to tell anyone, I will even wash your clothes."

"But what will I put on?"

"My shirt should cover you."

It was an intimate service that only a husband would perform for a wife. When he had washed her, he lifted her in his arms and carried her from the water. She closed her eyes and laid her head against his chest. With his heart thudding close to her ear, she felt as secure as a child in the womb.

Carolina stretched her bare legs toward the fire, savoring the rich, gamey flavor of venison soup. She felt cleansed by the smoke and the spicy, pungent scent of burning sage. Jacob had explained that sage smoke would drive the mosquitoes from their camp, and it seemed to be working.

Dressed in buckskin, Jacob relaxed against a log and watched his woman eat the meat he'd provided for her. In his heart, she was his woman, and her beauty stirred him. Her rich brown hair tumbled over her shoulders, while the firelight created an intriguing shadow play over her soft face. His blue cotton shirt reached only to the middle of her thighs, and her long legs were lovely.

Carolina set the cup aside and glanced up. She'd felt that he was watching her, and she could see the pleasure he was taking in it. "You haven't smoked since we've been here," she observed. "Did you forget your tobacco?"

"No." He patted his chest. "I have it. If I had my pipe, I would smoke that."

"This way of life fits you well. Would you be happy to live this way, here in this camp?" She would have liked to add, "With me."

"If my people could live this way again, I would be happy. Our life was more than hunting and preparing meat." He smiled at her. "And more than making love with a woman, although, when I'm with you, it's hard to remember what more there is."

"There's raiding the corrals and corn patches," she teased.

"Ah, yes, there was that." He chuckled.

"And what else, Jacob? What more?"

He seemed to be absorbed in the fire, entertained by the continuous flickering of its yellow magic. "It was all of us moving as one, sharing one life," he reflected. "There was none of this independence the white man seeks. We needed each other. But there was freedom. Times like this remind me of what it is to be a man among the Lakota."

"You can't go back, Jacob."

He glanced away. "I know that."

"But you are still a man."

"Am I? The men I live with think of me as less than a man."

"Why do you choose not to live among your own people?"

He stared at her now, knowing that there was no way she could know, realizing that even if he told her, she wouldn't understand. She had never seen his people as they had once been, and he dreaded the day when she would see them as they were now.

"It is not my choice. I would choose to go hunting with my friends, and steal horses, and raid the Mandan of their corn."

"Jacob—"

"But I do not choose to wait for the rations to come to the agency, or to trade land for whiskey." His attention drifted back to the fire. "The old men spend their days talking of old times, and the young men can do nothing to prove themselves. A man is required to prove himself, and the old men at least have done that. What are the young men to do?

"Now they have separated us by dividing up this land. The buffalo are gone, and there is no choice but to take what is offered so the women and the children will not starve."

"And you are not farmers," she echoed.

His wry smile reflected his distaste for the word. "We are not farmers. And now we are no longer hunters. Deer hunting does not make a man. We are without our purpose."

She tucked her legs under her and leaned forward. "You must find another purpose, then."

"I tried. I went to school, but I learned nothing that could make a difference for us. I should have learned about the white man's laws, which he uses against us, or of his medicine, which we need because our medicine cannot fight *his* diseases. Instead I learned to shoe horses and lay bricks. Bricks!" He laughed bitterly. "Our people have no bricks."

"You learned to read and write and speak English as well as any man, better than most. If you want to learn the law or medicine, you have the tools."

"But no opportunity. So I train horses for other men to use." He tossed a twig into the fire and watched it become a small torch.

"Why did you take the job?"

"Because they pay me to do it." He looked at her again and sighed. "I will tell you a story. We are great ones for telling stories. Soon after I returned from the East, I went with my father to claim the beef ration. The small bunch of scrawny longhorns were penned up in an area—" he made a corral with his hands "—a little bigger than this clearing. The soldiers entertained themselves by letting our men use their horses and rifles. The men rode around the pen as though they were hunting buffalo." The motions were imitated by his hands. "The game was played with half-dead animals by men who were half-crazy with longing for times past.''

Jacob stared into the fire as he punished himself with the pain of the memory. ''It isn't enough,'' he said finally. ''A man cannot live in the past while his family starves in the present.''

''But you're more man than any I have ever known.''

Jacob's deep, hearty laugh put an end to the somber mood. ''And how many have you known, little one?''

''I have been acquainted with several well enough to know that I didn't want to know them any better.'' He chuckled still, and she pouted. ''Would it matter if I had known a hundred? I know a man when I see one.''

He smiled, admiring her hair. It curved about her shoulders and looked burnished in the firelight. The reflection of the flames danced in her eyes. ''And I know a woman when I hold her in my arms. Come here, Carolina.''

She was drawn to him magnetically. The lacing hung loosely in the deep slit at the front of his buckskin shirt. She knelt beside him and spread her hands over the supple leather. He reached for her, drawing her shoulders toward his as he whispered, ''Kiss me, *wiwašteka*.'' Their tongues danced around each other in imitation of the flickering camp fire flames.

She stretched, sliding against him as he slipped his hands under the long tails of his shirt to clasp her buttocks. Their kiss was warm and wild, an equal proposition. With her hands planted on his chest, she levered herself away from him and took a deep breath. ''Lord, Jacob, if I stick my feet in the fire while you're kissing me, I don't think I'll even notice the difference.''

He kneaded her flesh. ''Would you be as delicious cooked as you are raw, little one?''

''Sometimes you're outrageous.''

"Always. It's my nature." In one swift motion he rolled her over on her back and hooked one leg over both of hers. "And you've become a demanding woman," he muttered against her mouth.

"You seem quite capable—" he nipped at her lips "—of meeting—" and her chin "—any demands I might—" and her lips again "—make."

"Quite capable," he assured her as he dispatched the first button on the shirt she wore.

His kiss sucked her strength away and replaced it with nerves that tingled everywhere and spoke of the need for more of him. She squirmed to get closer, and he rocked against her, promising that there would be more. He brought one nipple to a peak with his thumb and teased the other with his tongue. Lifting his head, he smiled as he moved his hand to caress the expanse between her pelvic bones. "How well are you acquainted with me, little one? Well enough to know whether you want to know me better?"

"Haven't I always known you?" she whispered. "Was there a time before I met you?"

"There is so much you don't know."

"About you?" He nodded. "Then teach me, Jacob. Please. I want to know everything."

He rose to one knee, lifted her and carried her into the tipi. With one hand he swept the shirt from her shoulders and let it fall to the ground. In the shaft of moonlight that shot through the smoke hole overhead, Carolina's body gleamed moonbeam white, its soft curves inviting his touch. He peeled his shirt over his head.

"Show me how this works, Jacob." She'd slipped her hands inside the front of his breechclout. He directed her to the single thong that held both breechclout and leggings, and she untied the knot. The strip of buckskin that was his clout fell away from his anxious manhood. She pushed the leggings down the length of his hard thighs and admired his body, as he did hers. They enjoyed the surge of longing, the sweet torture of waiting a moment longer. And then they reached for each other.

Carolina arched her back and pressed herself tightly against him, biting his shoulder as he lifted her on tiptoe. She turned her face into the hollow of his neck, burrowing past his heavy braid, and breathed deeply of the smell of buckskin and wood smoke. The leather pouches that hung around his neck were squeezed between them.

"Jacob," she said in a small voice, "I know what I need now. I need you deep inside me."

"And I need to be there." His voice was low and husky in her ear. "I have never wanted a woman as I want you—" he lifted her another scant inch "—now." Instinctively she moved her thighs apart and used his legs to brace herself as he supported her bottom in his hands. She gasped when he came straight home to her. He reveled in the feeling, but soon slid away, afraid he'd hurt her. He lowered her to the pallet and entered her again, devoting himself to filling all the empty places inside her with everything he had to give a woman, *this* woman. Stroking her inside, he gave his soul leave to touch hers. He wished her pleasure as his strokes quickened and deepened. He loved her well as he praised her in Lakota.

As the tide roared to a crescendo of release for both of them, Jacob lifted himself high off the pallet, and a guttural, triumphant cry erupted from deep in his throat.

Chapter Six

Jacob disentangled himself carefully from Carolina and covered her with a blanket. Tossing another blanket over his shoulders, he went outside to smother the embers of the camp fire.

His head throbbed. He knew this had gone too far. He'd meant it when he'd told her he had no place in his life for a woman. He had nothing to offer her, but he'd brought her here, and he'd taken from her. Oh, God, he had taken from her, and still he wanted more. He wanted a life with her. He wanted a life of his own making, one he could offer to share with her. But the future of his people plagued him like a festering ulcer. The gnawing pain was nothing to be shared with a woman. And yet he'd come this far.

His people would call him crazy, and hers would call him words for which there was no translation in Lakota. The Lakota did not curse. For all the trouble the white man had brought, Jacob gave him credit for providing words to describe it. No matter how bad a thing was, the white man had a word for it. There were English words for good things, too, but none so lyrical as the name *Carolina*.

Jacob stirred the dying fire and watched the coals break open for one last red hurrah. It seemed incredible to him that a woman had slipped past his shield so quickly, so easily, after all these years. He'd seen it coming and had been able to do nothing to ward it off. It was as though she had been sent to him, and Jacob was not a man to turn away anything his god had ordained. But what was the message? What was the purpose? Had *Ateyapi* somehow failed to see that the woman was white?

Impossible. His god would not have arranged such a thing for either of them. But she had come to him, and she was a balm of sunshine after so many dark, cold winter days. He had rubbed the balm over his skin and allowed the warmth to penetrate. Now she was with him, *within* him; he could not turn his back on her. There would be pain ahead, but tonight there was joy. Tonight they were together because they had come this far. That was the way it was.

He moved quietly. Slipping under the blankets, he drew her into his arms. She turned to hold him. "Jacob," she whispered. He smoothed her hair back from her face and kissed her softly. "Don't leave me," she mumbled.

"Are you awake, little one?" There was no answer, and her breathing was shallow and even. "I won't leave you. I should never have taken you, Carolina. You feel you are bound to me now, and I cannot make you my wife. In time I will have to let you leave me."

At daybreak Jacob stole from the tipi without disturbing Carolina's sleep. She had worked hard the previous day, and today there would be more work. He took his Henry repeating rifle and hung a pouch of shells around his neck. Dressed in breechclout and moccasins, with a knife sheathed at his waist, Jacob rode bareback. If his luck held, he would make his kill and return promptly.

Stationing himself above a bend in the river on a rocky knoll, Jacob faced the river and sang a morning song. His voice was as clear as the morning itself. The first note of his song reverberated deep in his chest. His voice rose to a high nasal pitch, and dropped abruptly at the end of the song. Now he would wait for the deer to come to him.

His patience was rewarded when a stately buck led three does and three fawns to the riverbank. His six-point rack branched beautifully, like a slender willow. While the others drank their fill, he stood guard, twitching his nostrils high in the air.

"I am downwind of you, my brother," Jacob whispered in Lakota. "Like you, I have women and young to feed."

He shouldered the rifle, aimed for a clean kill between the eyes and squeezed off a shot. There was a sharp crack in the morning air, and the deer bounded back into the trees as the buck dropped to the ground with a dull thud. Two young bucks darted from a chokecherry thicket and followed the herd. They would soon test each other, Jacob thought, and then one would take the fallen buck's place.

Jacob hoisted the buck over Sagi's withers and was about to mount behind it when he spotted a patch of prairie flowers amid a scattering of large rocks. Dropping the reins to ground-tie the horse, he smiled to himself as he headed for the flowers. He would be mocked by any self-respecting man who might see him returning from a hunt with a fistful of flowers, but he wanted to see Carolina's face brighten when he gave them to her.

Jacob Black Hawk was rarely caught off guard, especially by anything as predictable as a rattlesnake. There was no warning rattle, no movement in the grass, as he stepped over one of the rocks. It struck with a flash of fangs and tail. Jacob sprang back, and the rattler retreated with a slick swish through the grass.

"Son of a bitch," he hissed as he grabbed for his knife and dropped to the ground. He sliced deeply across the two fang marks on his left calf. He deserved this strike, he told himself. He sucked and spat, sucked and spat. The snake belonged to these rocks, and any hunter knew better than to thread his way among them on foot. He tied the thong of his tobacco pouch above the wound and limped back to the sorrel.

He was only about a mile from camp. When the pain stabbed him, he loosened the thong for a moment and willed the muscles to relax while he used his right leg on the horse. There were no small tooth marks around the two fang punctures, which meant the rattler had not gotten a good hold. Perhaps they had caught each other by surprise and the bite wasn't too bad. He steadied the buck and signaled Sagi for an easy lope.

Carolina's face appeared in the doorway of the tipi, and she smiled as she saw him coming.

"Bring me a rope!" he commanded. She ducked back into the tipi. When she emerged with the rope in her hand, the smile was gone. He gave the carcass a shove. Sagi pranced sideways as it slid to the ground. Jacob took the rope, fashioned a loop and handed it back to her. "Tie the hind legs."

Carolina tried to block the sun with one hand as she squinted up at him. "Is something wrong, Jacob?"

"Do as I say," he managed evenly. He'd done nothing to the carcass but let blood from the throat, and the kill must not be wasted. He tightened the tourniquet around his leg while Carolina secured the loop around the buck's stiffened hocks. When she was finished, she looked up, and he gestured for her to hand the end of the rope to him. He tossed it over a branch, got a good grip and used Sagi's power to hoist the carcass above the ground. Jacob's shaky dismount answered Carolina's question. She moved quickly to his side.

He steadied himself, fighting the encroaching nausea. "I need your help," he told her as he unsheathed his hunting knife.

The blood on his leg caught her eye. "Jacob, what happened? It looks as if you've cut yourself."

"The kill must be gutted," he said tightly. He pushed the heavy blade into the center of the animal's belly and hacked a path through the rib cage.

"You're hurt." She laid her hand on his arm. "I can do this, Jacob. Just tell me how."

He handed her the knife and braced his back against the tree trunk. "Pull out the viscera. Use the knife where they're attached to the bone. You've gutted chickens, haven't you?"

"Of course," she said as she plunged a hand into the still-warm carcass. But never a deer, she thought, and there was a good deal more to be handled. She worked quickly, turning her nose from the smell as the slippery inner parts fell into her hands.

"Save the heart and the kidneys," he told her. "Bring me a piece of the liver."

She did as she was told. He ate the slice of liver even though the process seemed to have left his face drained of its natural color. Carolina's stomach protested.

"Now cut a piece of meat."

She hesitated. Was he going to devour this carcass raw?

"Do it!"

She hurried to comply. "Is all this necessary right now? You need to see to that—"

"Bring the meat," he said between gritted teeth. When she did, he leaned on her heavily and indicated with a gesture that they were to walk. "Away from the camp."

"Jacob—" His scowl got her moving. "How far?"

"How far would you like to keep the ghosts from our camp?"

"Ghosts?"

"*Wanaǧi*. The departed ones." He drew his arm back and pitched the meat as he spoke a few Lakota words.

"Ghosts that eat deer meat?"

"They must be offered a piece of every kill." He nodded toward the tipi and hobbled in that direction, with Carolina serving as his crutch. "Otherwise they will make mischief in our camp tonight."

She hadn't seen him do any of this after yesterday's hunt, and she wondered whether these things were not usually shared with women.

"How did you cut yourself?"

They ducked into the tipi, and he couldn't straighten himself up. She helped him to the pallet. "What you cleaned from the deer must be taken away," he said. "But cook the—"

"Jacob!" She fell on her knees beside him when she saw the pain written in his face. "What is it? What happened?"

"Snakebite."

"What kind?" she asked, her breath coming in quick little bursts.

"Rattlesnake. I sucked most of the poison out, but I'm going to be sick."

"Oh, God in heaven." She touched his leg. "Jacob, a rattlesnake can kill—"

"It's not that bad. You must stay calm, Carolina. I need you."

She had begun to build a backrest for him by covering a saddle with a folded blanket. "We must keep your head above the wound and keep everything clean. Is there a remedy, Jacob? Do you have some medicine?"

He couldn't answer. His eyes rolled as the nausea finally overwhelmed him. She helped him lean to the side, and he retched violently and vomited. He was left trembling from loss of strength.

Carolina removed the soiled blanket and made bandages from her petticoat. His leg had already begun to swell. The wound bled again when she took the tourniquet off, and she washed it with soap and the water she'd been boiling for tea.

"Son of a bitch," he spat as she bandaged his leg.

"I'm sorry. Is that too tight?" When he clenched his jaw and shook his head, she continued, "It's swelling badly. I don't know what else to do."

"You seem to know what you're doing." His lips felt thick, and his tongue had grown heavy. "Snakebite can make a man crazy, but the madness will pass."

"I don't know much about snakes, but I've had experience caring for the sick." She touched his cheek. "You have fever."

"That will pass, too." He fought to keep her in focus, to hold back the swirling black wave that threatened to engulf him, but the effort was wasted.

Carolina knew how to handle fever. Outside, she picketed Sagi and disposed of the guts from the carcass as she'd been instructed. Why hadn't he simply left the thing and come back as soon as he'd been bitten? She hurried back to the tipi with cold water from the river, which she used to sponge Jacob's feverish body. The fever brought tossing, mumbling and, finally, raving, which came mostly in Lakota. Delirium wore him down until finally he only mumbled unintelligibly. During a quiet moment, she fetched fresh water.

She touched the cool buckskin sponge to his chest, and his eyes flew open. He stared wildly. She reached toward his face, and he knocked the sponge from her hand, shouting words she did not understand. She could only tell him, "It's all right, Jacob. You need rest. I'll take care of you while you rest."

For a moment he seemed to recognize her. He covered her hand with his. She turned her palm up and felt that his was hot and dry. He talked to her softly in Lakota, and she recognized the word *wiwašteka*. Then he closed his eyes, muttering, "Damned flowers."

She cooked the organs he'd had her save from the deer in the hope that he would want them soon, and that they would restore his strength. In the camp fire outside the door, a pile of sage burned beneath the paunch. Carolina decided that if it would repel mosquitoes, perhaps it would do the same with flies, and she wanted to keep the camp as clean as possible.

When she found Jacob shuddering with chills, she made a fire inside the tipi, wrapped him in a blanket and sat behind him, straddling him. His face was hot, his lips chalky, and he shivered in Carolina's arms with his head resting between her breasts. Carolina prayed as she rocked him and whispered, "Don't leave me, Jacob. Please don't leave me."

Carolina's head snapped up, and her eyes popped open in time to see a small, barrel-shaped woman step into the tipi. For a moment they just eyed one another. The woman wore a buckskin dress over her cylindrical five-foot frame. There were highlights of silver in her shiny jet braids, and her black eyes glittered at Carolina. She set her jaw in the image of a mother whose offspring was threatened.

Carolina tightened her arms around Jacob as though he might be wrested from her, and her heart pounded. "Are you Jacob's mother? Ina?"

"What are you doing to my son?" the woman demanded as she approached the pallet.

"He was bitten by a rattlesnake this morning." The woman frowned, and Carolina hissed and used a slithering hand to imitate a snake.

"Wagleza?"

"Rattlesnake, yes. He has fever." She touched Jacob's face, and the woman did the same. "And chills," Carolina added. "I was trying to warm him, and I fell asleep." She slid out from under him and laid her hand lovingly against his cheek again. "It seems worse."

The woman knelt beside her son and reached toward the bandages. Carolina drew them back from the swelling flesh and found that the wound had festered.

"Unhcela blaska," the woman said, bracing her hand on one knee as she pushed herself to her feet. Carolina had a fleeting thought that the words could be a death sentence, for all she knew. The woman leaned out the door and called, *"Cunks!"* Then she exchanged words with someone who waited outside.

The fever posed the most immediate threat. The whole tribe might be out there discussing her fate, but the important thing was that Jacob's flesh felt too hot.

"Mrs. Black Hawk—Ina—please help me carry him to the water. Sponging him down isn't enough."

The woman knelt beside the pallet again and touched her son's face as she spoke to him in their native tongue. Jacob opened his eyes and recognized his mother. He managed something of a smile, and he spoke briefly before closing his eyes and drifting off again. Agitated, his mother stirred the embers in the fire, then went outside for a handful of sage. When she had raised a billowing cloud of smoke, she wafted it over her son and chanted a prayer.

Carolina watched. Jacob lay between his mother and herself, but he could do nothing to help her explain her presence, or win this woman's acceptance of it. It was as though Carolina weren't there. When she repeated her plea, the woman regarded her with quiet suspicion.

"Ina." Without opening his eyes, Jacob took Carolina's hand from his chest and held it in his. "I trust this woman. Do as she says."

Between them they were able to carry Jacob to the water's edge and immerse him nearly to his neck. Carolina left her dress on the riverbank and sat with him, supporting his back against her chest. The cold water revived him. He tried to sit up, but Carolina held him fast. "Let me hold you, Jacob. Let the river draw the fever." She soothed him with her hands.

"You will turn my bones to ice, woman."

"The fever makes it seem colder than it is, but this is the way to chase it away."

"You didn't waste the heart, did you?"

She had to think for a moment. "I did as you told me. Everything is taken care of, Jacob."

He nodded and let his head drop back to her shoulder. "My mother speaks some English," he told her.

Carolina whispered close to his ear, "I don't think she likes me."

He found the strength for a quiet chuckle. "You are holding her baby, and she wonders where the hell you came from."

"Why don't you tell her?" She glanced quickly at the woman, who hovered like a blue jay at the water's edge, ready to swoop to her son's defense if this strange woman should step out of line.

"You tell her," he said. "My brain has become a mud puddle."

Ina had watched them long enough to understand that there was an intimacy between her son and this white woman, whose medicine had, indeed, evoked healing power from the river. He seemed lucid. *"Unĥcela blaska,"* she called to them and made a pulverizing motion in her palm with a fist.

"She's going to mash my head, Jacob!"

"She's going to mash some prickly pear and make a poultice."

"Oh."

A young woman appeared in the clearing, carrying a pouch. Jacob's mother met her, spoke with her and took the pouch. "My daughter will help you move him to the lodge," the older woman announced before she disappeared into the tipi.

The girl sloughed off her moccasins and hitched up her brown cotton skirt before she waded into the water. Her blue-black braids hung nearly to her waist against her blue calico blouse. She was beautiful.

"Are you Jacob's sister? What is your name?"

The girl looked down at her toes and wiggled them in the silt just below the water's surface. "I am called Ruth." She looked to be about sixteen. Her small face was heart shaped, and her tawny skin was clear and smooth.

Carolina looked up at her, smiling. "Help me, please, Ruth. We must dry him quickly after we get him out of the water."

"Woman, I am not helpless," Jacob growled.

Ruth supported him on one side, while Carolina maneuvered herself to the other. Jacob was able to bear some of his own weight while they gave him a brisk rubdown with one blanket and wrapped him in another, then took him back to the tipi.

Ruth added wood to the fire while Carolina went outside to get a cup of broth from the paunch. Ina was there, seated by the fire, grinding the cactus mash between two stones. The older woman refused to spare her a glance.

When Carolina got back inside, Jacob's skin seemed cooler. She set the broth aside and tested his chest and his face with a hand she knew to be cold. He looked at her through fever-dazed eyes.

"Is your leg very painful?"

"I have pain, but your medicine is good."

"The wound has festered, Jacob. That scares me."

"The poultice will draw that out."

She picked up the cup and blew into it, creating a cloud of steam. "This is heart soup." She smiled at him. "Can you hold it?"

"I have no appetite now."

"And you have no strength because the fever has sapped it all away." She offered the cup. "Please try, just a little at a time."

"The heart should be eaten raw, just like the—" He sipped and then protested, "First you freeze me, now you burn me! This medicine should kill the rattler's devil if it doesn't finish me first."

Jacob's mother heard the complaint as she came in the door. The humor was lost on her, and she hurried to his side, chattering in Lakota. Carolina saw that she had brought the poultice, and she turned to get clean bandages, unaware that she was being berated.

"*Hiya*, Ina." Jacob rolled his head from side to side. "This woman did not harm me. I was careless, and now I pay the price." Carolina was at his side again, and he reached for her hand. "She is called Carolina. She is a good woman, Ina. We will use English, so that she can understand us."

"She is your woman, *cinks*?" Ina asked in English, as he had told her.

Jacob's silence was his answer. His mother understood that he had done the unthinkable in allowing himself to care for a white woman, and she made no comment. For Carolina, it was a painful lack of what she wanted to hear.

"Then I leave her to watch over you. I will butcher the meat." The older woman handed Carolina the poultice and barked an order at Ruth, and they both left the tipi.

Jacob's silence was deafening. Carolina removed the bandages and examined the angry red flesh around the gash in his leg. When the cactus poultice touched his skin, he drew a quick breath between clenched teeth. Carolina put the pain from her mind as she applied the poultice and loosely bandaged his leg.

"Try some of this now," she offered, holding out the cup again. "It has cooled." After a few sips he shook his head, and she set the cup aside. When she started to get up, he caught her hand, and she settled back down, holding his hand in her lap. It felt clammy now, and still hot.

"Stay with me," he said quietly.

"I'm here, Jacob." She touched his face, and he looked up, smiling a bit. "You've broken a sweat," she told him. "That's a good sign. The water helped." She brought his hand to her lips, and he stretched his fingers to touch her cheek and her hair. "How about your leg? Is the pain...?"

"If a man puts pain from his mind, it becomes easier to bear, little one, but you continue to speak of it."

"I'm sorry. I'll put it from my mind, too."

With a groan, he shifted his back against the saddle. "It was those damned flowers."

"What flowers?"

"I saw flowers among the rocks and wanted them for you. I forgot all lessons about caution."

"You wanted to bring me flowers?"

"You fill my thoughts, *wiwašteka*. I imagined the way you would smile when I brought you the kind of gift white men bring their women."

She looked down at the brown hand she held in her lap, hoping he wouldn't see the woman's tears that had come quickly. She was betrayed by the one that escaped and splashed on his hand. He touched her chin with the tips of his fingers, and she lifted her head.

"I hoped that if I told you about the flowers you would smile for me anyway." She took a swipe at the tears with the back of her hand, and he whispered, "This crying makes my pain worse."

"There are some women who cry when something makes them very happy." She sniffed. "I seem to be a woman after all."

"Was there ever a question?"

She smiled at him through her tears. One of these days he would not be ashamed to claim her before his mother, to call her his woman in so many words. For now, she had the flowers he couldn't get and the words he couldn't say.

"Rest now, Jacob. You must build your strength."

"And you must put on dry clothes. You have a bad habit of standing around in wet clothes, little one."

His eyes drifted shut, and she realized that after she changed, she would be naked under her dress. She peeked through the door and saw Ina and Ruth at work on the buck. The damp camisole and pantaloons were peeled away quickly and hung up to dry. As she buttoned her dress, she felt that she was being watched. She turned slowly. Jacob's smile brightened his eyes.

"I see definite signs of recovery, Mr. Black Hawk."

He chuckled. "I thought all my signs were modestly covered." He closed his eyes, mumbled something about the sand in his clout and drifted to sleep.

Carolina tended him throughout the night. Chills alternated with fever, and it became a battle to keep him covered. At a distance his mother kept a watchful eye over her son, but she said little. Carolina wondered what Ina was thinking about her each time she glimpsed the old woman's unreadable look. Was it true that she was a strange bird in any language?

She catnapped the following day as Jacob's strength increased. Before nightfall he insisted on bathing himself in the river, and he would not be helped by anyone. He swayed when he got to his feet, and Carolina protested. He put his arm around her shoulders to steady himself and assured her, "If we were alone, you would be welcome to share my bath." But he hobbled down to the river on his own, determined to get the sand out of his clout.

Carolina and Jacob slept apart. In only two nights she had come to enjoy the warmth and security of sharing his blanket. She lay awake, listening to his mother snore, and counted five stars through the smoke hole. The fire was out, and she needed to keep it going. She heard his breathing apart from the others', and it was even now, not labored. He would take her back to the ranch soon, too soon, and she would count the hours again until another time for them came.

In the morning, Carolina shared tea and *wasna* with Jacob and his family while he gave them instructions to take the meat and the lodge home with them. He addressed Ruth as *tanksi*, his sister, and Carolina realized that the girl's English was more limited than her mother's. Carolina had insisted that he prop his leg up, and he sat with it stuck out awkwardly in front of him.

"How is my father?" He asked the question as though he did not want to hear the answer.

"He is the same," his mother reported. "The coughing is not so bad in summer. He says his body is weak, since there is no *ta canta*, no *taniga*, no *tanipa*. He has no taste for the *wasicun*—" she glanced at Carolina "—for the white man's beef."

"My father longs for the taste of buffalo meat again," Jacob explained. "My mother names the parts of the carcass that he would choose. But *tatanka* would not take away the *cahuwayazan*, the coughing sickness."

"Consumption?"

"There is another word...."

"Tuberculosis," Carolina supplied.

"Yes. It claims many of our people lately." It was a fact that required a time of silence in the conversation. Then Jacob asked another painful question. "How is my brother?"

"The same," his mother said. She shook her head. "*Iktomi* has a claim on that one, and he cannot leave the evil one alone. His woman comes to me with the little ones when he drives her away with his madness."

"Your brother is sick, too?" Carolina asked. It sounded like some form of insanity.

"He is sick with despair," Jacob said quietly. He watched the dying fire. "He drinks when he can get whiskey, and then he becomes a madman. Even his wife and two small sons are not safe with him when he's like that."

"They are safe with me," Ina said. "I took a stick to him last time. He is worse than a child."

"Is he your younger brother?" Carolina asked.

"I am twenty-eight years. Tokala is thirty-six. He remembers the old freedom better than I do, and it haunts him," Jacob said. "It haunts him," he echoed in a hoarse whisper. There was another period of silence before Jacob turned to his mother again. "Did the beef ration come?"

"We got some meat. There were a few animals. The rest died on the way."

"Like hell they died. Somebody got his cut along the way."

Ina hastened to smile for her son. "We got sugar this time, and coffee. Your father likes that. I would have brought you bread, but the flour—" She made a face, and Carolina laughed, thinking the woman meant to be funny. No one else joined her. Feeling foolish, she hazarded a glance at Jacob.

"Waglula?" he asked his mother. She made a sound that described her disgust. "Worms," he translated. "They expect us to eat it like that. If we have nothing else, we do."

"We have plenty now, *cinks*. You and your woman must keep some of this meat."

"We have no need, Ina. I will keep the *wasna* and regain my strength quickly. See that Ate, my father, eats well, and *tonśkapi*, my nephews, when they come. They must grow strong."

Ina studied her son's face and then his woman's. "You and this woman ... *okiciyuze*? The way of the white man in the church?"

"Hiya, Ina," he said, and the look he gave her warned her to say no more.

But Ina would not be cowed by either of her boys, and her Lakota chastisement quickly came down upon Jacob.

His eyes flashed at her. *"Hiya!"* he snapped. As he spoke further in Lakota, Ina turned to Carolina, and her face softened.

"My son tells me he is your first man," she said. Her tone had changed, and the warmth in her eyes was now for Carolina.

"Ina!" Jacob challenged.

"Haćib, cinks. Hold your tongue. I will speak to this woman in English, as you said. I worried when I saw this white woman holding you, and you so sick. The *waśicun*

brings so much sickness, and now the *wikośka*, that sickness between men and women that makes those who have it walk—"

"Ina, that is enough!"

"I will tell her my thoughts, *cinks*. They were bad when I saw her, but now you say you are her first man. She can bring you no sickness." Carolina's face turned crimson, and she cast her eyes down to her lap. The woman touched her arm in sympathy. "He tells me he has not married you, not the white man's way, not our way. He is wrong to use you like this. I am ashamed for what my son does."

"Please don't be," Carolina said quietly. "He made no promises to me, but I gave myself freely."

"Why have you done this?" Ina asked gently.

"Because I love him," Carolina whispered. There was nothing more to be said.

The meat was packed and lashed to the travois behind Ina's horse. Later she would return to take the lodge home. Now she turned a stern look on her son.

"You said this Carolina was a good woman, *cinks*. It is true. You treat her right. I raised you to know what that means." She turned to Carolina, taking her by the wrist. "You make more meat and feed this woman, *cinks*. Her bones show." Patting Carolina's cheek, she smiled. Soon, she thought, she would have her daughter-in-law and more fine grandchildren. "I will make a good dress and moccasins. We fix you up, and my son will be good to you. You'll see. He is a fine boy."

Together they watched Ina lead Ruth and the horse across the clearing.

"They need those hides," Carolina reflected. "I don't want her to use them to make things for me."

"It will please her to make a gift for you." He turned to her with a quick frown. "You would refuse them?"

"No, Jacob, I would never do that. I would wear them."

He shook his head with mock sadness. "My woman and my mother are two of a kind. They will do what pleases them, no matter what I say." He leaned on her shoulders, and they walked back to the camp fire. It seemed she felt the throbbing in his leg, for she propped it up immediately after he sat down.

"She likes me now, doesn't she, Jacob?"

"She likes you."

"At first she thought I was a loose woman, didn't she? I don't blame her. I know how it must have looked to her."

"Among the whites, it's only those women who look favorably at an Indian man. When there were fewer white people here and we had the upper hand, there was more respect. And it was fine for a white man to take an Indian wife. They say Yellow Hair had one."

"Custer?"

The look on her face made him laugh. "No one speaks of it. It would embarrass both of his widows."

"You wouldn't...you couldn't have more than one wife, could you?"

"A man has as many wives as he can support, little one, which is why I have none in these times."

She pouted. "I never know when you're teasing."

"Then let me tell you that what I will say now is true." She raised her eyes, and he looked through them into her heart. "I did not mean to tell my mother of the things that are private between us, Carolina, but I could not let her believe what she did about you."

"I know."

"My mother thinks that a new dress and an occasional deer are enough to offer a woman, that I could make a life for us this way. She knows little of the world as it is now."

"She knows that your father and brother are ill, and that the flour comes with worms."

"Still, the children must be fed."

"That's right, Jacob. She knows what all women know. She knows what's important."

Jacob could not comment. He knew what she waited to hear, and he could not say it. When a man declared his love, there was a promise in it, and he could promise only that one day she would turn to another man for the home and family every woman wanted. That thought gnawed at his gut. Another man would one day hold her, touch her. By God, he would kill any man who...

He reached for her suddenly and pulled her into his arms. Her startled look was not lost on him as he lowered his head like an eagle snatching a cornered rabbit. His groan gave voice to the ache in his heart as his tongue slipped past her lips and sought hers. They were both shaken when he drew back abruptly and pressed her head against his chest, holding her fiercely.

"My love is important to you, Jacob. You can't deny that now." She tightened her arms around him.

"Yes. It's important to me. I will give you what I can, little one, but your people must not know about us. I will not have you walk in shame."

"Jacob, Jacob, I could never feel shame."

"Before God, Carolina, when will you understand? You don't know what it means to be taunted by men who are not fit to crawl the earth on their bellies. To the victor belongs the spoils, they say. And what belongs to those who are defeated?"

"I don't know," she whispered against his chest. "I only know I belong to you."

"Your woman's heart is talking. I swallow my pride every day of my life when I am among your people, and I will not subject you to that. The women would make wide circles when they walked by you. They would hold their skirts to the side so that nothing would touch the woman who belonged to an Indian. And they would never let you teach their precious children."

"Do you think their acceptance is that important to me? They've never liked the woman I am. If you offer me a choice, Jacob—"

"I offer you no choice, because I have none. If there were any corner of this land left untouched by the white man, I would go there and take you with me. But there is no such place. The United States government tells me where I am to live, and I am not even a citizen of the United States. I am a citizen of the Hunkpapa, a dying society."

"Jacob, we are about to enter a new century. The strife between our people will soon be forgotten. After the war is over, there are no more enemies."

He rubbed her back and reminded himself that she was a woman, and they all thought this way. They were not warriors. They were soft, and they gave a man such a comfortable feeling when he let them lull away his hardness. He buried his nose in her hair.

"The Pawnee, the Crow and the Chippewa have been our enemies for centuries. I have read books about your wars, little one. It is the same with you. Long after the causes are forgotten, the suspicion remains."

"Sometimes," she admitted. "Not always."

"Not when the enemy is made childlike in his dependency? I doubt that I will ever be allowed to vote for the men who decide who gets what land and how much beef ration."

"I can't vote, either."

He laughed. "There, you see what a powerless pair we are? No, *wiwaśteka*, I will come to you at night, and I will hold you and make love to you. That much I can give you. but in the daylight I will protect your good name. That I can give you, too. And one day soon another man will come into your life, one who can give you a home—"

"There will be no other man," she countered firmly.

He held her away from him and looked deeply into her eyes. "When he does come, keep him out of my sight. If I see him touch you, I know that I will forget all I've said. And I will kill him."

Chapter Seven

No one was about when Carolina and Jacob rode into the yard at the ranch that evening. Carolina slipped down from the mare's back and handed Jacob the reins. "I plan to go back to the cabin in the morning," she told him. He nodded. "You will come to see me?"

"When I can." The throbbing had been almost unbearable during the last few miles as the blood pumped into his leg. If he didn't get off this horse soon he would surely humiliate himself. He glowered at her when he felt the light touch of her hand on his knee, but he couldn't scold her for the concern he saw in her eyes.

"Take care of your leg. Keep it propped up as much as you can. I'm sure that Charles—"

"Let me go, little one," he whispered. His anguish became twofold as she backed away.

No sooner was Carolina inside the door than Marissa grabbed her by the arm and pulled her into the bedroom. "Have you gone mad, Carolina? Where have you been? Do you realize what could have happened if anyone else had known about this?"

Carolina glanced away. "About what?"

"You've been with Jacob."

Carolina walked to the window, hoping for a glimpse of him. "Who else knows?"

"No one. I didn't even tell Charles. He thinks Jacob went hunting."

"How did you know?"

"I saw you ride up together, Carolina."

"Perhaps we just happened to—"

With a hand on her arm, Marissa pulled Carolina around. Carolina shrugged away, but Marissa would not back down. "I knew you were with him when I went to the cabin and you were gone. The tongues would fly, Carolina."

"Then keep it to yourself and let the tongues be still."

Marissa drew a deep breath and exhaled slowly as the two women eyed one another. "I don't want to see either of you hurt," she said evenly.

"We are two adults. We know all about life's pain."

"Listen to me, my friend. You are a white woman. Jacob is an Indian man. It is—"

Carolina's hands flew to her ears. "Don't tell me that, Marissa. I have heard it and heard it and heard it."

"All right." Marissa took Carolina's hands in her own and was permitted to lower them slowly. "All right, I won't talk about that. I'll talk about Jacob. You can't know the pain of this as he knows it, Carolina, because you have never—"

"He was bitten by a rattlesnake."

"What?"

Carolina squeezed Marissa's hands. "A rattlesnake bit him. He took me hunting with him, Marissa. That's where we've been. His mother and I were able to do the right things for him, but his leg is still badly swollen."

"My Lord! He might have died!" Marissa exclaimed. "And his mother was with you?"

Carolina nodded, knowing how much better that made things sound. "And his sister, Ruth."

"Then he's all right now?"

She nodded again. "I think so. He was very sick for a while."

Marissa led Carolina to the bed, and they both sat down. "Carolina, you must be careful. If people see you with Jacob, they'll be getting the wrong impression."

"And what is the wrong impression?"

Marissa considered Carolina's face. There was defiance there, and pride, and a readiness to defend the one for whom she obviously cared. "It's too late for all my warnings, isn't it?"

"If you mean—"

"I mean it really can't matter anymore whether he's an Indian or a prince."

"You're an Indian, Marissa," Carolina reminded her stubbornly. "Does that matter to Charles?"

"No. Between the two of us those distinctions ceased to exist long ago." Carolina looked satisfied. "But, as far as anyone else is concerned, I'm not much of an Indian. I'm my husband's wife. Don't you see, Carolina? I am not Lakota anymore, but Jacob *is*. That will never change."

"It shouldn't have to change."

"No, it shouldn't." Marissa sighed. There were times when she was uncomfortable about her ancestry. There were other times when she felt a vague loneliness, a deep tugging that pulsed to the beat of some distant drum. "Jacob walks a narrow fence," she said finally. "He's educated, wise to both worlds, and he could be a bridge from one to the other for his people. But the people around here would give him trouble—and you—if they knew."

"So I've been told." Carolina's eyes burned as she turned toward Marissa. "It's not hopeless, is it?"

"Would it make a difference if I said it was?" Carolina shook her head. "Of course not," Marissa continued. "The man you love is the man you love. We women know that. And if he's a good man, there's hope in that fact alone."

"He says he can't offer me anything. I don't need things, Marissa. I need Jacob."

Marissa pulled a lace-edged hanky from her sleeve and handed it to Carolina. "He does have a job," she reasoned. "Over the years Charles has often paid him in horses, but he's had a time getting Jacob to keep any for himself. Jacob is forever giving them to relatives who need bride gifts or whatever. But Jacob does have some fine breeding stock and a good reputation for training horses. So he could support himself. And you."

"Being in business would probably go against his grain."

"Maybe at first. I think that Jacob feels he must suffer whatever his people suffer, and yet he can't be idle. He can't abide the useless feeling that is strangling so many of the young men."

Carolina blotted her tears and dabbed at her nose. "He has land."

"He's one of the few who understands what that means," Marissa said.

"But he hates the idea of using it."

"He'll have to get used to it. He knows that. The Lakota are accustomed to working for the good of the group rather than each man making his own living."

Carolina chuckled as she heard his voice in her head. "And he is not a farmer."

"No, but he's taken the first step. Working here helps him keep his self-respect and gives him a way to help his family. Besides horses, that's where his pay goes."

"He'd like to learn a profession," Carolina remembered as she rose from the bed. She went to the washstand, poured water into the lavabo and continued. "Like the law or medicine, so that he could help his people."

"I'm sure he would. Then he could give himself to them, lock, stock and barrel. He has no ambition to acquire property or money, but he has his pride."

Carolina cupped her hands in the bowl. "He disdains pride," she said as she brought the water to her face.

"There's pride and there's *pride*. He would have to be able to provide for a wife and family himself, and not let the government do it for him."

"Why doesn't he think he can?" The water dribbled from her chin as she dipped her hands for more.

"You have to see it, Carolina. The people waiting in line for their rations."

"He doesn't have to do that."

"But *they* do. Jacob is one of the few who knows how our system works, but his heart tells him the old way is better, even as his brain tells him the old way is dead and that the bones are strewn across the prairie to prove it."

"He's caught in the middle," Carolina acknowledged as she dried her face. "I'll wait," she said quietly. "And I'll be there whenever he—" Her face flushed instantly beneath the towel.

"Whenever he wants you." Marissa walked up behind her. "I love my man that way, too. We're fortunate. Some women never know how that feels."

"I know." Carolina hung the towel on the bar. "I'd like to use your mare, if you don't mind, Marissa. I want to go home soon."

"You're welcome to the mare." She put a hand on Carolina's shoulder. "Don't hurry off, Carolina. Get some rest. The men are out behind the barn butchering the beef for the barbecue that will follow the branding. Please stay for the doings."

Carolina turned, smiling wistfully. "I've learned a lot about butchering in the last few days. Do you think I could learn to brand a calf?"

"I think you could learn to fly to the moon if you got stuck on the notion, my friend."

There was a carnival atmosphere about branding, which was an event that brought neighbors together more than it was a chore. All the cattle that could be rousted out of the coulees had been rounded up and herded in close to the corrals. The calves were chased into several large wire pens. Fires burned in each pen, and branding irons were thrust into the coals to heat. Men raced around on horseback to rope the calves. When he had one on the line, a cowboy would throw the animal to the ground and tie its legs while his horse backed up on the rope to keep it taut.

Other hands carried the hot iron to the calves and sizzled hide and hair with the Bar MAC brand. Clouds of acrid smoke filled the air. Calves bawled, cows bellowed, and cowboys cussed, barked orders, joked with one another and showed off their skills in as obvious a manner as possible.

The women were in the house preparing a feast. They shared the latest gossip while they made dinner. Little girls shrieked while little boys chased them and pulled their braids. Then the girls ambushed the boys for a buss on the cheek. All but the calves considered the whole affair to be good fun.

Carolina met the Friedricks, who had two strapping blond-headed boys of fourteen and eleven years, Rolf and Willy. Wilda Friedrick told Carolina that if the two misbehaved in school, she was to take a stick to them. Carolina took one look at the angelic expressions on their faces and knew she would have to catch them first. Their mother excused them, and they ran to torment pretty little Nancy

Laughlin. At twelve, her soft new curves attracted more attention than she knew how to handle. Her older brother, Tom, was in for many a battle over her. There were also two younger Laughlins who would be in school: Sarah, who was nine, and seven-year-old Michael.

The Rieger family also had four school-age children: Maddie, John, Adolf and Dierdre. They were particularly well-behaved, and fifteen-year-old Maddie, who considered herself to be too old for school, explained that she would be there this year only to see that the younger children got to school and back safely.

The school would be built at a spot where the boundaries of the four families' land came close to meeting. Charles was the only real rancher in the group. The others had a few head of cattle, but mainly they were farmers, which was not an easy vocation in this mid-Dakota land.

Carolina made polite conversation with the women while they turned Marissa's kitchen into a food factory. Marissa had baked bread and pies in advance. The beef was roasting in a large pit outdoors. Now the women boiled a bushel of small red potatoes. Vegetables, some fresh and some put up in jars the previous summer, were steamed in great kettles. Hilda Rieger contributed her famous prune kuchen. She had pans of pastry dough spread on the table, where she and Maddie worked together as a mother-daughter team to add the filling.

Marissa was in her glory. This was the time of year when the neighbors got together to help one another with big jobs like this. Later there would be threshings. The MacAllistairs' was by far the biggest branding, but with many hands to do the work, the labor became a festival, with Marissa as hostess. She played her role well. She had a way of making each woman feel that, above all others, she was particularly welcome.

At dinnertime Charles came bounding into the kitchen, his eyes still watering from the smoke. He was a gentleman rancher who generally let the cowboys do the dirty work, but he knew his business, and today he enjoyed being in the thick of the activity. He was a tall, trim, handsome man who looked distinguished even in his dusty denim pants and battered brown hat. His gray sideburns hinted that he was somewhat older than his wife, who glanced up from the kettle she was removing from the stove to offer her husband a warm smile.

"We're hungrier than a pack of wolves, ladies," Charles announced. "The boys are digging the beef out."

"Everything is ready here. How's the gravy doing, Mary?"

Mary Laughlin looked up from her stirring. "Bubbling up like a hot spring."

"Well, ladies," Marissa said, "shall we feed these wolves before they go after our children?"

The women filed from the kitchen carrying steaming kettles, each one offering its own tempting aroma. A long serving table had been fashioned from planks. They set the kettles there with a stack of tin plates and a box of silverware. The children swarmed around a large vat of apple cider, while the men surrounded the water pump, hoping to cool off as much as to clean themselves up. Charles was overseer for the carving of the beef, which had been roasted in quarters and now was hoisted to a huge wooden slab near the serving table. The rich aroma of roast meat overshadowed all other smells. All noses were drawn to it, and all mouths watered.

The men were served first, followed by the children. The women served themselves last, when the others were working on dessert.

"Carolina," Marissa hailed loudly, "one of the men is laid up with snakebite. Would you be a dear and take some dinner to him?"

No one asked why one of the children wasn't sent, but everyone knew that none of the men would be asked to run errands on branding day. Everyone but Culley.

"I'll take a plate out to the Injun, Miz MacAllistair."

Marissa hadn't noticed that Culley was still hanging around the table, but now his eager nose suddenly appeared at her shoulder. She turned, smiled and allowed her eyes to harden. "I believe the tack room is off-limits to you, Mr. Culley. Anyway, we have no intention of asking a hard-working man to help us serve dinner."

He shrugged and shoveled more pie into his mouth.

Carolina prepared a plate, covered it with a napkin and headed for the barn. She pulled the creaking door open and wondered if Jacob had been sleeping. If he had, he wouldn't be now. At the door to the tack room she called out, "It's Carolina. No weapons are necessary." With a sweet smile she sauntered into the tack room.

He was sitting up on the cot, his back against the wall, with his bad leg propped up. A cigarette hung from the corner of his mouth, and his hands were busy with some leather work. He looked up from it slowly, his eyes cool. She could just as well have been one of the cowboys, she thought. Her smile faded.

"I brought your dinner. How is your leg?"

He drew on the cigarette, plucked it from his mouth and swung his hand down off the side of the bed. He wore only a clout and moccasins. He hadn't expected visitors.

"I told you to stay away when there are people around." He blew a gray cloud, and his eyes glittered behind it.

"Marissa asked me to bring this to you, Mr. Black Hawk. You're lucky it's me. It could have been Culley." She approached him with a tentative smile. "There's a lot of commotion out there. No one's paying much attention. You have to eat sometime, you know."

"The fine ladies out there would choke on their apple pie if they saw you in here with me, especially dressed like this."

"I'm sure none of them is about to come in here, so let's not waste time worrying about that prospect. I want to know how your leg feels. Is the swelling going down?" She handed him the plate and sat on the big wooden box near the bed. He took another deep drag of his cigarette before snuffing it out in the jar lid on the floor.

"It hurt like a son of a bitch last night." Maybe if he played the role of the crude cowboy she would get herself out of here, he thought. "But as soon as I can get my pants on over it, I can get back to work."

"I'll change the bandage after you eat."

"I can do that myself."

"I'm already here, Jacob, and I want to see for myself whether the infection is gone."

"Have you been meeting your future students?" His look was stony. "If you're here to teach, you must have students. You won't have any if you stay in here much longer."

"It's amazing what a different person you are when you're here at the ranch. You talk differently, act differently."

He shrugged. "The two faces of Black Hawk. You should know them both if you're going to insist upon—"

"This one isn't you," she said quickly before he could say something hurtful.

"Yes, it is, Carolina. I told you how it must be with us, and you must accept that. I cannot see you here. I will see you when I can, but not here."

She sighed. "Eat your dinner, Mr. Black Hawk. I won't argue with you. But I will change that bandage, and if you try to stop me, there will be a wrestling match between us, I can assure you."

He could imagine just that happening, and he had to laugh. "You are a stubborn woman, Miss Hammond." He proceeded to eat quickly, so that she could do what she was determined to do and get out. From the corner of his eye he watched her rummaging through his saddlebags, where she had packed the bandages herself. He could have told her that a woman did not meddle with a man's property, but he hadn't gotten far in telling her to leave.

She took the plate from him. "I wish I had brought whiskey, too," she said as she leaned over the bandaged leg.

"Do you want to make me crazy?"

"Not for drinking. It can also be used for cleaning wounds."

"Then it serves only one good purpose," he grumbled as he watched her cut the bandages away.

"I should boil some water and wash this," she decided as she examined the wound. The flesh had begun to knit itself together.

"That would call for a fire, little one. There isn't time."

The endearment made her smile. He was softening. She went to the stove and laid a small fire. "If I sneak back into the house through the front door and emerge from the back door, people will probably assume I've been in the house for some time. Will that satisfy your sense of propriety?"

"You will regret your lack of respect for my decisions if I have to become strict with you, woman. Disobedience is not tolerated among the Lakota."

She put a pot of water on the stove and went to kneel beside him. Her hand was drawn to touch his chest. Her touch was feather light, and her eyes were warm with love. He started to speak, but her fingers flew to his lips to silence his objections. "What would you do to me, Jacob? How strict would you be? I only want you to touch me. You wouldn't beat me for that."

His hand closed over hers, and he kissed her fingertips. "I would never beat you, little one. And I ache to touch you."

"Touch me, then."

"I could not stop at that."

"Kiss me just once, Jacob."

"Don't do this, Carolina," he warned gently. "Not here. Not now."

She dropped her head to his chest. "I need to know you want me as much as I want you."

He groaned. "Move your hand just a little lower if you need proof."

She turned her lips to the satin of his skin. "Neither of us could hold back if I did that." He swallowed hard and stroked her back. "Jacob, give me your promise that you'll find a way to come to the cabin as soon as you can ride."

"I have said I would."

"I shouldn't ask," she whispered. "I know that. A woman shouldn't ask."

"Why not?"

"My behavior is shameful."

"There is no shame between us." He brought her hand to his lips for another kiss, the only one he dared give her now. "I will come to you only if that's true."

She looked up. "No shame between us," she echoed. "I'm not ashamed to want you."

"Then I will come as soon as I can ride. Now leave me before I lose touch with my senses, little one."

She cleaned the wound and bound it, satisfied that the infection was no longer a problem. "Everything must be kept clean, Jacob, the wound, the bandages—everything.

Keep this leg up as much as possible, and the swelling will soon be gone.''

"You women get too bossy when a man is laid up for a while. You're all the same.''

"Then any one of us should do nicely for any one of you.''

He laughed. "Life would be simpler if that were true.''

"No, it wouldn't,'' she decided. "It would be much more complicated in the long run.''

She prepared to leave him to his leather work. Then she hesitated. "Jacob...''

"I'll be there, little one. We'll talk then.''

"Take care of your leg.'' He nodded, and she hurried out the door.

Chapter Eight

Carolina's precious plantings had wilted in the interim. Reviving the garden would take more than a miracle, but she poured water into the little irrigation troughs she'd dug until most of the parched plants rallied. Like most newly transplanted women, she'd brought the seeds of an Eastern flower garden along with her, and every container she could find had been planted. Her morning glories were already at home with the wild grass, and the marigolds and portulaca were hardy, but the petunias were fading. It took her best efforts to bring them back to life. She wished for a tree in the yard, just one tree. The stand of cottonwoods was too distant, and it left her little cabin looking naked.

North Dakota was not New England, she reminded herself as she loosened the crusty soil around the Juneberry cuttings she'd planted. She didn't want it to be. North Dakota was a new state. Surely here a woman didn't have to pretend she might wilt like one of these plants if some man didn't tend her. Jacob didn't expect her to be a shrinking violet. He welcomed her honest responses to him and did not judge her for her lack of feminine wiles. Their only problem seemed to be that he didn't think she could withstand the rejection of a few snippy matrons and most of the white male population. She'd tried to tell him that she had ignored their foolish notions for some years now.

In time he would see the stuff she was made of, she told herself. And they had time. He had promised to come to her when he could. Meanwhile she tended her garden, prepared lessons for her students and sewed. She made a divided skirt for riding astride, which was the style she planned to use in the future. If Marissa could do without a sidesaddle, then Carolina could, as well. As far as she could tell, her friend's femininity had not been in any way compromised by riding with the horse between her legs.

The shirt she made for Jacob was a labor of love. She used a soft lawn fabric the color of ivory. Remembering the beadwork designs on his moccasins, she embroidered a similar pattern on the sleeves from shoulder to cuff.

Nearly a week had passed. It was dusk when she heard the mare nicker and another horse respond. She saw him through the window, and her heartbeat accelerated as she sailed out the door. He slid down from the horse's back, still favoring his left leg, but he had, indeed, gotten into his pants. Carolina stopped just short of throwing herself into his arms, but she couldn't help grinning foolishly at him. He grinned back, his eyes brightening at the sight of her.

She moved closer, but felt suddenly shy. "It's good to see you, Jacob."

He laughed. "How good?"

She leaned into his arms, nestling her face in the side of his neck. "How do the Hunkpapa say *good*?"

"Wašté." He slid his hands along the length of her back.

"How do you say that something is *very* good?"

"We say *lila wašté.*"

She tightened her arms around his waist. "Seeing you is *lila wašté,*" she whispered.

"Woman, I have missed you," he breathed against her hair.

Sagi interrupted with a plaintive whinny and a toss of his head. The mare nickered again. Jacob chuckled, nodding as Sagi curled his lip back over his nostrils and sniffed. "The urge is that great, is it, old friend? What happened to your dignity? Your proud bearing?" The horse lifted his muzzle to the sky, and Jacob shook his head. "There's no help for it, is there? She's too close, and your need is too great." He smiled at Carolina. "Our one great weakness."

She laughed. "I beg your pardon. I think some men have a few more."

"For Sagi, the weakness is for this mare until the scent of the next one reaches him." He cupped her cheek in his hand. "I have only one weakness, little one. I cannot stay away from you."

"Don't try."

He lowered his head in obedience, giving her the kiss that had been in his mind for days. It was like coming home. At his back the stallion protested, and Carolina smiled against Jacob's mouth. "Let him have what he wants, Jacob." She shifted her eyes without turning her head. "The mare is as ready as he."

"Is she?" He glanced toward the corral. "Then it's decided. Marissa will have a new foal."

He turned Sagi in with the mare and led Carolina to the cabin. She stood behind him while he lit the lamp and turned the wick down. He took the time to admire her prim, high-necked blue dress with its little tucks and the tiny buttons that marched in a line between her breasts all the way to her waist. Her hair was fastened properly in a bun at her nape, but there was nothing prim or proper about the look of anticipation in her blue eyes. It was she who crossed the distance between them, moistening her lips with the tip of her tongue. He smiled at the gesture, but when she reached him, he took her by the shoulders and turned her around.

He wanted to touch her long silky hair, and he felt for the pins and plucked them out. Her hair waved softly as he combed through it with his fingers before smoothing it aside for a kiss just beneath her ear. Something warm surged through her body when he reached over her shoulders and unbuttoned her dress. He tucked his hands inside, crossing them over to cup a breast in each one while he nuzzled her neck. She leaned back against him and closed her eyes.

The dress fell to the floor, but there was more clothing underneath it. "Carolina?" he whispered.

She shivered with the feel of his breath on her neck. "Hmm?"

"How long does it take you to dress?"

"Not as long as it's taking you to undress me." She unfastened her petticoat and let it fall atop the dress. His chuckle rumbled in his chest as he whisked her into his arms and carried her to the bed.

He watched her remove shoes and stockings, suppressing the amusement he always wanted to express when he saw *wašicun* shoes. He unbuttoned his own cotton shirt and freed it from his pants. Watching her slide her little bottom toward the fluffy pillows, he tossed his shirt aside and unbuckled his belt. In a moment he was again as he had been at the camp by the river—naked except for his clout.

Carolina giggled. "A breechclout under your denim pants?"

"I didn't laugh at your shoes, woman." But he laughed now. "What would you have me wear? Those long drawers? I take what I like from the white man. What I don't like, he can keep." He planted one knee on the bed and loomed large above her. "I like you."

He dispatched the rest of her ribbons and strings quickly, and she was again as she had been at the camp by the river— a pink blush tinting her creamy skin. And she was his.

He came to her slowly, nuzzling her breasts. She found the knot that held his breechclout, freed it and pushed the buckskin away. He raised his head and teased her with a sparkling grin.

"I like you, too." Coquetry danced in her eyes as she took a thick braid in each hand and pulled his head down. He opened his mouth over hers, and she responded to his tongue with her own. She gave him kiss for kiss. When he nuzzled his way along her neck, she pushed his hair back and caught his earlobe in her teeth. Hot and hard, he throbbed against her thigh. He tasted her breasts with his tongue and slipped his hand between her thighs. Her legs parted for him, and she arched herself against his palm.

A high-pitched equine squeal sounded outside the cabin.

"Jacob," Carolina breathed, "is that animal teasing the poor mare as you are me?"

"No, he isn't." He touched her nipple with the tip of his finger. "But his pleasure is brief, and it makes no difference to him whether the mare shares in it." He took the nipple in his mouth.

"Take me with you to the sun, Jacob."

"To the stars, this time," he promised as he rose above her. "To a place of our own."

Jacob wondered at finding such peace in a cabin, in a spool bed and in the arms of a white woman. It was like being in a cocoon for two. Here he could empty himself of everything he had kept to himself for so long, and she refilled him with her love. Everything about her was unexpected. He wove his fingers into her long, luxuriant hair and lifted it away from her. Who would have believed that the tight knot she wore at the back of her head was really made of this beautiful stuff?

"Jacob," she whispered simply because she loved the sound of his name. "Jacob Black Hawk."

"What would you have me do for you, little one?" He gloried in the touch of her hand over his chest. "Name anything."

"Talk to me. Tell me all there is to tell. From the beginning."

He laughed. "The beginning of Black Hawk? You would have to ask my mother, and I would take my nephews hunting while she told you her mother's tales."

"Tell me about the other pouch, then." She lifted the small buckskin bundle and weighed it in her hand. "What's inside it?"

"Things that mean something to me, that recall my vision and my name. I cannot name them. It is my medicine, and it protects me."

She laid it carefully back on his chest, willing it to continue to do its job. "What is the name your mother calls you?"

"*Cinks*. It means *my son*. And *cunks* means *my daughter*."

"What did you call Ruth?"

"*Tanksi*. My little sister. *Ciye* is my older brother."

"Don't you call each other by your names?"

"Not within our family. It is our way to speak of our relationship when we speak to each other. Anyone can call a man by his name, but only a special person calls him *son* or *brother*."

She had dismissed her estrangement from what family she had left as good riddance, but now she felt cheated. "And do you address all your relatives that way?" she asked.

"My mother's brother is *lekši*, my uncle, and my father's brother is also father to me, which is *ate*. It is the same with my aunts. My mother's sister is also my mother."

"Why is that?"

"We have no orphans. If a father dies, his brother becomes father to his children."

"What do you do for the children of a father who doesn't want them?"

"A person like that is not a man. Every man wants his children."

"Not *every* man," she said quietly.

He thought this over for a moment. "Among my people, there would always be a father for such a child. Our families are more than parents and children. We are aunts, uncles, cousins, grandparents, and we are together in all things."

"All in one tipi?"

"No. Together in good times and bad times, in making our way. We are a circle, little one. Family means a great deal to us."

"It means nothing to my father," Carolina said. "He loves business." She laughed bitterly. "He says it's a *family* business, but it's a poor substitute for what you describe. It must be a secure feeling to be a Lakota child."

"When I was a young boy, life was good for us. Things have changed very much since then." He thought about his nephews and the threat of his brother's madness. "We are people, too, Carolina, like your people. There are the strong and the weak. Among us there are the bad tempered and the patient, the selfish and the generous, the cowardly and the courageous. And with all that, we had a good life once."

Resentment niggled at her. He was part of something else, even though much of it was a memory. Her way of life had crowded his out, and the life of his people was lived in dreams. She wanted to be part of the dream because he cherished it so. She could not be part of the memory, but perhaps she could make a place for herself in the dream.

"Do you think in Lakota or in English?" she asked him. She had studied Latin and French, but they were only part of an academic life.

"Both," he told her. "It depends on what I'm thinking about. I have spent much of my life speaking English, and what I have learned from the white man is in my mind in English. But I see the earth and the sky as a Lakota. What is closest to my heart is in my mind in Lakota."

"And how do you think of me?"

His arms closed around her possessively, and he drew her to him. "You are *wiwaśteka*. Beautiful woman." His lips brushed her forehead, and his fingertips moved slowly along her spine. "You are *skuyēla*, sweet, and *skuya*, delicious. You are *wankala*, tender and soft. I think of you in Lakota, little one. You have become part of me."

Her heart soared. To be part of him, *part* of him. "I was hollow inside before I met you. You've filled me, Jacob."

"I knew emptiness, also. You have given me much joy."

It was not the time to suggest to him that this joy could last a lifetime if they stayed together. He was at ease with the past, but not with the future. And the present felt good. It was good to lie there beside him and feel warm in his arms. It was good to plant small kisses on his chest, listen to his heartbeat and feel his breath on her forehead.

"Do you want me again, little one?"

When had she clamped his thigh between her knees? "I don't seem to be the proper lady at all anymore." His laughter sounded deliciously wicked, but she protested. "Don't laugh at me, Jacob. You make me feel—"

"I make you feel like a woman. I'm not laughing at you. I am laughing at that proper lady who stands in one corner of your mind and shakes her finger at the rest of you, just like another teacher I knew long ago."

Carolina smiled. "Did she shake her finger at you?"

"Yes." He hooked his leg over hers and drew her closer. "Often." She moved her hand over his back, and he continued, "I thought it a rude gesture. Tell that lady in your mind to go to sleep for a while. I'm going to make love to my woman."

When Carolina awoke the following morning, he was gone. Remarkably, she did not feel lonely. The bond between them was still there, even though Jacob was not. He had, indeed, become part of her. It was more than just romantic talk. This new insight into the capacity of the human heart buoyed her spirits through the next several days. She was busy with her needlework one morning when Marissa's one-horse buggy appeared out front. Carolina hurried outside and found Culley trailing on horseback not far behind.

"Marissa! It's good to see you," she called out happily, and then, with less enthusiasm, she added, "And Mr. Culley. What brings you up this way?"

He tipped his dusty hat as Marissa offered the explanation. "That Charles. He has a protest for me every time I go out of the house these days. Mr. Culley was on his way out to ride fence, so he volunteered to see that I got here safely."

Culley swung down from his horse and sidled up to the buggy to offer Marissa a hand. "Really, Mr. Culley, this isn't necessary. Don't let me keep you from your chores."

"Fence'll keep a while, ma'am. Maybe Miss Hammond needs some help around here. Woman oughtn'ta be out here alone, doing her own lifting and toting."

"Thank you, Mr. Culley, but I don't need—"

"See you done some wash," he said. "That tub need to be emptied?"

Carolina's glance followed his to the clothes that flapped on the line behind the cabin. She didn't want him looking at her under things, not even on the clothesline.

"Yes, Mr. Culley," Marissa put in. "Do empty the water on Miss Hammond's garden, and then be off to do your job. We have girl talk to tend to."

Culley grinned like the schoolboy appointed to dust erasers for his teacher. His spurs jingled on his bowed legs as he ambled off to do the ladies' bidding.

"He wouldn't be satisfied unless we let him do something," Marissa whispered.

When Culley returned, Carolina was watering the buggy horse. He broke into a funny little trot. "I coulda done that, Miss Hammond. You shoulda let me—"

"I don't want to keep you from your chores any longer, Mr. Culley." Carolina managed a smile. "I know what a long day you must put in."

"Cowboy's work is never done," he quipped. "Boss says to see you back home, Miz MacAllistair. When do you want me to swing back this way?"

"In a couple of hours."

"But you'll stay for—"

Marissa cut Carolina off with a warning glance. "No, no, we have to get back to the ranch in time for dinner. Just a couple of hours, Mr. Culley."

"Yes, ma'am." He bent the brim of his hat in a farewell gesture and rode away.

"You almost saddled yourself with him for dinner," Marissa said as she watched Culley make his unhurried retreat.

"I only intended to invite you."

"Yes, but *I'm* saddled with his escort service for the day." She shaded her eyes with her hand and smiled. "Let's get out of the sun and have some tea."

They headed for the cabin. "I was thinking of visiting you today," Carolina said. It was only a half-truth. She had thought of it, but ruled it out.

"I needed an outing, but I'm afraid Charles will start prohibiting them soon."

"How are you feeling?"

"Wonderful. Pregnant and wonderful." Marissa settled at the table while Carolina set about making tea. "I'm afraid there's going to be trouble between Jacob and Culley."

Kettle in hand, Carolina turned from the sideboard. "What do you mean?"

"Jacob was working with a beautiful red roan early this morning, and I went out to watch him work. He's such a master with horses, Carolina, and this horse... Well, anyway, Jim Bates joined me, and we were watching when Jim saw Culley and called him over. He told Culley he wanted him to ride fence up this way today. Culley got a grin on his face like a cat who's been told to clean the bird's cage."

Carolina rolled her eyes in disgust. "Or perhaps the chipmunk who's found the key to the peanut bin."

"Carolina, this is serious. I could see Jacob's reaction. He was livid." She hastened to add, "Of course, no one else was paying any attention to Jacob at that point, but that's when I said I was coming up here. Otherwise I knew Jacob would come, and then you would have seen the fur fly right on your doorstep."

"Heaven help me," Carolina groaned as she sank into a chair. "For the first time in my life I'm attracting male attention, and I'd rather continue to go unnoticed."

"Except by Jacob."

Carolina smiled. "Except by Jacob. Marissa, please mention to Mr. Bates that Mr. Culley seems to be a bit taken by me and that I'm uncomfortable around him. Maybe Mr. Bates would—''

"He probably would. I think Jim's a bit taken by you himself, truth to tell."

"Oh, no," Carolina groaned again.

"And I'm sure there will be others. Unmarried women are hard to come by around here. Eventually Jacob will either have to show his hand or watch in silence while others try to court you."

"I can discourage would-be suitors very effectively myself. You'll notice that I remain unmarried."

"For how long?" Marissa wondered aloud, and then she caught herself. "Oh, that was a stupid question. I've been telling myself to discourage this romance because it's so impossible. I keep thinking of Romeo and Juliet."

"It's nothing like that," Carolina protested.

"Of course not. At least they were both Italian."

Carolina set tea in front of Marissa. "It's hardly so dramatic. We have a private relationship, and I plan to avoid this stampede of suitors you predict by being my usual cold self."

"Jacob may be pushed into a confrontation, my dear, and a confrontation between him and a white man would be disastrous. If violence occurred, Jacob would be held responsible."

"It could happen with Culley," Carolina reflected. "Please ask Mr. Bates to keep him away from me, Marissa, just as he does with Jacob."

"That might be difficult at the picnic." Marissa noted Carolina's puzzled expression over the rim of her cup as she sipped her tea. "Our Fourth of July picnic. I did tell you—"

"No, Marissa, you didn't."

She clucked to herself as she set the cup down. "We have it every year. We don't even invite people anymore. They just come."

"Jacob wouldn't go, then."

Marissa sighed. "Probably not. He'll either ignore the fact that it's a day off, or he'll go home."

"Or he'll come here," Carolina said slowly, a smile dawning in her eyes.

"Carolina—"

"Just do this one favor for me, Marissa. Let Jacob know that I won't be at the ranch for the picnic, that I'll be here."

"You want me to play nurse to your Juliet," Marissa concluded.

"Not exactly." Carolina grinned. "We'll have no weeping and mourning if you'll be sure to get the message straight. I know he'll come."

Carolina was up before dawn on the Fourth of July. She wanted to be ready. She set bread dough to rise and put a honey cake in the oven. Then she dressed. Her blue taffeta skirt with the wide black sash was her favorite. Her white blouse with its mutton-leg sleeves had delicately crocheted eyelet trim around the collar and cuffs, with blue ribbon laced through it. She kept her hair down, because he liked it that way, but she fastened the sides up with her mother's hand-carved ivory combs. At her throat she wore her mother's blue-and-white cameo. Her hand mirror said that she looked pretty, and because she felt pretty, she decided that it must be true.

She was removing the cake and putting her bread in the oven when she heard the sound of hoofbeats. She hurried out the door. Resplendent in his buckskins, Jacob sat tall on the blanketed back of his spirited sorrel. The sky behind him was streaked with pink and gray as the sun rose above the line of a square-topped butte. His back was to the rising sun; his face was shadowed. He was a breathtaking silhouette.

It was a role the Lakota male played to the hilt, and Jacob enjoyed it. He was the warrior, the hunter returning at daybreak to the woman who waited for him. Sagi's prancing gait was part of the design, and both horse and man had been carefully groomed for the moment. Like the courting grouse, Jacob expanded his chest on a deep breath and held his shoulders as square as any butte. His hips rolled smoothly with Sagi's light-footed prancing.

The rising sun glowed on her face. Her hair snatched glints of red and gold from the bright new morning, and Jacob's heart slammed against his ribs. His role became secondary. She was a vision that a man might see after days of fasting and prayer.

He stopped near the corral and slid from the horse's back with quicksilver grace. It was only then that Carolina took note of the second horse, the one he led. The red roan was smaller than Sagi, with a small head, tapered neck and slender legs. The lower legs, mane and tail were all black. Jacob held the reins of both horses as he turned to the rising sun and sang his morning song. Carolina stood quietly, honoring the moment and the free and natural relationship between Jacob and his god.

His resonant voice dropped on the final note. He took a pair of *parfleches* and the blankets from Sagi's back and turned him loose in the corral. Then he stood beside the roan and waited for Carolina to come to him. It was a wordless greeting, a heartfelt embrace. His kiss was that of a man who'd hungered for days for the soft lips of his woman. Hers was that of a woman who'd waited, watched and kept faith.

"What did you sing about?" she asked.

"I thanked the One Above, *Ateyapi*, for the vision he gave me this morning. It was only when you came into my arms that I could believe the vision was truly flesh. I've brought you a gift."

She smiled up at him. "What have you brought?"

"You cannot see, little one? The sun is in your eyes."

"The horse? This horse is for me?"

He beamed with pride. "This mare is mine to give, and I have trained her for you. She is yours."

Carolina stepped closer to the mare, reaching a tentative hand toward the sleek neck. "Oh, Jacob, she is the most beautiful animal I've ever seen. But I couldn't. She's just—"

"Couldn't what?"

"I couldn't take her. She's much too—"

His eyes lost their luster. "You would refuse me?" he asked quietly.

"No, Jacob, I would not refuse *you*, but you mustn't give this beautiful horse away."

"If you refuse my gift, you refuse me, Carolina. I am courting you."

"Oh." Her eyes widened, their blue brightening as her face grew pink. "I didn't understand. In that case, what is the proper way for me to accept?"

He answered with a hearty laugh. "Take the reins and lead her into your corral so that I know you have accepted my gift. If I were a proper Lakota suitor, I would hold my blanket around both of us, covering our heads, and we would talk. In a little while I would leave. But since we are beyond that stage, and since I smell bread—"

"You'll stay." She kissed his lips quickly and followed the custom. Her heart felt light as they walked to the cabin hand in hand.

Carolina rescued the golden-brown bread from the oven in timely fashion. Jacob leaned against the wall with his arms folded and watched her bustle about. She was a sweet sight.

"White women wear foolish clothes, but you look beautiful anyway, *wiwašteka*. You should be going to a party. You should be celebrating your Independence Day."

"I am," she said happily. "By sending my regrets. I am dressed to receive a special gentleman caller."

"And I am dressed to court the woman who haunts my days and nights with the memory of her beauty. Look at us." He chuckled. "Who would guess that I am your gentleman caller, and you are my woman?"

She cracked an egg on the edge of her skillet. "No one would. Our secret is safe."

He came up behind her and put his strong hands at her waist. "That may be it is, little one." For now, he added mentally. He worried her earlobe with a small nip, and she tipped her head back, smiling. "Is this ready?" he asked, indicating the teapot on the sideboard. He found cups, and, at her affirmative reply, poured the tea as she slid saucers under the cups.

"You people keep so many useless things in your houses," he commented as he took his cup to the table. "The cup is enough to hold the tea."

"But what if it should spill?"

He shrugged. "Something would get wet."

Serving him breakfast seemed an intimacy to her. She'd made Juneberry preserves and fried his eggs hard at his direction. The butter melted quickly on the warm bread, and the smell of bacon made this truly the morning ritual shared by couples.

"What are these?" he wondered as he poked at a breaded slab on his plate.

"Green tomatoes. Don't you like them?"

"Not much," he said honestly. "I've never tasted tomatoes like this."

"My mother used to fix them this way." Her voice tightened. "Don't eat them if you don't like them."

He looked up, and his eyes softened. "It's just a strange taste for me. I like the rest."

She was disappointed. "I wanted everything to please you."

"Everything does, except the tomatoes. I've gotten used to strange tastes before, and I might even get used to these." He poked again with his fork and mumbled, "But I doubt it."

"Just ignore them."

He laughed. "The differences between us will make our relationship more interesting. You said that, remember?"

She raised a prim brow. "I made the preserves from Juneberries."

"They're good, little one. A man could grow fat in your lodge. Your bread is better than any I've tasted." He did not want his day ruined over some damned tomatoes! He wanted to see her smile. "Where was your mother's home?"

"She was from South Carolina. Hence my name. My father met her when he was there on business. Her family was ruined by the war, and my father bought their land." She chose not to use the word *carpetbagger*, but others had called him that. "My uncles still run the plantation for him, and the cotton is shipped north. My father has a textile mill."

"Then he helped your mother's family in return for marriage to their daughter?"

"It was profitable for him, but he did make it possible for them to stay on the land they loved."

"Your father made a good marriage. Both families benefitted from it."

"Is that what marriage is? What about my mother?"

"Was she not pleased to do this for her family?" he asked. He saw that some good things had come about from her parents' marriage and thought she needed that consolation.

"My mother was a beautiful woman," Carolina recalled wistfully. "Small and fragile, like a porcelain figurine. She was so pale that the blue veins in her arms and neck seemed to be covered only by tissue paper. And tiny. When I was ten years old, my hands were larger than hers."

"Did she have eyes the color of the egg in the nest of the *siśoka*, the red-breasted bird? Eyes that draw a man's heart from his chest?"

"Her eyes were the same color as mine, but my father's heart stayed where it was—in his bank vault."

"Perhaps he loved her in his way."

Carolina sighed. "Maybe at first. But she hated Boston, and the cold winters killed her. Only when she talked of South Carolina and the times before the war did she feel warm and look happy. Her memories..." She heard what she was saying, and she saw the sympathy in his eyes. "We can't live in the past, Jacob. When the world changes, people must change with it or—"

"Or die inside when they cannot live with the way things are."

"Good memories should be kept and treasured, but the present must be lived, and the future must be anticipated."

He permitted a ghost of a smile. "Keep the memories in the bank vault, then?"

"And let your heart be with me now."

He reached for her hand. "Carolina, you must understand that there is a single spirit among my people, and I am part of that spirit. If I were taken from them, I would die as your mother died."

"I would not take you, Jacob. Just your heart."

"And you have done that, *wiwasteka*. But you cannot wear it on your sleeve. I want to live in whatever world is left for me and for the survivors like me, but it is not a world I would share with you."

She carried his hand to her lips and pressed a kiss to his fingers.

"My soul is part of the Lakota, and I cannot turn my back on the dying ones, even though I choose to live. Something in me is dying, too."

Fearful of his words, she looked up at him. "Don't let me take anything from you, then. Let me love what lives in you. Let me nurture that."

"The man must nurture, too, little one, or he ceases to be a man. With the coming of the white man, we lost our livelihood, and now, without him, we have nothing to eat. We must find a way to feed ourselves, or we will become..." The thought was too horrible. He had seen too much, and he hated knowing what he knew. He had no way to prepare the others. "I don't know what we will become."

He scraped his chair against the plank floor as he stood to leave the table. He opened the cabin door and leaned against the door frame as he breathed deeply of the morning air. Rolling himself a cigarette, he watched the horses in the corral and listened to the plates click together behind him as Carolina cleared the table. He heard the rustle of taffeta, and then her arms came around his waist. A heavy sigh cleared his lungs of smoke as he welcomed the slight pressure of her weight against his back.

"No sympathy, Carolina," he said quietly. "I am a man, and I don't want sympathy. I want one day's peace of mind. Be my woman, just for today, and let me be your man."

"For today only?"

"We must take each day as it comes." The smoke tasted bitter, and he ground out the cigarette before turning to take her in his arms. "God help me when the day comes that you are no longer mine."

"That day will never come unless you take me far out into the desert and leave me there. Otherwise, I swear to you I shall find some way to be with you, Jacob." She pulled his head down to hers and demanded sustenance from his mouth.

With one hard, possessive kiss he tried to ensure that what she said was true, even as his good sense railed against it. She was smiling when she backed away.

"I have a gift for you, too. I hope it turns out to be better than the tomatoes."

She seemed to float to her knees in front of the trunk as the blue skirt billowed around her to the floor. Lifting the lid, she withdrew the shirt she'd made and presented it to him. He touched the embroidery as though it might be a delicate part of her. When he unfolded the shirt and held it at arm's length, Carolina felt a sudden urge to take it back and hide it. It wasn't good enough.

"You don't have to wear it, Jacob," she whispered. "It's probably foolish, like white women's shoes. I just wanted to make something for you."

"I like this, Carolina." He hiked his buckskin shirt over his chest and peeked at her before peeling it over his head. "Truly." When he put the ivory shirt on, he ran his hands, first with one, then the other, over the embroidered sleeves. He looked up at her and grinned. *"Wašte yelo."*

"That's *good*," she remembered. "What does *yelo* mean?"

"It is what a man says to show that he is convinced of what he says." He buttoned the embroidered cuffs.

"Then you like it?"

"I have said so."

"The designs and everything?"

Her eyes were bright with excitement, and he knew that she would make a good Lakota. She was a gift-giver. "My mother will be delighted with your handiwork. Now we will see what you think of hers." He produced the pair of *parfleches*. "My cousin brought these to me yesterday. My mother sent them for you."

Carolina opened one packet and found a butter-soft, white buckskin dress. There were long fringes at the ends of the sleeves and hem. The entire yoke was beaded with blue, yellow, white and black beads.

"Oh, Jacob, it's beautiful. How did she make this so quickly?"

"She made that long ago." He watched Carolina hold the dress up in front of her and touch the fabric in the way of women and new dresses, and he remembered seeing his mother wear this one in times past. "You are taller than my mother, but it would please her to see you wear it. If you wear it for me here, I can tell her that—"

"So pretty, Jacob." She touched the beaded yoke, tracing a triangular design. "It's obviously a special dress. Why would she want me to have it?"

"I have taken your virginity, little one, and now I am—in her eyes, you are my wife. Nothing I say will convince her otherwise."

Carolina looked up. "Why doesn't she worry about all those differences everyone else sees?"

"She is my mother," he said simply. "She worries. But she knows only that her son has taken a maiden, and that makes us married."

"It does?"

He laid his hands on her shoulders. "In her eyes it does, *wiwašteka*, and so you have a mother. You will be loved as a daughter. If you wish, you may call her *uncíši*, which means *my mother-in-law*. That would also please her. But her beliefs do not bind you to me, Carolina. You are as free as ever."

When would he know her? Without comment, she opened the other *parfleche* and found moccasins, belt, hair ties and leggings, all beaded to match the dress. "The moccasins and leggings are new," he told her. "Ina made those to fit your long legs."

"And my long feet?" She giggled with gift-laden glee. "Help me put them on, please, Jacob. How do they go?"

"If I help you undress, it may be a while before I help you dress again."

"Behave yourself, now." She had already removed the cameo and was unbuttoning her shoe. "I have a new dress, and I can't wait to try it on." When she got down to her camisole and pantaloons, she looked up at Jacob.

"No." With a teasing smile, he shook his head. "Lakota women do not wear those things." He reached for her drawstring.

She spun away laughing, and then spun back again. "Then what do they wear?"

"Something like a breechclout."

"And how would you know that, Jacob Black Hawk? Do you and your friends hide in the bushes while the girls bathe?"

He shrugged. "Someone must consider their safety."

"I see. Well, I have no breechclout, so these will have to do."

He reached for the small buttons on her camisole. "They wear nothing over their breasts except their dress."

The frivolity stopped. Carolina shivered when the camisole fell away and he stood there loving her breasts with only his eyes. Something inside her began churning slowly, moving deeper, getting warmer. The dress would wait.

She echoed a question that had once embarrassed her. "Do you want me again, Jacob?"

His eyes burned with the answer. "I need you, *wiwašteka*. If I touch you now, I will not let you go."

Their eyes did not waver as she lifted his hands to her breasts and whispered another echo, "Touch me, then."

With his kiss he hungrily sucked her breath away. It seemed that her feet had long since left the floor when he lifted her into his arms and carried her to the bed. Impatiently, he removed their clothing. He loved her body with his kisses, spreading warmth over her breasts, her belly, sending her senses on an upward spiral that emanated from the depths of her womb.

Jacob knew her need, and he wanted to augment it, to drive her mad with it. His words said that she was not bound to him, but his body claimed her for its own. It was his body that insisted upon reminding her, time after time, that she needed him, that she belonged to him, that only he could make her feel this way. As his tongue played over the soft plane below her navel, he thought how good it would be to quicken her belly with the life of his seed. He hoped that white women knew what Lakota women knew of avoiding conception, but his desire quickly crowded that concern from his mind.

He moved her legs apart, and his teeth gently tortured the tender inside of her thigh. Her soft mewling enflamed him, and he wanted to know more. He had never done this for any woman, and his conscience said *no*, it is for her husband. But the answer came back in his mind, *I am her husband*. In the heat of his drive to possess her, he said aloud,

"Nimitawa ktelo," and he offered an intimacy that was beautiful only because his love made it so.

Her eyes flew open, and his name was on her lips, but no protest followed as she shuddered in release. Then he slid over her, and, at the moment of their joining, he whispered, *"Wana . . . nimitawa ktelo."*

"Yes," she whispered. "Oh, yes, Jacob, yes. . . ."

And they became one flesh.

They lay in each other's arms for a long time, telling one another with little touches, small caresses, what could be told in no other way. Finally he whispered against her hair. "I will dress you as a Lakota woman now, *waśtelakapi.*"

"What does that mean? *Waśtelakapi?*"

"It means *beloved*. It means that I love you, Carolina."

She pressed her face against his shoulder and held him close. "I have held my breath each time we've been together, hoping you would say it."

"I know you have. I tried to keep that much from you, even though it was no longer mine to keep. Come." He moved away from her regretfully. "Let me see you in my mother's dress."

She watched him dress in his own white breechclout and leggings. He smiled when he saw that she had not moved, and he went to the washstand and prepared a damp cloth for her. Then he turned discreetly to pull his buckskin shirt over his head and retrieve the other clothes from the floor, folding his new shirt and laying it aside with special care. Then he handed her the pantaloons.

"Come, little one. You were anxious to try the dress."

She laughed as she went to him. "You distracted me, I believe."

"We could argue about who did the distracting, but I want you to ride the mare. So put these on."

It seemed almost a ceremony to him to dress her in his mother's dress. He tied the belt around her waist, added the leggings and moccasins, and then he braided her hair, using the buckskin hair strings that were decorated with beads and fluffy white down. When he stepped back to admire her, he said, *"Mitawin."* Her eyes asked for the translation. "It means that you are my woman." *My wife,* he added in his mind.

She slipped her arms around him. "And what did you say to me before when you . . . made love?"

"I said what I had no right to say, Carolina. I said, 'now you will be mine.' "

"Say it again," she whispered near his ear. "In Lakota."

"Nimitawa ktelo."

"It sounds beautiful in Lakota. Why do you deny yourself the right to say such a beautiful thing?"

"A man does not take a woman if he has nothing to give her."

"Stop it, Jacob. Listen." She formed the words just as she'd heard them. *"Nimitawa ktelo.* Is a woman permitted to say the words?"

"Yes."

"And would it be true?" she insisted.

"That my heart is yours?" He hesitated, but no lie would come. "Yes, you know it's true."

"I have nothing, Jacob. My father's property will go to my brother. There will be no wedding gifts from my family." She paused to draw a cleansing breath. "This cabin belongs to someone else. If I were to provide a lodge, I would have to build it with my own hands. I may be a woman, but I have a good head on my shoulders and able hands, and by God—"

"Shh." He touched a finger to her lips and smiled sadly. "You are yet respected by your people, little one. You have a life." He touched his forehead to hers. "Don't let me take that from you." Straightening, he took her face in both his hands. "I can give you love, but I cannot offer you a life with me. I have no right to call you mine."

Covering his hands with hers, she lowered them from her face. None of this made sense. "I have required no promises from you, Jacob. I asked only that you let me be with you as long as you love me. If our love is a burden to your conscience, then you may leave me."

"You know I cannot do that."

"Then I know where I stand. You cannot marry me, but you cannot leave me. You cannot do what you cannot do. I accept that for now. For both our sakes, I hope that you will soon realize what choice must be made. There is only one that will bring us both happiness. In the meantime, remember this: in my heart, I belong to you."

"I have heard you, little one. Now come. Let us see how well you can ride your mare."

She rode with only a blanket, because Jacob said that she must learn. "You cannot be one with the horse if you put a saddle between you."

"But I keep losing my balance," she complained. "I feel as though I'll slide off the side."

"You remain stiff while the mare is in motion. Your balance will come when you move with her."

He watched them as they established a more fluid physical rapport—the graceful roan mare and the slender, strong-willed woman. Carolina struggled to coordinate her movements with the horse's. He saw her shoulders and back relax when her hips found the easy rhythm of the lope. The tenseness vanished from her face when she knew the feeling was right.

"*Wašte yelo!*" he shouted, grinning at her as she passed. Her face lit up in response to his compliment, and she was a glorious sight in beaded white buckskin, fringe fluttering from her sleeves and her braids bouncing on her breast.

"Oh, Jacob, she's wonderful!" Out of breath, she slid down from the mare's back. "She must have a Lakota name. How do you say tornado?"

He laughed, his eyes crinkling at the corners. "*Tate iyumni.* By the time you said that, you would forget why you called her. *Tate* means wind. That is a good name."

"Yes. Tate. But you and I will know that her *full* name is Tate Iyumni." She nuzzled the mare's cheek. "You are Tate, as fast as the wind."

"She is a gentle breeze," he assured her. "Otherwise I would not trust her to carry you, *waštelakapi*."

Carolina laid her hand on Jacob's cheek. "Thank you for Tate, Jacob. Now that I have accepted your gift, how shall our courtship proceed?"

"Among my people, a man is not allowed to marry until he proves himself by counting coups, touching the enemy. The next time someone gets a war party together, I will go along."

"Weddings must be rare occurrences these days." She kept her tone light as she dropped her hand to her side.

"Old customs die hard." He took the reins from her and scanned the hills. "There were three men who painted themselves for battle about a year ago. They dared one another to count coup in the old way—by stealing a horse. They got drunk first. Naturally they were caught. No one had been harmed. All property was recovered." He turned a stony look on her, and she caught her breath. "All three *hostiles* were hanged. One was my cousin."

"I'm sorry, Jacob. I'm sorry for all of it." She put her hand on his arm. "If one white woman's regrets mean anything—"

"Let's ride together, Carolina. I see that you will not accept the way things are until you see for yourself."

"Where are we going?" Wherever it was, she was ready.

"Your Independence Day is for picnics and family gatherings. I think we will take a picnic with us and visit my family."

"Oh, yes! Shall I wear this?"

"If you're comfortable. It's a long ride. We will stay the night, if you consent."

"Consent?" She kissed him and tugged on his hand. "Help me find a gift for your mother. Tell me what I have that she might like."

He smiled. Here indeed was the spirit of the Lakota within a white woman's body.

Chapter Nine

Carolina refused to admit she was tired. She'd been trailing Jacob for hours with little conversation between them and few chances for him to notice that she was perilously close to losing her seat. If she landed on the ground with a soft thud, it occurred to her that he might not even notice. He seemed totally absorbed in the journey, and she bit back all temptation to complain.

They rode along a ridge overlooking the river, near the place where they had camped weeks before. Jacob reined his horse in and dismounted near a clump of buffalo berry bushes. He picketed the sorrel and deposited the blanket and *parfleches* downwind of the bushes. Finally he noticed that Carolina hadn't followed his lead.

"The mare is trained to be ground-tied, but she should be picketed now so that she can graze."

"Yes, well..." She knew her legs would turn to jelly the minute her feet touched the ground, but she tried to gear herself up to perform a graceful dismount. Despite her best efforts, her foot dragged itself across the horse's rump as she attempted to lever herself down. Jacob's hands were suddenly at her waist, and she let him take her weight. "I guess my muscles need to be conditioned for this kind of riding."

"A little walking will help with the stiffness. Come. We'll picket the mare."

He made her walk for several minutes, and then he showed her how to flex her feet and legs after a long ride. When they sat on the blankets, she served sandwiches and honey cake with cold tea from a canteen.

From the vantage point of the ridge they could watch the narrow river cut a blue-gray path across the rolling prairie. It twisted and turned several times before it disappeared behind a hill and emerged a distance away on flatter ground. The ridge sloped away behind them, a rippling wave of green and brown buffalo grass that rolled to the edge of the earth. The sun was high overhead, and the wisps of white clouds cast a patchwork of pale shadows over the land.

"You will be a red woman before this day is over," Jacob observed with a wry smile.

"You've said that I need color in my face."

He touched the pink patch that had blossomed high on her cheek. "Why do white women shade their faces from the sun? Do they want their men always to think they are sick?"

She laughed. "Have you ever had a sunburn, Jacob?"

"Sometimes in the spring, if I'm careless. But I've seen white men browned from the sun." He frowned as he puzzled over the phenomenon. "I've also seen white women with flour on their faces, and I realized they put it there. Our women use vermilion on their faces. White reminds us of death."

"Fair skin is fashionable." She didn't want to explain that fashionable people did not labor in the sun. The concept would disgust him. "I've been criticized for not being fashionable, so a little sun is fine with me. The only problem is..." She touched her nose and found it warm.

"You will shed your skin like the snake."

"Not like a snake!"

He flopped on his back and laughed. "I'll have to put bear grease on you, little one. I don't want more snake-bite."

"I didn't think a bonnet would suit this dress."

He propped himself on his elbow and grinned at her. "Probably not. But that dress has been fashionable for many generations. Before the white man brought beads, we used porcupine quills much the same way." He pulled his tobacco pouch from under his shirt. "The dress you wore this morning—is that fashionable?"

"Not really. Have you seen the bustles women are wearing?" By his laughter, she knew that he had. "I agree. I would be no more comfortable in a bustle than you would be in long drawers. Did you like what I wore this morning?"

"Yes."

"Then it's fashionable enough. I wanted you to like it."

He licked the edge of his cigarette paper and smiled at her. "It was fashionable because you were wearing it. Now the buckskin dress is in style."

"It's really up to us, isn't it?"

He chuckled. "You are a rebel. A bad trait in white women."

"And in Lakota women?"

"Lakota women have much to say, little one. I think your God put you in the wrong skin."

"What does it mean, anyway? They call you a red man, but your skin turns brown in the sun, and mine turns red. We're just people, Jacob. I think God wanted variety."

Jacob sat up and cupped the cigarette in his hand as he drew deeply on the smoke. He gestured with his chin toward the valley below them as the smoke escaped his lips.

"What do you see down there, Carolina?"

She surveyed the valley. "Land, grass, river. Oh, there's a little prairie dog town over there."

"I see those things, too, but I see more. When I stand on a hill like this, with the warm summer wind blowing against my face, I can see much more if I let my mind have its way."

She leaned forward. "What do you see?"

"I see myself as a very young boy. I am with my brother, Tokala, and our uncle, whose duty it is to scout ahead for a good campsite. He shows us what to look for—water, firewood." He pointed toward the cottonwoods and the glistening river. "But he reminds us that we must camp on the open ground and not in the timber, where we might be ambushed. We listen closely, because someday this may be our duty."

He took another puff of his cigarette and glanced back at her. "Shall I tell you what else I see in the valley?"

"Yes, please do."

He stretched his arm out over the land. "There are the people, moving as one. The women's horses pull their lodge poles and travois, and the women chatter with each other and shoo the children along. The children have their games, and the people indulge them, because a child's laughter is like music. The men are proudly mounted and positioned defensively. They wear the symbols of their accomplishments—the eagle feather, the scalp lock and the medicine bundle. The older boys bring up the rear, herding the horses. Other scouts are out looking for buffalo, and there will be a hunt soon.

"By August, we will have made our way south to *Paha Sapa*, the Black Hills, where we will see old friends from other bands. Some of the older boys and the men will make the *Wiwanyank Wacipi*, the Sun Dance. Our life moves, and this land lies before us, open and free. It *moves*, Carolina. Do you understand?"

"Yes," she said quietly. She knew what he meant, but she realized that he felt differently about moving than she did, and so she added, "I think I do."

"My dream, as small as I am, is to be like my brother, growing tall and preparing for manhood. And then I want to be like my father and my uncle, who have counted coups many times and are greatly honored. That dream is still with me, even now that we're told to live on this reservation. I have memories of freedom."

"It must have been a long time since life was that way for you. Yet your memories are vivid."

"The dream is strong because the seed was planted in a young mind. You cannot know who I am unless you know the man I dreamed I would one day become. And you must also know what happened to the men who were once willing to slow their steps so that I could tag along behind them." He saw her wistful smile and knew that she had a mental picture of the child he'd once been. "We are great ones for story-telling," he reminded her.

"And I'm a good listener. Tell me more."

Jacob draped his forearm over his upraised knee. "Times became more difficult. I was still very young when several bands of Lakota—Hunkpapa, Oglala, Brûlé—joined with a few allies from the Cheyenne and Arapaho and killed Custer at the Greasy Grass River. I remember that time." He looked into her eyes. Even now his people rarely spoke of the great battle, because the reprisals had been grievous.

"I was playing near the river with some of the other boys when the first attack came against the Hunkpapa camp." He chuckled, remembering. "We ran like a pack of jackrabbits. We hadn't heard the warnings of *eyapaha*, the one who cries out the news to the camp. My mother had been looking for me, but there was no time for a scolding. Crazy

Horse rode through the Hunkpapa circle on his buckskin paint, and we cheered for him.''

Carolina was fascinated. This was the terrible massacre at the Little Bighorn of more than twenty years ago. ''I remember reading an account that numbered the warriors at four thousand and the soldiers at six hundred.''

Gazing out over the prairie, Jacob smiled. ''I think the newspapers spoke of 'murdering red-devils,' not warriors. If you call the women warriors and you count the bunches of terrified little boys they were trying to herd to safety, the account might have been nearly correct. And if Custer had waited for the other two columns of soldiers, they could probably have matched us man for man.'' Jacob shook his head slowly. ''It was not like the defenseless village he had attacked on the Washita River. This time, Custer was met by armed warriors, who rode out to defend their families. When I saw my brother, Tokala, paint his face to ride with our cousin, Gall, I wanted to go, too. The victory was sweet, even though we struck camp and scattered before there was time to celebrate. More soldiers were coming.''

He dragged on his cigarette as though it gave him the fuel he needed to finish the story. ''We scattered, and we ran. Those were bad times, hungry times. They chased us through the winter. My family went with Gall and Sitting Bull to Canada, but we grew homesick and finally submitted to the reservation. I agreed to attend school. My mother said we would have to deal with the white man and his strange ways, and she thought the missionaries were better than the soldiers. So I learned from them. A few years later I was sent to Carlisle.

''I returned in the summer of 1890. I was crazy with loneliness, and I found that the Lakota had become crazy, too, crazy with the dream of dancing back the buffalo. The hunger for the old life was worse than the hunger in their bellies. My father danced the Ghost Dance. He believed it would bring a savior to us, that the buffalo would return and the white man would disappear. The missionaries said the people were confused about the Savior, but Tokala said only women listened to that talk. He had counted coups, and he was a man.

"I looked at my father and my brother, and nothing had changed for me. They were the men I wanted to be. I danced, too, even though I did not share their pathetic last hope. Nothing would bring back the buffalo or the woman I had lost—"

"What was her name, Jacob?"

His eyes narrowed at the question. "One does not speak the name of a dead loved one. It would bring her ghost to haunt me."

"I'm sorry."

"Has my story become too long?"

"No. Please tell me what happened."

He paused, letting the last of the smoke trail slowly from his mouth as he ground the cigarette into the dirt. "I danced the Ghost Dance so that I could be with my father. The Ghost Dance, the pitiful last gasp of the Lakota, sent the genteel white settlers running to the forts again. The army used the Indian Police to help restore peace by murdering Tatanka Iyotaka, whom you call Sitting Bull. And then the brave soldiers slaughtered a freezing band of half-starved men, women and children at Wounded Knee Creek."

"Children, too?" she whispered.

He turned to her. "Did the newspaper accounts neglect to mention the children? Did they mention the Gatling guns, or the white flags that were ignored?"

"Oh, Jacob—"

"The greatest honor for a Lakota warrior is to touch the enemy—*touch* him—count coup and ride away. By the time we understood that a white soldier took as much honor home from waving a baby about on the end of his saber, it was too late for us."

"But Jacob, surely not *all* of the soldiers did that." Tears scorched her throat as she heard her mind scream, *Please, God, not all.*

Closing his eyes, Jacob sighed. He could recall the sound of the bugle that had hounded them through the winter and the gnawing pain of hunger, the kind that made a boy's head feel light. "Surely not all," he said. "But they came to kill, not to count coups."

"And did you continue—" She went hoarse. "Did you continue to dance?"

He shook his head. "Not if we wanted to stay alive. That didn't bother me. I never believed that painted shirts could stop bullets, or that the buffalo would return. But they took away the Sun Dance, too. I wanted to seek new visions, count coups some new way and earn the respect of the people, as my father and my brother had."

He looked at her again, and his eyes glittered. "How can my people let go of the old life? This new way offers nothing but empty promises and rations and scratching furrows in the dirt and wondering how a man is supposed to get something to eat out of that. We have been stripped of our manhood just as surely as if we had been castrated."

"Oh, no, Jacob, you are more man than—"

"More man," he repeated, and then gave a sardonic laugh. "More man than who, Carolina? Those old men you talked about? The ones your father sent? More man than yellow-haired Custer? More man than Culley, who noses around the women at every opportunity?" He rose to his feet and towered over her, gesturing wildly. "You compare me with *white* men. I am Lakota!"

She stood and reached out to him, beseeching. "Jacob, I don't know those men. I know you, and I believe—"

He gripped her arms. "Let me finish my story before you tell me what you believe. I've never told anyone this much in my life, but I want you to know it all now—all of it—before you see where my people live, where *I* truly live. I want you to know about my father and my brother, who have proven themselves to be men in my eyes."

He paused, and he saw that she was willing to listen. The words came more quietly now. "*Atè*, my father, is dying. The sickness in his body will soon bring him relief from the pain in his heart. And Tokala, who was named for the swift gray fox, was once a fine warrior and bore himself proudly. Now he cannot feed his family, and he uses whiskey to dull his pain. I have seen him retch from it until I thought he would bring his stomach into his mouth."

He stared at a spot somewhere behind her, and Carolina would have put her arms around him, but his grip on her did not permit that. She could only listen and try to imagine the shape of the things he told her.

"Tokala loves his wife and his boys as much as any man does." Each time Jacob said the words aloud, he tried to believe them. "But when he's drunk, they run from him and hide. It is the madness that drives him to hurt those he loves most. The *madness*. Do you understand this, Carolina?"

He shook her once, and she nodded dumbly. Tears coursed down her face, and she trembled inside.

"How can you understand? You look down and see nothing but land and prairie dogs. A man who has stood on the hill and watched his people, strong and free and on the move, cannot live with the government handouts and the reservation. My brother shames himself before his people when he is so drunk that he falls on his face in his own vomit. It doesn't matter to him anymore, because the shame of our people has already torn him apart inside."

She sucked her lower lip between her teeth and suppressed any sound, but the tears slipped past.

Jacob scowled. "I want no pity from you, woman—none for my family, and none for myself."

"It isn't pity, Jacob." She wanted to wipe the tears away. She wanted to move closer to him, but she could do neither. He held her fast at arm's length. "I see these things as you tell me about them and I feel pain, too. I feel shame. My people did these things." She watched his face soften slowly, and she squared her shoulders. "Shall I be held accountable, Jacob? I have done nothing but love you."

"No. No, not you," he whispered. He shook his head and drew her to him. "Not you, *waśtelakapi*."

"I share your pain, my love. I do."

"That is not what I would share with you. I only want you to know why I cannot—"

"I need your love, Jacob."

"You have my love." He tried to envelop her completely, tucking her head under his chin. Let nothing harm her, he prayed. And then he withdrew from her, hoping to temper the intensity of what he felt by offering a wry smile. "What you do not need is a Lakota husband."

"Perhaps I don't need any husband." She wiped her tears with the heel of her hand. "We agreed. You are my man, and I am your woman—for today."

With his forefinger he claimed one tear from the well beneath her eye. *"Mitawin."* *My woman.* He had to clear his throat to suggest, "Let us show Ina how we have fixed you up, little one."

Jacob's parents had a small cabin built on open ground about a quarter of a mile from the riverbank. His brother's log house was within sight, about another quarter of a mile downriver. A small cornfield stood knee-high near Tokala's house, and in Ina's yard there was a full-fledged garden.

Jacob's mother sat inside what appeared to be a primitive gazebo. Four posts supported an overhead frame, which was covered by willow branches. More branches formed three walls, and the open side faced east. Jacob took the reins from Carolina's hand as they watched the old woman come to her feet. Carolina grabbed his forearm before he could move away. "I don't want to say or do anything wrong, Jacob. I'll follow your lead. Give me a sign if I start to do something improper."

After he picketed the horses, he turned to her, and his eyes brightened with his smile. "My mother is not the Queen of England. Be yourself. You won't offend anyone. She's the only one who speaks much English, anyway."

His mother emerged from the willow structure, her round-faced smile encroaching upon her eyes. "My mother likes you," Jacob said as he took Carolina's hand. "You have nothing to worry about. Ina!" he called out as the woman hurried toward them. "You have a guest."

Her hands shot up to give Jacob and Carolina equal attention as she managed to pat each one's cheek at the same time. "*Cinks!* I see your leg works. Your woman has good medicine. And you look fine, daughter." She touched the yoke on the dress she'd beaded long ago. "My son keeps you happy?"

"Yes, *unciśi*, your son has made me very happy."

"He takes care of you good now?"

Carolina nodded toward the horses. "He gave me this wonderful mare."

Ina turned to Jacob. "She has no father?"

"Carolina is alone here," he explained. "I offered her my best horse, and she accepted."

"My husband gave my father many horses in my honor," Ina boasted. She peered past Carolina for a look at the mare and finally nodded her approval. "These days, one good horse is about the same."

"*Unciśi*, these clothes are lovely. I am honored to wear them." She took a small wooden box from her saddlebag, turned a key and opened the lid. The tinkling music made the old woman smile. "This is for you."

Ina acknowledged Carolina's appreciation and her gift with only a brief nod, as was the custom. "*Cińks,*" she said, "tell your father that you have brought your woman." She jerked her chin toward the tipi that stood a short distance from the cabin. "Come, daughter. I will show you how to make the lodge." She tucked the music box into a leather pouch that hung from her belt.

Carolina glanced at Jacob, but he was quick to heed his mother's instructions, and Carolina was left to follow Ina to the cabin. She stepped over the threshold and let her eyes adjust to the dusky interior. There was one small window in the south wall, and the glass was encrusted. She could smell the packed clay beneath her feet and the sod that covered the beams and branches overhead. It looked more like a storage shed than a home. Articles of leather hung from pegs on the wall, and there were several piles of hides and blankets stashed in the corners. A piece of stovepipe came down through the roof and ended abruptly in midair, where it must once have been attached to a stove. Ina grunted as she dragged a bundle away from the wall, and Carolina bent to help.

They moved the heavy tipi cover outside. Ina pointed to the poles that lay near the cabin and then to a spot twenty yards away. At that point the tipi would form a circle with the other structures. Carolina did much of the moving. As she straightened from the last pole, she glanced at the other tipi and wondered when the men would decide to come out and help. But the only help came from Ina, who set up a tripod of poles, laid more poles on the tripod and covered the skeleton with the tipi skin bearing Jacob's symbols. Carolina dogged Ina's steps, lifting, lowering and learning as she went.

As they carried a load of firewood to the tipi, Carolina asked, "Where is Ruth, *unciśi?*"

"She is with her sister-in-law, making meat." Ina dropped her load and straightened her back slowly, clearly not without pain. "You take this lodge with you back to your ranch."

"I think Jacob still needs it for his hunting trips. We should probably keep it here."

"What kind of house you got?"

Carolina remembered that it was for her to provide the home. "A cabin," she said. "Much like yours."

"Too hot in the summer." Ina waved her hand at the cabin in disgust. "In winter, they stink."

Carolina heard Jacob's chuckle, and she turned to find that he'd joined them. "The tipi is much cooler," she admitted. "I would like for you to teach me the leather work and the beading, *unciśi.*"

"Can you sew, daughter?"

"She is very good with a needle," Jacob said. "And she can grow vegetables and cook. She also teaches children, the way the missionaries do."

Ina heard these things and gave a nod to each qualification. "It is good. My son reads," she told Carolina. "If they give us a paper and tell us to sign, I tell them my son will read this to us first." She went through the motions, handing an imaginary paper to Jacob, who smiled at her. "It is written in English—this one reads to us in Lakota." She passed her hand in front of her own face. "They get such long jaws on them, those white men, and their big eyes—"

Ina slid a quick glance at Jacob and hurried on. "I have a real cookstove, too. My son gave me this. Come and see."

As they followed Ina toward the willow structure, Jacob explained, "I bought the stove from Charles when he put a new one in his kitchen. What a job it was to get it out here!"

The aroma of boiling venison filled the willow house, and Carolina saw that the stove was vented out the back wall. "How wonderful to have a stove here in this cool place. I'd love to have a willow house in my yard for this purpose."

"This son made mine," Ina said, tapping Jacob's chest. "He can make one for you. You got a good stove?" Carolina assured her that she did.

"Is your father feeling well, Jacob?" Carolina asked a little while later. "Shall I be permitted to meet him?"

"He waits for me to bring you to him."

Carolina followed Jacob outside, but he walked slowly and took time to explain. "He will not speak to you, Carolina. A man never speaks to his daughter-in-law, and you will not speak to him. Even though you know he will not understand, that doesn't matter." Jacob hesitated a moment as he reached for her hand. "He is very sick. I am going to ask you to do something for me."

"My mother suffered from a lung ailment, as well. Perhaps I could—"

He shook his head and waved her offer aside. "He would never consent, little one. But it would please him to see us mingle our blood in the old way." When he saw that the idea shocked her, he took her thumb in his hand, and his voice became a gentle thing. "He would make a small cut across your thumb and mine and put them together. It is important to him that we keep the old ways alive. This much I would do for him . . . if you would agree."

"What would it mean?"

"It would mean something to my father." His eyes did not betray any feeling of his own. Why couldn't he admit that it had meaning for him, too? Carolina looked down at their clasped hands and knew she would not refuse this custom, even though it was not the one her traditions had prepared her for.

She expected a stern face and a wasted body, but such was not Jacob's father. His leathery face was wrinkled with age, but he sat straight-backed, with his shoulders perfectly square, in front of a small fire. His long braids were still jet black, and his eyes, though aged, were the image of Jacob's. Rows of beads trimmed his tan buckskins, and a large claw was suspended from a thong around his neck. He seemed to ignore Carolina as he puffed on the carved stem of his red stone pipe, but he addressed Jacob as *"cinks,"* and apparently told him to sit down.

"Women sit on the left side of the tipi," Jacob instructed with a gesture. Carolina took her place and listened to the lilt of the Lakota that was passed with the pipe between the two men. It irked her when they laughed and she knew nothing of the joke they'd shared. She was certain she'd become completely invisible.

The old man stood abruptly, and Jacob followed suit. Carolina made ready to do the same, but Jacob raised his hand. "I will have a sweat with my father now. You'll wait here for us."

She watched them leave, and then she set her chin in her hands and wondered how they planned to sweat. She thought a short run would produce the desired effect. And then would her bridegroom come to her with his body bathed in perspiration? She remembered how she'd struggled with his chills and sweats, and she wondered what such a thing could signify in a marriage ceremony. And was that even what they were to have?

They could have run to the ranch and back in the time it was taking them. They should have thought to leave her a cup of tea. Had the pipe been left behind, Carolina thought she would have tried it. A glass of water would have been tasty. She eyed the door. Perhaps she might slip out and return before they came back. But she waited. When they returned, she wished she had been given the option of a bath, for they were obviously refreshed.

Jacob removed his knife from its sheath and put the blade in the coals. Jacob's father sang with the haunting nasal solemnity Carolina had come to regard as the sound of prayer. Jacob handed the knife to his father, who used it to slash the ball of Jacob's thumb. Carolina lifted her eyes to Jacob's face and stretched out her hand. She felt the bite of the blade as she willed Jacob to see the depth of her commitment in her eyes.

She watched as their thumbs were pressed together and wrapped in a strip of rawhide so that the blood of each might become one with the other. Stunned by the sting and entranced with the procedure, she was startled by the first note of Jacob's song, which began low in his chest and rose sharply in praise or petition, she could not guess which.

The ceremony was simple and brief. Carolina's heart was lifted above the restrictions Jacob had placed on them. She had heard no restraint in his song. The visit continued, and Carolina was again ignored. She realized that Jacob's father was seeing her without ever looking at her directly. She challenged herself to follow his example, but she found herself sneaking furtive glances from time to time. His cough was under his tight control, and his demeanor was scrupulously dignified.

The old man leaned forward to tap the ashes of his pipe into the fire. Jacob stood quickly and walked to the door without a word. Carolina scrambled to her feet and followed without looking back.

Jacob went directly to his tipi. Carolina lengthened her steps as she followed. She saw Ina's face in the shadows of the willow house and flashed her a grin before ducking into the tipi behind Jacob. He laced the flap closed and turned to enfold her in his arms.

"That was not what I intended in bringing you here, little one, but he is dying. I could not refuse him."

"Then how could he manage such a long run?"

"Run?"

"For sweating."

Jacob's eyes danced, but he did not laugh. "We use hot rocks to make steam in the sweat lodge. We talked and prayed together, and when our bodies were purified from sweating, we bathed in the river."

The thought made Carolina shiver. "Did he say what he thought of me?"

Jacob smiled and kissed her brow. "He said that you were well behaved and easy to look at. He hopes we bring each other much pleasure and many..."

"Children?"

He hesitated. "Yes."

"Are we married, then?"

"In the way of my people, we are. Divorce is quite simple, too. You need only say, 'I divorce you,' and it is done. That is, if you ignore the missionaries, who insist upon complicating everything." She smiled, hoping he wouldn't qualify his answer more. "It was good of you to do this for me, *waśtelakapi*. It goes easier with my father now."

"Does it?" She pressed her face against his shoulder. "I'm not that easy just to look at, am I, Jacob?"

"Not when I think—" He started to pull back from her, but she clung to him.

"Don't think," she whispered. "Don't look. Just hold me for a little while."

Both households shared supper in the willow house. Ruth and Anptaniya, Jacob's sister-in-law, had returned with the deer hide they'd cleaned after preparing the venison to be dried. They'd also brought Juneberries to be made into a fruit soup called *wōjapi*.

Ruth touched the sleeve of Carolina's dress and smiled. *"Waśte,"* she said. "You . . ." With a glance she asked Jacob for help.

"You look pretty," he coached her, and she repeated the words. Carolina called Ruth *"wiwaśteka,"* which brought a mixture of encouragement for Carolina and good-natured taunting for Jacob.

When one of his small nephews darted into the circle, Jacob snatched him off the ground and swung him in a diversionary arc. "Watch how you flatter your woman, boy," he warned in English. "She may blurt it out one day in front of everyone, and you will feel foolish and proud at the same moment." He sent Carolina a sparkling smile, adding, "As only a man in love can feel."

Carolina exchanged her charged smile for his. As the group took their places on the blanket, she wondered where Tokala was. Apparently they would not be waiting for him. The men were served their venison soup, and the women and children followed. The *wōjapi* was served with round slabs of unleavened bread, fresh from an iron skillet.

Anptaniya, whose name recalled the first light of day, had a cheerful round face and small, sparkling eyes. She had broad shoulders and the square hips of a young mother. All three women were dressed similarly in dark cotton skirts and calico blouses, but Anptaniya's skirt fit her poorly. She patted the small bulge beneath her waist band and smiled at Carolina.

Carolina nodded. "I hope you have a little girl. A baby sister for your boys." She turned to Jacob. "How do you say *girl*?"

"*Winyan.*"

Carolina gestured toward Anptaniya's belly. "*Winyan?*"

She giggled and gave Jacob her reply. "She would be grateful for a little girl," he translated. "The two boys keep her running after them all day long."

"But when they're old enough, you will be charged with training them," Carolina recalled.

"That is my responsibility." The younger boy dodged his mother's restraining hand and snatched a piece of bread. Jacob laughed. "And my privilege," he added.

After supper the women took Carolina in hand while Jacob and his father disappeared into the old man's tipi. The women spread a blanket in the yard, and Ina explained that Carolina was to learn a game. It was played with plum pits and a basket, and the object seemed to have something to do with matching the markings painted on the pits. The fact that Carolina was in the dark about the rules only added to the fun, and all four women soon found themselves giggling uncontrollably. Each time Carolina's turn came, Ina teased her by listing a new rule, which provoked more girlish giggles. Carolina finally fell back on the blanket and held her sides as she laughed.

The laughter stopped. Carolina opened her eyes and saw a man looming above her. He seemed to duck his head beneath the swirling clouds as Carolina peered up at him. She sat up quickly and tried to compose herself as she pushed herself to her feet. The man looked haggard, his hair straggling from his braids, but his face and build reminded her of Jacob. This was Tokala.

He leered at her through eyes that refused to focus. Carolina stood her ground, forcing herself not to gag from the stench that hung in the air between them. He reached out suddenly, grabbed one of her braids and examined the hair string. Carolina needed no facility with Lakota to know that he slurred the language when he spoke. He clapped his other hand over her shoulder and ran his thumb over the bead-work that covered her collarbone, shouting at her as he steadied himself on her shoulder.

Carolina stared at the man. She heard Ina's voice and knew she was scolding him. The scolding was ignored. At length Carolina managed to croak, "Are you Tokala? Jacob's brother?"

He gave her a quizzical look, which grew cloudy as he gripped her shoulders and shouted something at her. He shook her hard, shouting into her face again with hot, sour breath.

"Ciye!"

Carolina caught a glimpse of Jacob and Ruth behind him, but she regarded the man again, letting him know that even without this assistance, she would not have cowered.

"Hiya, ciye!" Jacob clamped a hand over his brother's shoulder, and Carolina was released straightaway. The brothers stood toe to toe, and the language she had thought melodic became warlike. Carolina inferred Tokala's disdain for the *wasicun* and took it to heart. She watched Jacob curl his hands into fists, but when his hand shot up, it was to steady his brother, whose tirade had rocked him too far back on his heels.

Jacob spoke calmly, using the term *mitawin*, and Carolina knew that he had claimed her as his woman. Tokala backed away in shock. Scowling, he turned to bark orders to his wife before he stalked off in the direction of his own cabin. Anptaniya took both boys in hand and followed him. The children, who had run merry circles around the entire group since the moment they had arrived, now followed like silent automatons, the older one with his thumb in his mouth.

Carolina licked the dryness from her lips as she watched them walk away. "What did he say about me?" she asked quietly.

"He was surprised to see you in our mother's dress."

She dreaded the look she might find in Jacob's eyes. She was the only *wasicun* present. The warmth of his hand against the back of her neck drew her head around, and she saw nothing of the resentment she'd feared.

"Forgive him, Carolina. When he is drunk, we say *Iktomi* owns him."

"*Iktomi?*"

"*Iktomi* is a spirit who teases us, tricks us with good feelings that turn sour. His mischief is to be avoided, but those who use whiskey give up their power over themselves and cannot resist him." He jerked his chin in the direction of Tokala's cabin. "First he becomes happy-stupid, and then this madness consumes him."

"What did you say to him?"

"That you are my woman."

"He didn't like the idea."

"He likes very little these days. Himself least of all." With a hand at her back, Jacob guided her toward their tipi. "I want you to see him when he's not drunk, Carolina." They stepped inside, and Jacob laced the flap. He turned to her, his brother still on his mind. "If you could see him on a horse. If you could hear the way he tells a story. He laughs before he tells a joke, and it warms your heart and makes it ready for the humor."

"You'll introduce us another time." She touched his cheek, and he gave her an unguarded look. "I'll make our bed," she said.

"And I will make the fire."

When the work was done, Jacob sat and stared into the center of the fire, where the logs blackened slowly. Hissing spirals of steam marked the damp spots in the wood. He tossed small sprigs of sage into the flames and watched them curl and turn to smoke.

Carolina removed her moccasins and leggings and took the belt off her dress. "I love that smell," she said as she knelt behind Jacob and slid her hands over his shoulders and down to his chest. "We had such fun playing that game with the plum pits. I think the women in your family like me. Don't you?"

"Why do you worry so much over whether *they* like *you*? Have you thought about whether you like them?"

"Yes, of course. I liked them immediately." She laid her cheek against his hair where the braid began. "I'm the one who's different, and I want them to accept me."

"In your world, I am the one who's different, and I am not accepted."

"This is your world," she reminded him. "You've brought me to your home, and you're testing me somehow. Be fair with me, Jacob, and tell me what you're looking for."

He took her hand from his chest and held it in his open palm. It lay smooth and soft against his calluses. "You surprise me at every turn. You never turn away. That's why they accept you, little one."

"And you?"

He brought her hand to his lips and rubbed it against them. She felt the flicker of his tongue.

She moved her knees apart and gave herself more contact with his back. She saw herself becoming a shell over his back, but she spoke of other things. "It would be terrible to send the boys away to boarding school at this age," she said.

"Tokala refuses to hear of that, but very soon I think he won't care what they do."

"And there will be a third child soon."

Jacob took up another handful of sage and tossed a sprig into the fire. "I remember when she told him of their first child," he said. "For days he talked of nothing but his dreams of a son. I had just returned from the East, and he teased me about my clothes and my hair, but he showed me that nothing had changed between us. He shared his dreams with me. We would dance back the buffalo, he said, for his sons and mine." His sardonic chuckle left Carolina with a cold chill. "When Anptaniya told him of the child she carries now," he continued, "he struck her."

They shared long moments of silence while Jacob tossed the last of the sage into the fire. "I see you in the fire, *waśtelakapi*. Like the wood, you ask to be consumed by something that will feed on you and die." He arranged her arms into a necklace for himself, and he held it close about him in what he knew to be a selfish gesture.

She laid her cheek against the top of his head. "Jacob, you are not Tokala."

"Neither am I Jacob."

"What do you mean?"

He shook his head. "It's not important." He pulled her around to the front of him and cradled her in his lap. With one hand he began untying her braid. He smiled as he loosened her hair and raked through it with his fingers.

"There," she murmured as she touched the corner of his smile with her fingertip. "There is the look that warms my heart. Keep looking at me like this, just like this."

Her hair lay in his hand in liquid ripples. "This is like the winter pelt of a beaver, softer than down to the touch. You are soft and fine all over, and you are the kind of woman a man needs to hold and protect."

She pulled the lacing from his buckskin shirt and slid her hand into the deep V, seeking his smooth chest. "You are the kind of man who makes a woman feel safe and secure. And beautiful. Your eyes tell me I'm beautiful."

He lifted her, lowered his head to meet her and muttered against her mouth, "Beautiful and mine."

Something like the curling sage burned slowly in Carolina's belly. She opened her mouth for his tongue's penetration. Their kiss sparked another conflagration, and she drew up her knees involuntarily. He shifted to one hip and rolled her on her back as he moved his mouth over hers and then kissed her randomly all over her face and neck. She pulled his shirt up and caressed his back.

"I have fever," he told her. His voice had become gravelly. "Woman, when you touch me, you make me drunk with the need for more touching."

She tugged at his shirt. "Take this off. Give me more of you to touch."

He laughed when she fumbled with his drawstring, and he turned away, rising to his knees to make shorter work of the job himself. But she snaked her arm around him from behind and caressed his hard belly until his breechclout fell away. When she found what she wanted, she nuzzled the back of his neck. "Is it good when I touch you?" she whispered.

"Wašté yelo." He directed her hand. "This makes it better."

"Will this make you happy-stupid?"

He groaned. "If we're not careful, it will finish me." He took her hand and rubbed it over his belly again, and then over his chest as he turned to her. "I have places to take you tonight, little one." He pulled her dress up from the bottom. She raised her arms over her head, and he smiled. When her breasts were exposed to him, he held the dress where it was, trapping her arms. He dipped his head to taste one nipple. It beaded nicely under his tongue, and he took the other one the same way.

Carolina arched her back and thrust her aching breasts toward him, but he teased and tortured until she whimpered in frustration. The dress was whisked away, and he lowered her to the pallet. He levered himself above her and found a perfect fit. He rotated his hips, and she grasped his buttocks and made the loving more exquisite.

"Is that what you want? Are you ready for me, *waśte-lakapi?*"

She reached for him and guided him home.

Carolina awoke during the night when Jacob stirred in her arms. Somewhere in the darkness an old man's body was wracked by coughing. She started to sit up, but Jacob's arms tightened around her. "Nothing can be done, little one," he whispered. And so she held him and shared his heartache, just as she had shared his joy hours before.

Chapter Ten

The schoolhouse raising brought the four families who had hired Carolina together at the chosen site on a Saturday three weeks into the month of July. With the renovation of her cabin, the construction promised Carolina a sense of belonging in this place. The schoolhouse would give her a place to carry on her work. The cabin was her own place to be. The prospect of being mistress over her own small domain was exhilarating.

The crew converged shortly after sunrise. Each family hauled its contributions to the project in the back of a buckboard or lumber wagon. Charles had ordered most of the exotic components. He was the only one who could afford the slate, the glass, the stove and its fittings, and the kerosene light fixture. Those would arrive later. Gustav Friedrick's carpentry skills would be applied to the furnishings.

Carolina arrived at the site on horseback. Already the flat rock had been laid for the foundation and the sill was in place. One of the Bar Mac hands was heaving planks off a wagon, and each one clattered with the others on the ground. Piles of cut sod lay waiting to form the roof, and there was talk of planking and shingles for the roof next year. The log structure would have a plank floor and two windows with a southern exposure.

The children were devising a game that involved climbing on the sod, but they were quickly banished from that area. They dashed past their mothers, who were improvising a plank table, and ran off for unclaimed territory. As she turned her head to follow their retreat, Carolina realized that Jacob was there.

It had been nearly three weeks since she'd seen him, but there was his big sorrel picketed on a knoll. The children ran a wide circle around the horse and disappeared as Carolina took a quick survey of the crew in the hope of spotting him.

"Carolina!"

Marissa squinted into the morning sun and waved. Carolina waved back before she dismounted at a spot where the mare could graze on the tether she had handy. As she unbuckled the flank strap on her saddle, she heard Culley's voice behind her. She ground her teeth.

"Let me help you with that, ma'am."

She pulled the heavy saddle down herself. "I have it, Mr. Culley. Thank you, anyway."

He dogged her steps after she deposited the saddle out of the mare's reach and headed for the congregation of women. "Nice day for a school raising," he offered.

"It certainly is."

"Book learning is a good thing," he declared, and then he tried to think of a reason, but couldn't quite come up with one. "I sure do think it is."

"I agree." Carolina scanned the group, nodding at each one she passed. No one had time for much more than "hello"—no one but Culley.

"Myself, I can't read." He chortled. "But then, neither can my horse."

"It's never too late to learn." She noticed several of the hands assembling logs for the walls, and she waved at Charles. Where was Jacob?

"It ain't? Think I could get some lessons somewhere?"

Carolina paused and looked at the man. What he'd said began to register with her. He wanted to learn to read. "I don't know, Mr. Culley. I haven't discussed the possibility of adult classes with Mr. MacAllistair, but the idea is a good one."

"It is?"

"It would take a good deal of effort on your part."

"Effort?" he repeated. She saw that something behind her had attracted his attention. "I guess if an Injun can learn to read, I oughta be able to handle it."

Carolina followed the direction of Culley's squinty gaze. Jim Bates was handing a keg of nails down from a wagon into Jacob's arms. "I seen him do it," Culley said.

"What?"

"Read. I seen him do it myself. Otherwise I'da never believed it."

"Mr. Black Hawk has a brain just like yours, Mr. Culley." She shook her head and laughed, feeling clever and mischievous and ecstatic all at once. "Well, not *just* like yours. But they undoubtedly bear some resemblance to one another." She couldn't resist recalling Mr. Darwin's book and imagining a chimpanzee labeled CULLEY.

Culley went away convinced that he'd been flattered.

As the work continued, Carolina stayed close by the women. There was talk of bringing a circuit preacher in once a month to hold services in the new building, and Carolina promised to supervise a Christmas pageant.

When lunch was served, Carolina exchanged a look with Jacob over the buffet. She knew she risked his anger in seeking even this much contact, but his eyes reassured her that he was not angry. He had missed her, too. He took his food and moved away from the group, hunkering down on his heels with the wheel of one of the wagons at his back for a windbreak.

"Bring your lunch over here, Miss Hammond." Carolina turned and saw Jim Bates sitting on the tailgate of another wagon, his smile lifting the deep grooves in his craggy face. "You won't be eating so much dust over here."

She glanced around her. Culley hovered nearby, and Bates's wagon was parked not far from where Jacob was dining alone. Bates's company would discourage Culley's. With a smile, she joined him on the tailgate.

"We missed you at the Independence Day doings, Miss Hammond." Bates lifted a forkful of beans to his mouth.

"Several of the others have expressed the same regret," she responded pleasantly. "People seem to form a close bond here quite readily."

"All we've got around here is each other." His gesture indicated that the whole community stood within these few yards. "Who else was asking after you?"

"Mr. Culley, for one."

"Miz MacAllistair said he was bothering you quite a bit, and I told him to keep his distance. You weren't sick, were you, ma'am?"

"Sick?"

"On the Fourth."

"Oh, no." She shook her head quickly and cut into a pickled beet. "I'm a private sort of person, Mr. Bates. Large social gatherings make me uncomfortable."

"I know how you feel. Miz MacAllistair, though, she sure likes to have a big to-do now and again."

"Marissa is a wonderful hostess."

"Miz MacAllistair's been the only real lady around here for a long time." Bates surveyed the group as though making sure he hadn't missed one somehow. "Now you come along. You kinda make an old fella like me realize what a lonely life he's got."

Carolina made herself busy with her food, but out of the corner of her eye she saw Jacob shake a line of tobacco into a piece of rolling paper.

"Guess I'm not really so old," Bates continued. "How old do you think I am, Miss Hammond?"

"What?" She read his expectation. "Oh. How old? I would guess you might be maybe . . . forty?"

Bates beamed as though she'd undershot the mark by a mile. "Be forty-two in September. Came out to Minnesota in seventy-five."

"Have you ever been married, Mr. Bates?"

"Was once. We had a little place down on the Minnesota River. The wife died with the first baby. Lost the baby, too. Didn't have much luck farming after that, so I headed west and started punching cows."

"Maybe you should have a ranch of your own."

It wasn't a novel suggestion, but he took it as encouragement. "I've thought about that a lot lately. I've got some money saved. Think I'd move farther west." He bit into a ham sandwich and thought it over again. "You don't think it's kinda late to start over?"

"I don't think so. This is a land of opportunity." She smiled. "I hope you find yours."

"Things work out right, I just might."

The conversation continued with Carolina's mechanical responses taken at face value. Bates was too pleased with her company to notice that she was listening with only one ear. For the most part she looked past him, watching the man who leaned against the wheel of a nearby wagon and lingered over a cigarette.

The contributions of many hands made for quick work. One team of men notched logs, while another hauled on the ropes that brought them up a pair of log skids and then set them in place. The clay soil provided ready material for chinking, and the children were more than happy to help mix it with water and straw, wedge chips of wood between the logs; and plaster the cracks shut.

When the food was put away and the dishes were clean, Carolina and Marissa joined the plastering party. "Don't overdo it, Mrs. MacAllistair." Both women turned from their work. Charles brushed a spot of mud from his wife's chin and showed his love in his smile. "I'm giving you half an hour to play in the mud, and then it's back in the wagon with you."

"Oh, Charles—"

"And I have a surprise for you," he told Carolina. "A walnut teacher's desk is on its way from Minneapolis."

"Oh, how lovely!" The two women said in unison, and Marissa added, "How about my credenza?"

Charles laughed. "Do you think I'd dare buy the teacher a desk without ordering that credenza I've been hearing about for months? And Gustav will have the tables and benches ready for the children by the time you're ready to start school."

"The primers should be here by early September." Carolina had ordered the books herself, insisting upon McGuffey's latest editions.

"You can start with the younger children as soon as you like, but the older ones will be needed in the field until after the harvest."

"I'm going into town tomorrow for supplies," Marissa said. Charles was ready with an objection, but Marissa nudged him and offered a convincing smile. "I haven't seen

Mother since the weekend of that terrible storm. Spend the night with us and come along with me, Carolina."

"I don't know, Marissa. I have some things—"

"Please say yes. You're becoming such a hermit." A mischievous smile edged its way into Marissa's eyes. "Charles can't go along, but I've asked Jacob to drive. He said he wanted to get some things for his mother."

Carolina plunged her hand into the bucket that stood between them. "I would be able to purchase some yard goods," she said as she examined a handful of mud. "And Bismarck is the only town I've seen since I came here."

"Well, Shields isn't Bismarck, but we do have a store."

"Where Marissa enjoys spending my money."

Carolina watched Marissa receive Charles's peck on her forehead and thought it a relief to have her *own* money to spend. "Will it be an all-day jaunt?" she asked.

"Pretty much. In another month I'm going to prohibit Mrs. MacAllistair from taking any more trips until after the baby is born. You'll see that she doesn't wear herself out on this one, won't you, Carolina?"

"I'll try."

"Haul 'er up!" came the order from another side of the building. Carolina took a couple of steps back and shaded her face with her arm as she squinted into the sky. Balanced on a rafter, Jacob hauled on the rope hand over hand, his sleek brown back taut and gleaming with his effort.

Jacob pulled the buckboard up to the house promptly at daybreak. It would be a long drive, and he hoped Marissa was ready. He was rarely asked to do this chore, but Marissa had approached him herself, and he did want some decent flour for his mother and some Bull Durham for himself. He wanted a cigarette now, which meant he was restless. He usually didn't smoke on an empty stomach, and his stomach was empty because he'd skipped breakfast. Carolina was here.

He figured she'd agreed to help out with the cooking or something while Marissa took the day off. He'd lain awake half the night thinking about her being in the house and thinking about the bath she must have taken before she went to bed and the nightgown she must be wearing and...Bates. He thought about Bates and his damned talk about his loneliness and his dreams of a ranch. Bates was old. Bates was losing his hair. Bates had been a farmer, and once a farmer, always a farmer. Bates was ... a white man. And a fair one, at that. At least he was someone Jacob knew, a man who shunned whiskey and women whose favors were for sale. Carolina would be safe with him, and he wouldn't have to worry that her husband was... Her husband. Carolina's husband. Since yesterday Jacob hadn't been able to get past the urge to break both of Bates's arms.

When Marissa came out of the house, Carolina was with her. Their good-mornings were full of feminine smiles and wiles, and Jacob refused to respond. He took the basket Carolina handed up to him and then leaned down to assist Marissa. She backed away.

"I forgot the lemonade. Go ahead, Carolina. I'll just be a minute."

He straightened slowly. Carolina stepped in front of Marissa, lifted her chin and met his stony stare. She refused to cower. He refused to bend. It was only after she had placed her foot on the hub of the front wheel that he offered her a hand. She settled on the wagon seat, and Jacob sat down beside her as Marissa shut the front door.

"You didn't know I was coming, did you?" Carolina asked quietly.

"No."

"Do you object?"

He said nothing as he stared straight ahead between the two horses.

"I appreciate all the work you did on the schoolhouse yesterday."

"It was part of my job."

"Was it? Did Charles tell you to help?"

"No." He wasn't sure why he'd gone to the schoolhouse raising. Self-torture, perhaps, just as this trip would be. He would be rubbing thighs with Carolina and thinking it might be a privilege Bates would be accorded one day.

"Then I thank you for helping," she insisted.

Marissa returned, and Jacob helped her into the seat, took up the reins and clucked the team into an easy trot.

"Are you hungry, Jacob?" Carolina asked. "You missed breakfast, so we brought ham and biscuits."

"I've got my hands full, Miss Hammond."

"Don't be unpleasant, now, Jacob," Marissa put in. "I planned this myself. We're going to have a lovely day together, and no one will be the wiser."

"Wiser about what, Mrs. MacAllistair?" Jacob slanted her a cold look. "Do the three of us share some secret?"

"I just thought the two of you would enjoy spending the day together practically alone."

"Since you suspect we enjoy each other's company, you must know we've been able to arrange to spend time together without your help," he said quietly. "And since I prefer *completely* alone to practically, perhaps I will leave you along the road somewhere, *hankaśi*."

Marissa squared her shoulders and clucked her tongue. "Honestly, Jacob—"

"What's the matter, Marissa? Shouldn't I call you *cousin*? Should I take care not to use the term in town at the same time I'm taking care not to appear to be too familiar with the new teacher?"

"Jacob, please," Carolina said. "Marissa meant no harm."

"I don't like the feeling that I've been maneuvered."

"It's all right, Carolina." Marissa leaned forward. "Jacob and I understand each other."

"No, Marissa, we do not understand each other. I have no time for games like this. I have no taste for playing the role of the Indian hired man."

"But we couldn't go to town unescorted."

Jacob gave Marissa another hard look. "Jim Bates would have been the proper choice for an escort. Cousin or not, I am the hired Indian. In town that's the role I must play." He turned his attention back to the team. "No, Marissa, I don't foresee a 'lovely day'."

"I see your point, *sic'esi*. I didn't think of it that way. I'm sorry." There were several moments of silence before Marissa asked in a shy tone, "May I call you *sic'esi*? My cousin?"

"You just did."

"I may yet learn to speak Lakota," she said with a smile.

He chuckled. "Don't let your mother hear you use it. She's worked too hard to make you white."

"I am who I am, Jacob." She shrugged. "My grandfather was French and my father is a Swede."

"Your grandmother was Lakota."

"Do you remember her?"

He nodded. "She gave me a candy stick once when my mother took me to the trading post."

"My grandfather used to say he never knew a woman who could nag in so many different languages."

Jacob leaned his elbows on his knees and felt some of the tension melt away. He looked at Carolina. Her hair was caught softly in a single braid down her back. The stray wisps around her face shone with the red-gold of the morning sun. The expression in her round blue eyes was artless.

"How many languages do you know to nag me with, little one?"

His eyes sparkled, and hers took the cue. "I can tell you about the Gallic Wars in Latin and serve up a meal in seven courses in French, but I probably couldn't conjugate any good nagging verbs except in English."

"That should do."

"I do think you should eat something, Jacob. Marissa made wonderful biscuits, and they should still be warm."

Laughing, he flexed his shoulders and stretched his back. Then he shot Marissa a glance. "English works well, doesn't it? Yes, Miss Hammond. I'm hungry."

Carolina delved into the basket for the ham and biscuit sandwiches she'd carefully wrapped in layers of toweling. She held one to his lips, and he devoured it, growling playfully as he tore the ham with his teeth. After he'd eaten his fill, he slowed the team to a walk, secured the reins over the dashboard and reached for the canteen.

"I thought your hands were full," Carolina remarked.

"The team will hold the road at a walk. If I let you pour water down my throat, you'll have me soaked." He tilted his head back for a deep draught and then grinned at her. "But the attention was welcome."

"A casual observer might think you have the stoic Jacob Black Hawk eating out of your hand, Carolina."

They turned their heads, Carolina craning her neck for a look at Marissa's bright smile.

"Be careful, *hankaśi*," Jacob warned. "I could still put you out along the road."

Swenson's Drygoods had once been Dubuque's Trading Post, but Marie Dubuque Swenson had long been the source of its charm. As a child she had minded her father's store, and now she was minding it under her husband's name. As soon as she saw the buckboard, she hurried outside to greet her daughter. Marie was the epitome of the typically handsome blending of French and Indian blood. Her dark, graying hair was pulled back into a twist, and her tawny skin complemented her delicate bone structure. Marissa launched herself into her mother's arms before Jacob had time to secure the reins and help her down.

He would have felt more comfortable if the women had made less clamor and fuss over seeing each other out there in the street. Carolina waited for his assistance and then suffered Marissa's exuberance over introductions while Jacob took inventory of the quiet streets. When the noisy women went inside, he remained in front of the store and had a cigarette. Three cowboys emerged from Kelly's Tavern. Apparently they'd been there all morning. They hung on one another and shared some humor amongst themselves before they crossed the street in the direction of the store. Jacob leaned against the hitching rail and took a deep pull on his cigarette.

"Swenson's must be a *ci*gar store now, boys." The big, blond cowboy peered hard at Jacob as they passed. "Got one o'them *ci*gar store Injuns right out front." The blonde turned his head on a rubbery neck as the three let themselves inside.

Jacob ground the cigarette butt under his boot. The cowboys were whiskeyed up, and Carolina was inside. That was all he knew, and all he needed to know. He went into the store.

Marie lifted a box of shotgun shells down from a shelf while one of the cowboys selected a sack of Bull Durham. The blond cowboy eyed Jacob. "You want this Injun in here, ma'am?"

"Certainly. He works for my son-in-law. Now, are these what you're looking for?" She placed the shells on the counter.

Jacob's intention was to blend quietly into the background until the cowboys left the store. He stationed himself near the door and feigned interest in a chessboard, on which a game had been left in progress. He smiled. The local German immigrants often challenged Swenson, the Swede, for a line of credit. Swenson always played white. As usual, he was winning.

"What do you think, Jacob?" He looked up, and a bolt of blue yard goods was shoved in his face. "I want to make something for your mother and for Ruth. Would they like this or something brighter?"

He raised his chin and stared, dumbfounded. What was wrong with this woman?

Carolina's smile was, as always, perfectly innocent. "Well, what do you think?" There was absolute silence in the store as he stared right through her. She looked confused.

"You choose," he said, almost inaudibly.

It suddenly struck Carolina that she had embarrassed him, and she felt her face grow hot. The cowboys completed their purchases. The blonde reached the door first, and he turned to Carolina with an insolent smirk on his face. "You that new school teacher out to MacAllistairs'?" There was no answer. "You sure got yourself a nice buck there, ma'am."

The three laughed after the last one out had closed the door behind them.

Without a glance at Carolina, Jacob strode to the counter and gave Marie his order. She totalled the bill, and he tossed the money on the counter. He turned to Marissa.

"Send for me at the blacksmith's when you're ready. I'll load the wagon."

And then he was gone.

Carolina stood quietly, clutching the bolt of cloth. "He warned me so many times," she muttered. "I didn't . . . I simply didn't . . ."

Marissa was at her side with a comforting hug. "It seemed innocent, but you must be on your guard, my dear. These cowboys have their own silly set of ethics."

"Ethics?" The word hardly fit the behavior she'd just witnessed.

"Where women are concerned," she explained. "We're either saints or sinners. Don't worry about them. Jacob can take care of himself, and we're going to have tea with Mother."

Carolina was not good company. Her perfunctory contributions to the conversation did little to hide the fact that the cowboy's remark still stung. When Marissa announced that it was time to hunt Jacob down and load the supplies, Carolina was on her feet immediately and on her way to the door.

"Carolina, it might be better if I—"

"The smith is just down the street, isn't he?" She pointed in the general direction. "I believe I saw the sign. I'll find him."

Carolina surveyed the row of buildings across the rutted street. The afternoon had grown oppressively hot, and the town had all but gone to sleep. The guests at the hotel must have been keeping cool inside, and the tavern was probably doing a brisk business. Carolina located the LIVERY AND BLACKSMITH at the end of the street. Each clop of her heel against the plank sidewalk echoed in the plank- and log-front canyon. The dust lay undisturbed in the street.

She stepped off the walkway at the end of the block. A sign on the side of the smith's barn pointed to an entrance in the back. She could hear the clang of mallet and anvil, and she wondered now whether her appearance at the back door would anger Jacob even more.

Suddenly she was jerked from behind. Her shoulder was wrenched painfully as her body reeled backward and her feet skittered against the compacted ruts in the street. She stumbled back against a big body, and her feet churned in futile rebellion. Craning her neck, she got a glimpse of the blond cowboy. A dirty, callused hand cut off her short screech, and she was dragged across the alley and behind a pair of rickety outhouses.

He reeked of whiskey and sweaty flannel. "Be still now, little lady. If you want it bad enough to be getting it from a redskin, you're sure as hell gonna like what I got here."

She pulled at the hand that covered her mouth and kicked up with her heels. He laughed and slid his feet apart so that his shins were out of reach. Carolina sank her teeth into his hand, clamping her jaws until she tasted blood. The man yowled like a whipped dog and slammed her face-first into the back wall of a privy.

"Feisty bitch!" He spun her around, and her neck snapped back. She hit her head against the wall, and it bounced forward again, only to receive the back of his hand across her cheek.

Carolina's senses reeled, and her vision was murky. Her shout for help was cut off again as he pinned her against the wall with a breath-stealing hand on her chest. He fumbled under her skirt with his free hand. "No more noise, now," he ordered. "Be a good little squaw and I'll let you get back to your sewing."

She fought to push his hands away. His weight became unbearable, and then it was suddenly lifted from her chest.

Gasping for breath, she slid down the wall. Two bodies dropped to the ground in front of her. As she struggled to orient herself, she heard a fist-pounding thud and a grunt. Another deep breath cleared her vision, and the first thing she saw clearly was the rage in Jacob's eyes as he pummeled the man beneath him. Carolina gave herself over to a flooding sense of relief. Straddling the cowboy on the ground, Jacob got both hands around the man's thick neck and uttered a low animal growl in his throat as he rocked back and forth in fury. A gurgling sound issued from the cowboy's throat.

"Jacob, no!" Carolina crawled on her hands and knees in his direction. "You'll kill him, Jacob. Stop!" When she reached him, she grabbed his arm. He turned his head, saw her face and released the inert cowboy. They looked down at the man together. "Is he dead?"

Jacob flexed his hands to release the tension in them and then felt for a pulse in the man's neck. "No. He lives."

Carolina closed her eyes and shuddered. She wasn't sure whether she was sorry or relieved by the news. Jacob touched her cheek, and she winced with pain. "He struck you," Jacob said in a voice that was like thunder's low warning. Carolina felt a rush of shame, and she couldn't meet Jacob's eyes. Without another word he stepped over the unconscious man and lifted her into his arms. The pounding inside her head matched the pounding in his chest as she dropped her face against him. He carried her to the back entrance of the store and kicked the door open to gain admittance.

Marissa came running. "Oh, my God, Jacob! What happened?"

"That white bastard did this to her." Carolina's head lolled against his shoulder, and he was afraid she'd lost consciousness. "The blond one."

"I'll get the doctor," Marissa offered. "Mother, we need a doctor!"

Marie's face had appeared in the kitchen doorway, and her eyes widened instantly. "Put her in there, on the bed. What happened?"

"That cowboy!" Marissa answered as she hurried out the front door.

Jacob leaned over Carolina and examined the welt on her face. "Where do you hurt, little one?"

"Inside," she whispered.

"Inside?" The word tore through his gut. He'd seen no sign—the man's pants were buttoned—Carolina's clothes were—but his hand, his scavenging hand had been beneath her skirt! Rising slowly, Jacob tasted bile and smelled blood.

Carolina snatched his hand and held fast with both of hers. "Stay with me, Jacob."

"I cannot let him live."

"Jacob, no! I'm all right. I'm just shaking inside, and my head—" He was looking down at her as though he couldn't quite focus. "I'm all right, Jacob," she whispered again. "Nothing happened. He didn't have time."

"He didn't—"

She shook her head and tugged on his hand. He sank to his knees beside the bed. "I should have stayed."

"No. I embarrassed you, and I'm sorry. You could not have foreseen this."

"I should have gone after him when he spoke to you as he did."

"There were three of them," she reminded him.

"Do you think I can't handle three drunken white bastards? Do you think your honor means so little to me? If I am to be hanged as a murdering savage, or spat upon as a coward, I will choose—"

She covered his lips with her fingertips. "Neither. There must be another choice—Jacob!" Pain shot through her as she moved. "My shoulder hurts."

Marie set a bowl of water and a soft cloth on the bedside table. Jacob could see that the intimacy she witnessed surprised her. He turned away from her frown, and she said nothing.

Carolina winced when he touched the wet cloth to her face. "I'll probably be black and blue for a while," she said. "The worst part was that filthy paw over my mouth and the taste of it when I bit him. I wish I could inject poison, like a rattlesnake."

He washed the purpling welts with warm water. There was no change in the tender expression on his face, though anger roiled inside him. "If you are attacked by an unarmed man, the hardest blow you can land in his groin will be your best defense."

"That's good advice, Miss Hammond, crude as it sounds." A gray-haired man in a dark suit approached the bed. "I'm Doc Wells. Mind if I take a look?"

Jacob moved away from the bed, and the doctor sat down. Marissa and Marie looked on from the doorway. Carolina felt as though she might have been a curiosity in Mr. P.T. Barnum's museum. She would have preferred to crawl off by herself to lick her wounds.

The doctor tested her shoulder. "That hurt?" Carolina turned her face away. "The sheriff has Sanderson over at the jail. He was beaten pretty good. Couple of broken ribs. Looks like he had it coming, to my way of thinking. How about your head?"

"It hurts."

He probed through her hair with his fingers. "Nasty bump. Does your vision seem blurred?" She shook her head. "I'll leave a powder for the headache. Nothing seems to be broken, but that shoulder might be wrenched pretty bad."

Doc Wells rose to his feet on creaking joints and turned to Jacob. "I'd stay out of sight for a while if I were you. Sanderson's a troublemaker."

"I should have killed him," Jacob said quietly.

"Then they'd have hung you, boy. No, I'd say Sanderson got just what he had coming. You lay low for a while and let the talk die down."

The doctor sent everyone out of the room and examined Carolina more thoroughly. When he left, Carolina called for Marissa.

"We must leave town as soon as we can," Carolina insisted. "Jacob has been pushed to the limit."

"You need to rest, dear." Marissa mixed the powder the doctor had prescribed and brought it to Carolina's bedside. "We'll leave in time to get home before dark."

"Doctor Wells could see how it was with us." Carolina accepted the glass. "He didn't seem terribly shocked."

Marissa watched her friend drink the painkilling potion. "He's a good man, Doctor Wells. He's worked among the Indians. There's so much illness among them, and he's tried to help." She knew that Doctor Wells felt pity for the pair rather than disdain, but she kept that to herself. Carolina needed rest, not more admonition.

Intending to close her eyes for just a moment, Carolina drifted into sleep, which her battered body welcomed. It was late afternoon when a light tapping on the door brought her awake. Groggy, she got up to answer. Every movement brought another aching muscle into play.

"The sheriff is here to talk to you," Marissa whispered through the crack in the door.

Sheriff Pritchard was an older man with few social graces, as his cheekful of tobacco made evident. "Wanted to see how much Sanderson roughed you up, ma'am."

Carolina gingerly lowered herself into a chair in the front room. "You see my face, sheriff. The rest you will have to accept on faith."

He gave her face a beetle-browed perusal. "What do you think he had in mind, Miss Hammond? Sanderson, I mean."

Carolina's lips thinned as she folded her hands tightly in her lap. "What he had in mind was a violation of my body, Sheriff Pritchard."

"He told you that?"

"Yes," she clipped. "In no uncertain terms."

"Did the Indian pull him off you, or did Sanderson back off first on his own?"

Carolina swallowed and fixed her eyes firmly on the man's face. "He was crushing my chest with one hand and lifting my skirt with the other when Mr. Black Hawk jumped on him from behind."

Pritchard's eyes widened. The lady didn't mince words. "I guess Sanderson's got a little jail time coming."

"How much?" she demanded.

"A while. Long enough to let things cool off a bit." He braced a hand on his knee and leaned closer. "Take my advice, Miss Hammond. Be mindful of your station in life. People start thinking there's something going on between you and Black Hawk—" He raised his hand to deflect any objections. "Now I know Black Hawk sounds almost white when he talks, but that don't make no never mind. Sometimes Easterners don't understand the way of things here, and I'm just offering a piece of advice. Years ago the Indians around here gave us a lot of trouble, and folks don't forget easily. The Sioux have been keeping to themselves lately, and that's the way we like it.''

Carolina stared so hard that the man's features blurred. She ignored his curt leave-taking. Marissa saw the sheriff to the door, then joined Carolina.

"Are we ready to leave?" Carolina asked.

"In a few minutes. Why don't you lie down now, dear?"

"The sheriff thinks I brought this on myself."

Marissa frowned. "Pritchard is an old prune face. Don't worry about what he thinks."

"I feel dirty, Marissa. I hate this feeling."

Marissa took Carolina's hands and drew her to her feet. "You need quiet time, my dear." Carolina allowed herself to be led to the bedroom. "Just wait here. We're almost ready to leave."

Carolina stood before the mirror and pulled her hair back tightly from her face. Jacob's reflection joined her own, and the door closed softly behind him.

"Not like that, *wiwašteka*." He stood behind her and freed her hair from the pins. "Your hair must not be tied up in a knot like that."

"Are we ready to go?"

"Soon." He smoothed her hair with both hands. "Do you have much pain?"

"No."

It was a lie.

He moved his hands to her shoulders and then slowly, patiently, slid them up and down her arms. The truth came in the tears when they spilled in silence over her cheeks. Jacob knew them to be a good sign. He turned her around and took her in his arms. He ached to tell her that this would never happen again. He wanted to promise that his protection was all she would ever need, but such was not the way of the world. If he hadn't come outside today, if he hadn't been there to hear her cry out . . .

"I misunderstood when you told me you had pain inside."

"I know. But I'm really all right." She shuddered with the words.

"No, you're not. I feel it, too, *waśtelakapi*." He pressed his lips against her hair and then whispered, "I love you, and I feel your pain."

It felt good to cry. It was a relief to be able to let the tears flow and let his shirt absorb them. "What if . . . if he had succeeded?" She took a deep breath and swiped at her tears. "If I had been violated, Jacob, would you still—"

"I would love you, and I would weep with you as I do now." She looked up quickly, and he gave a sad smile. "Inside."

"You're not angry with me?"

"I am angry, little one, but not with you."

She blinked away more tears and managed a smile. "According to Doctor Wells, you fixed that wretched man but good."

"I would gladly fix him the way he should be fixed and feed the trophy to the vultures."

"Jacob!"

"My people could teach yours some lessons about justice." He touched her chin and kissed the welt on her cheek with soft lips and the delicate flutter of his tongue. "Let me take you away from this place."

She could think of nothing she wanted more.

Chapter Eleven

Carolina spent several days at the ranch. Because her bruised face would have been a topic of discussion, she avoided the kitchen at mealtime. Jacob did not seek her out, but Culley did. He appeared just inside the kitchen door one morning after breakfast was over.

"I, uh, I come back to get..." He pointed to the table, then back over his shoulder toward the mudroom and finally thrust his hat forward. "Forgot my hat." He shifted his weight from one bowed leg to the other and made no move to leave.

"Something else, Mr. Culley?" Carolina asked as she dropped a handful of forks into a drawer.

"I see it's true." He gestured with his hat again. "You got a bruise on your face there."

Carolina shut the drawer.

"We heard about Sanderson, ma'am. We heard he was drunk, and he tried to do something bad."

"It was an unfortunate incident, Mr. Culley, and I hoped it would be forgotten quickly."

Marissa came down the steps, stopped at the kitchen door and cocked her arms, slamming her hands on her hips. "Mr. Culley, I fed you once this morning."

"S'cuse me, Miz MacAllistair, but I heard about the terrible incident in town, and I had to come and see for myself. No self-respecting man on the place should let this pass without doing what's right by Miss Hammond." He waved his hat in the air like a pointer. "Now I know that Injun was prob'ly the only hand the boss could spare that day, since the rest of us have important jobs to do, but I always say, never send a redskin out to do a white man's job."

"Mr. Culley—"

"Two fine ladies out for the day with no man to look after them, and look what happens. Now, I intend to see that snake Sanderson make proper amends for what he done. I surely do."

Carolina had taken another handful of silverware from the dishpan. The water dripped on the floor as she stood staring at the man. "That will not be necessary, Mr. Culley. Ja—"

"The sheriff took care of Sanderson," Marissa put in quickly. "Miss Hammond is anxious to put this behind her."

"Well, I don't blame her, such a fine lady. She offered to teach me how to read, Miz MacAllistair. Did you know that?"

"No, I—"

"Mr. Culley, I said I—"

"You don't need to worry about Sanderson," Culley promised as he backed out the door. "He's got some paybacks coming to him."

The two women looked at each other after the man was gone. "You offered to teach him to read?"

"I said I would ask Charles about an adult class." Carolina let out a huff. "I'm thinking maybe Jacob should be the one to teach it." She tossed the dish towel on the counter.

"Marissa, you were right. I need some quiet time. I'm going back to the cabin."

Marissa was content with Carolina's decision only after she agreed to return to the ranch for the weekend.

In the days she spent alone at the cabin, Carolina grew stronger. She had vegetables to harvest and put up, flowers to tend and seeds to put by for the following year. Being alone after dark was another matter. Shadows and sounds in the night were hard to identify. As long as she kept busy, she was fine, but when she lay still in her bed, she remembered the grabbing, the shoving, the smell of that hand.

Her skin crawled, and she needed Jacob to take the crawly feeling away. Soap and water didn't help. Thinking reasonably didn't help. She needed to know that he was not disgusted by her now, as she was with herself. It was not sensible of her to feel this way. The man had been stopped. But not by her. She had not fought him off, and he had succeeded in invading her privacy. She carried the taste of his hand and the smell of his breath in her head, and because of those things the invasion continued. In the daylight she was strong, but at night she hated herself.

On Friday night the disgust turned to terror. Carolina lay in her bed with the covers pulled over her head. She was sweating all over, and the air under her blankets grew stale and stagnant. When she could no longer stand it, she stuck her face up for air, but the howl of a coyote sent her back under the covers. The coyote was joined by a mate, and soon they had a pack of yowlers sending up cries that at times sounded like tortured children. Carolina huddled under her blankets until dawn. Then she carried her blanket with her to the window and peeked outside. The sun rose laughing.

Payday for the ranch hands meant a night on the town. Even Jim Bates decided it was time he listened to a little piano music and had a few belly laughs. Soon after quitting time, the hands were gone. Carolina sat on the veranda with Marissa while Charles and young Charlie perched on the corral railing and watched Jacob work a spirited two year old.

"Why hasn't he come to see me, Marissa?"

Marissa's chair creaked as she rocked. "It's only been a few days. He asked me if I would go check on you, but I told him you were coming back for the weekend."

"I think he's disgusted."

"Disgusted?" Marissa turned her head against the high back of the rush rocker. "With you?" Carolina nodded. "Don't be ridiculous. He's furious with Sanderson is what he is."

"I don't know, Marissa." She studied her hands. "I'm disgusted with myself. It's silly, I know."

Marissa laid her hand on Carolina's arm. "You need to be with your friends now."

"Everyone here was staring at me, pitying me—even judging me. And Jacob stayed away."

"I think he blames himself for what happened. I've watched him brood over it."

"He should have come to see me. If he—"

"Don't push him, dear. Have you thought about where all of this is leading the two of you?"

Carolina watched the activity in the corral. "Of course I have. He says we can only have one day at a time—no future. I only know that when I am not with him, I'm miserable."

"And you want a future with him." Carolina turned to Marissa. A look was all that was needed to confirm the statement. Marissa smiled. "Let's go join the men."

The gray colt planted all four feet firmly in the dirt and tossed his head in objection to the steady pressure Jacob applied to the hackamore. He rode bareback, and his moccasined heel was buried in the animal's right flank while he spoke softly in Lakota. His patience was rewarded when the colt finally circled to the right.

Charles put his arm around Marissa's shoulders. "The gray didn't even offer to buck. What do you say we make him Charlie's horse?"

"You mean it, Papa?" the boy squealed.

"If Jacob doesn't find any fault with him, he'll be yours." Charlie clapped his hands and threatened to tumble off the corral rail until his father steadied him with a "Whoa, there."

They watched Jacob apply his tactics to reverse the colt's direction. Charlie applauded again. "He's a good horse, isn't he, Jacob?"

"He will be."

Charles turned to his wife. "Looks like you'll have your milk cow soon. She's working on that calf."

"You mean my Lily's finally going to freshen?" Carolina's questioning look elicited an explanation. "Charles brought this Jersey heifer home from Minnesota last year. I think she's going to be a good milker."

"Jacob," Charles called out, "what do you know about pulling calves?"

"Not much." Jacob rode closer to the railing. "I've watched them do it. You people go to a lot of trouble for cow's milk."

"Don't you like milk?" Carolina asked. She needed to say something to break the ice.

Jacob swung down from the colt's back, his eyes suggesting that there was humor in her question. "It makes me sick. Like snakebite and green tomatoes. We're meant to drink the milk from our mothers, and my mother is not a cow." Carolina brightened as he approached her. "How are you, Miss Hammond?"

"Much better, thank you."

"That looks like a sensible dress." Carolina looked down at the divided skirt and back up at him, smiling. "Is it made for riding?"

"Yes."

"Is the mare working well for you?"

"Yes, she is."

"Then let's take her out in the pasture. The colt will work better with another horse along." He turned to Charles. "How soon must we do this thing with the milk cow?"

"No contractions yet, but there's swelling, and she looks worried."

Jacob laughed. "She worries about someone pulling on her teats every day after this is over." He handed Carolina the colt's reins between the rails. "Hold him while I get your mare."

Carolina touched the colt's velvety nose and smiled. Her own worries had suddenly taken flight, and she turned her smile on Marissa and then Charles. Her eyes were beacons of joy.

"He's a fine man, Carolina," Charles said after Jacob had disappeared from sight. "One of the finest I know. But I'm afraid you're letting yourself in for a lot of trouble. I hope you know what you're doing."

The beacons shone on. "I know exactly what I'm doing. I'm going for a ride with a fine man."

They shared a quiet ride at a leisurely pace across the vast, undulating prairie. Carolina surprised Jacob by mounting her horse from the right, Indian style. It was a good time to share with her, he thought—the cool of the evening at the end of a hot day. A breeze kept the mosquitoes at bay, and even the gray seemed to enjoy the outing. He was responding well to the subtle shifts of his rider's weight. The horses were drawn to the smell of water as they reached the banks of the little creek that snaked its way across the grassy flat.

Jacob dropped to his feet and let the gray dip its nose into the water. He watched Carolina follow his lead. "You're quiet this evening." She turned from the mare and looked up. He brushed his hand across her cheek. "The mark is almost gone."

"I had hoped you would come to the cabin."

He drew his hand back and turned away, staring across the creek. "Is that why you left the ranch? To give me a chance to follow you there?"

"That's partly why. I was also uncomfortable with the attention I was getting, with the way people looked at me."

"How did they look at you, Carolina?" His voice was flat and distant.

"As though they wondered what *really* happened."

"You don't enjoy those stares."

"No, I don't."

"I don't enjoy them, either." He looked down at the reins he held in his hands. "How will it be when the eyes tell you they know you've been with an Indian?" She didn't respond. "It becomes more difficult to tell me it doesn't matter, doesn't it?"

"Being with you is not the same. That man tried to rape me, Jacob."

His eyes were hard as they bored into hers. "No, it would not be the same. They pity you for his actions because you resisted and called him an animal. They would despise you for mine because you accept me and call me a man. I stayed away from the cabin knowing you must realize that now."

"The only thing I realized was that you stayed away from *me*." His eyes softened instantly, and she stepped closer.

"Don't turn away from me, Jacob. Not unless you don't want me anymore."

One fist tightened around the reins, but his other arm surrounded her shoulders and pulled her to his chest almost as a reflex. "A man needs to protect his woman."

"You did," she whispered into his neck. "Thank God, you were there. Oh, Jacob, the nights have been terrible."

"I know."

"I thought you were angry with me."

"No, *wastelakapi*, no."

"I hated the way he made me feel, Jacob. Make that feeling go away."

"If I killed him—"

"No!" She kissed the corner of his mouth and spoke with her nose touching his cheek. "If you touched me your way, I would forget his."

He lifted her face in his hand and angled his head for a long, slow, possessive kiss. He slipped his tongue past her lips, and she welcomed him with a soft sound of female satisfaction. He stiffened and raised his head.

"Jacob?"

"Not here, little one," he whispered. "Not now. My way would take all night."

"Another night?"

He pressed his lips against her temple. "Yes."

"You'll come to the cabin?"

He closed his eyes. This could not go on. But he admitted, "I can't stay away as long as I know your door is open to me."

"And I can be shameless with you again." Her laugh came from somewhere deep in her throat. "It's such a good, good feeling to be shameless."

"Yes," he whispered, then kissed her. "Yes, it is." He closed his mouth over hers and sipped her sweetness. This could not end.

When they rode back into the yard, they heard the unmistakable bellow of a cow in trouble. Charles appeared at the barn door and waved for Jacob to come inside.

"How will the calf be pulled?"

Jacob opened the corral gate and took the mare's reins from Carolina. "We'll tie a rope to the front legs and use a horse to pull it. It's necessary sometimes with a first calf." She turned her mouth down, and he smiled. "Go inside now."

"I'll make coffee."

He nodded and led the horses into the corral. Carolina went to the house and found Marissa resting on the settee in the living room.

"I'm so glad you're back," Marissa said as she swung her feet to the floor and sat up. "That bellowing is driving me to distraction. I know what poor Lily's going through, and I keep thinking pain, pain, pain."

"Think baby, baby, baby." Carolina sat next to Marissa and squeezed her hand. "Did you have a difficult time with Charlie?"

"Terrible time." She rested her neck against the rosewood carving on top of the settee. "I'm small, and he was a big baby. The pains went on and on for hours. *Days.*"

"Are you scared?"

Marissa raised her head and met her friend's worried gaze. This was a woman's blessing, and it was her greatest anxiety. The latter was not for men's ears. "I try not to be, but I am."

"It should be easier this time, since you've had one."

"I've had three," Marissa corrected. "I've lost two."

"We'll keep you off your feet this time. I'll help you all I can."

Marissa pouted. "How can you help me when you're up there in that stupid cabin?"

Carolina tilted her head, considering. "I have an idea. If Jacob consents, let's ask his sister, Ruth, to stay here for a while. She could help you while I'm at school, and we could teach her more English."

"Do you mean you'd stay here at the house?"

"There will be times, yes. When the weather's bad, when your time draws near—"

"I don't really know Ruth."

"She's your cousin, too."

Marissa looked down at their two hands. She made a practice of avoiding the sun, and she knew that Carolina did not, but Carolina's skin was lighter. Even Charles's was lighter than hers was. She liked to tease him about the white strip across his forehead.

"She's a lovely girl," Carolina said. "Of course, I don't know that her parents would permit it, but I do know Jacob's mother encourages her children to learn to read and to speak English."

"Perhaps I could learn some Lakota."

That brought a smile from Carolina. "I have several motives. Jacob tells me that the Indian children are sent away to boarding school under the present system. It occurs to me that we need some more teachers here."

"Like Ruth?"

"In time, perhaps even Jacob himself."

Marissa's eyes widened. "Oh, my friend, you are a conniver. But who would pay them?"

Carolina shrugged. "Money doesn't seem important to Jacob, which would make him well suited to the teaching profession. It's just an idea. Meanwhile you need some help."

"I would love to have her stay. I wish I had your wonderful sense of independence, Carolina, but I really hate being alone."

"I won't leave you alone." She tugged at Marissa's hand. "Not if you'll come into the kitchen with me. I promised coffee."

"And I have apple cake in the pantry." Marissa licked her lips and rolled her eyes saucily. "I've been dying for another piece."

"So, it's true." Carolina led the way, heading for the coffeepot. "Expectant mothers do prowl the kitchen at night."

"We have our quirks. We're sick half the time, tired *all* the time, moody, and finally—" Marissa puffed up her cheeks "—fat. About the only good part is being spared the monthlies."

Carolina stared at the pot as though it were sprouting a tail as awareness raised its head in her brain. She hadn't thought about that in some time, not since she'd promised Jacob that she would tell him when it happened. She hadn't told him. It hadn't happened.

"I always end up in bed," Marissa went on. "I get terrible headaches, awful stomach cramps. Do you?"

"Stomach cramps? Um . . . no, not usually."

"How lucky."

Carolina put the pot on the stove and stood back to study it. "Do you get sick right away, Marissa? When you're pregnant, I mean."

"About the third month with me. Some women don't get sick at all." She set the cake on the counter. "I get all the symptoms."

"Are there others?"

"Sore breasts. Nothing you wear seems soft enough."

Carolina turned from the stove and found Marissa staring. Carolina gave a quick smile. "No one explains these things to an old maid. I know the scientific aspect, but science is not concerned with what a woman feels." Marissa still looked skeptical. "The books are all written by men," Carolina added lightly.

"And men get women with child. You *do* know that, don't you, dear?"

"Of course." She flashed a naughty smile. "And I think the man who got you that way is coming in the door."

Lily had successfully delivered her calf with Jacob's and Charles's help. They celebrated with cake and coffee, and Carolina decided that the feeling among the four was friendly enough to broach the subject of giving Ruth a job. Charles was delighted with the idea, and Jacob promised to discuss it with his family. The men went back to the barn, and the women lingered over their coffee and their plans. Bedtime came too early for Carolina. She found that sleep eluded her again, but this time fear was only a small factor.

She spent several days at the ranch and then returned to the cabin. She decided a doctor would only tell her what she already knew, but she would have to make arrangements for an examination sooner or later. Someone would have to take her to town, and she had eliminated all prospects but Jacob. He had to know. She wrangled with herself over the prospect of telling him, burdening him, trapping him. But the ethical choice was clear to her, and she intended to tell him. He had promised to come to the cabin, and she waited nearly a week. Still he did not come.

It struck Carolina that the ranch was napping in the late afternoon sun as she trotted her sleek roan across the yard.

She turned the mare loose in an empty pen and considered the barn door and the advisability of storming it.

"Afternoon, Miss."

With an inner groan Carolina turned to face Culley. He and Bill Tanner were approaching the corral on horseback, and Culley wore a wide grin. "You just ride in?"

"Yes, I did. How are you, Mr. Tanner?" Bill Tanner touched the brim of his hat and muttered a greeting. "It seems quiet around here."

"You missed all the excitement," Culley told her as he swung down from his horse. "Sheriff was out yesterday. Arrested the Injun."

Carolina's pulse rate surged. "Arrested...Jacob?"

"Yeah, ol' Blanket Bottom himself. Left here trussed up like a turkey."

"Never seen a man fight the cuffs as hard as he did," Bill said quietly.

"Did my citizen's duty and gave the sheriff and his deputies a hand." Culley tucked a thumb in his belt and postured proudly. "Nobody else'd lift a finger to help."

Carolina turned to Tanner. "What reason? What charge?"

"Murder."

"Bud Sanderson," Culley supplied.

"Sanderson? That terrible man who—impossible!" She headed for the house.

"Got himself some real trouble now," Culley crowed.

"Where is Charles?"

"Boss is gone," Culley called after her. "Off to Minneapolis on business."

Carolina burst into the house. Her hands were shaking, and her mind was dazed. "Marissa! Is it true? Where's Jacob?"

Marissa hurried from the kitchen. "Oh, Carolina, I didn't know whether to send for you or—" She raised her hands in a beseeching gesture. "I couldn't stop them, and Charles is gone—he should be in Minneapolis by now. They put him in handcuffs, Carolina. They. . .they. . ."

The women embraced one another. "When did this killing take place?" Carolina asked.

"That's just it. It happened Saturday night, the night they pulled the calf. All the other hands were in town."

"But Jacob was here." Carolina drew back. "Did it happen in town?"

Marissa nodded. "He was knifed. They found him behind the blacksmith's barn."

"But Jacob was here!" Carolina gripped Marissa's arms. "Didn't you tell them that?"

"I told them everything—about the calf and having coffee. That night Jacob went back out to the barn with Charles, and that's the last I saw of him."

"But he was with *Charles*."

"They said they'd have to hear that from Charles, himself. They said Jacob was the best suspect they had."

"Why?"

"You know why. The fight. Jacob said he wanted to kill Sanderson after—"

"I wanted to kill him, too!" Carolina dropped her arms and turned away. "I'll tell them I was with him."

Marissa grabbed Carolina's shoulder and pulled her back around. "Jacob won't want you to expose yourself to any more speculation, and they might not—"

"Expose myself! Good Lord, Marissa, this is a trumped-up murder charge. I'll tell them whatever I have to."

"And they won't believe you. I'm not even sure the sheriff will telegraph Charles as I asked." Marissa rubbed her hand over Carolina's back. "I'm sending Jim into town to wire a message. Let's try to stay calm until Charles gets back. I know he can take care of this."

"I'm going with Mr. Bates."

"Oh, no, Carolina, that's not—"

"I have to see Jacob."

There was no question of changing her mind. Marissa saw the determination in her eyes. "Tell Jacob not to do anything or say anything. He could be lynched. They've done it before."

"I know." Carolina's voice did not waver, nor did the look in her eyes.

"He must try not to give them any excuses. You'll stay at my mother's, and you will not stray from Jim's sight."

Carolina held the edge of the wagon seat tightly in both hands and kept her eyes on the rutted road. The trip was made longer by her own anxiety and Bates's uneasiness. Small talk was impossible. There were too many big worries, big questions. After several false starts, Bates finally voiced the one that loomed largest for him.

"I guess a fella has to wonder why you'd be going to see Jake Black Hawk in jail, Miss Hammond."

"I guess wondering is a person's prerogative."

He kept his eyes on the spot between the lead horse's ears. "You understand, I got nothing personal against his kind." There was a moment of tolerant silence. "Jake's about the best wrangler I ever seen." A moment of silent admiration passed. "But I think a lot of you, too."

"I wouldn't make much of a wrangler, Mr. Bates."

He glanced at her and took note of the set of her jaw. "Maybe not, but I think you'd make a fine wife for the right kind of man."

"I think so, too." She didn't want to be angry with this man. She needed his help.

"I know I'm some years older than you are, but I've been thinking..."

"Mr. Bates, if you tell me what you've been thinking, it will make us both feel even more uncomfortable with this situation than we do now."

He fixed his attention on the lead horse again. "White women don't take up with Indian men, ma'am. It just ain't done. You think Jake's in trouble now, but I guarantee, something like that would bring on—"

"I know. I would be ostracized by my own...kind."

"Those people are different from us, ma'am. Working together is one thing, but when it comes down to what's right and proper for a lady like you, well...there's plenty of good white men to choose from around here. And Jake, he needs to find him a nice Indian girl."

"Mr. Bates—"

He shook his head and expelled a pent-up breath. "Look, I know that didn't come out right. Jake's in a tough spot. He's a good boy. He's had schooling, and if it wasn't for those braids, he would look damn near—"

"Human?"

"White."

They looked at each other, and their separate perspectives were clear. Jim Bates sighed. "I'll get you in that jailhouse, Miss Hammond, and I'll give that deputy a stiff warning against any gossip about your being there."

"Thank you, Mr. Bates."

"And just take what I've been saying as friendly advice. You're gonna need friends, Miss Hammond. So is Jake."

It was not yet dark when they arrived in Shields. Jim suggested that they avoid the sheriff's office until after nightfall. Carolina agreed that the telegram was more urgent than her visit, and she asked to be left with Doc Wells. As long as she had the time, she said, it wouldn't hurt to have him look at her shoulder. When Jim called for her again, she followed him to the jail without a word. He imagined she'd never seen the inside of a jail cell and that the prospect had finally hit home with her. When they came to the door, he asked, "You sure you want to do this?" He received only a quick nod.

Carolina peered through the bars into the darkness of the tiny cell. The deputy's lantern cast eerie shadows on the floor, and the moon's white light glowed through the barred window. A blue-black figure stood in the shadows beside the window. Carolina saw the outline of his profile in the moonlight as he blew a stream of smoke into the night air beyond the bars.

"You got company, Injun." The deputy set his lantern on the floor and fumbled with his keys. Jacob shifted his weight from one leg to the other. The ash on his cigarette glowed near his face. The keys clanked, and the lock clicked open, but Jacob did not turn from the window.

"May we have a few minutes alone?" Carolina asked quietly. At the sound of her voice, Jacob turned slowly.

"Guess it can't hurt." The door creaked as the deputy swung it open for her. "Got to lock you in, though. Get your business done quick. I could get in a lotta trouble for this."

Carolina stepped inside. Jacob dropped the cigarette and crushed it under his boot as he took a step toward her. The door clicked shut behind her back, and the lock ground into place.

"Thank you," she said, but her eyes were riveted to the shadowy outline of Jacob's face. They listened to the deputy's footsteps as he shuffled back to the office, taking his lantern with him.

"Why have you come here?" His voice was low and even, and there was an angry edge to his question.

"I had to see you." She stepped closer.

"You didn't have to see me here. This is a cage for an animal."

"This is a terrible mistake, Jacob. When Charles gets back, he'll tell them where you were that night."

"I have told them." The moon cast a halo on her hair, and he wondered what she was thinking as she looked up at him with those beautiful round eyes. Was this the humiliation that would drive her away? "I have also told them that I wanted to kill the bastard myself, but if I had, they would not have found the knife in his back."

"Please don't say anything more to them, Jacob. There are people who would hang you without a trial."

She stood so close that he could smell the flower-scented soap in her hair. He ached to touch her, but this place had made him feel unclean.

"A trial?" He gave a bitter laugh. "Where I would be told to swear on their Bible before I told them again that I did not kill anyone? My word means nothing to them, with or without any Bible." He turned his face to the window. "You should not have come here."

"I have something to tell you," she said quietly as she laid her hand on his arm. She felt his muscles tighten. "You must not antagonize them, Jacob. We've telegraphed Charles, and he'll be here soon."

"I can't stay in this place," he told her. "It stinks of the men who have been here before, men like Sanderson. Their lice infest the blankets."

"I'll bring you a clean blanket, Jacob, please—"

"When a Lakota is locked up, he loses touch with his spirit. Sometimes the only way out is—"

She sealed his lips with her fingers and whispered, "No!"

He closed his hand around hers and lowered them both to his side. "You must go."

She stepped close, took his hand in both of hers and pressed it to her belly. In the moonlight she saw his face, saw the question in his eyes. "I carry your child, Jacob."

His hand trembled as though a current of electricity flowed between them. He pressed it firmly against her, and he lifted his other hand to cup her cheek. His eyes softened, and his gaze did not falter. "My child," he whispered. The words sounded wonderful, and they terrified him. Her smile told him that she was too much woman to be terrified, but he was only a man. He had the wisdom to know that the courage for childbearing lived in a woman's heart and that he spoke with a man's cowardice when he said, "Ah, careless woman, why did you not prevent this?"

"The only way I know that I could have prevented it would have been to refuse to let you touch me." She slid her arms around his back and drew herself against him. "I would sooner have prevented my own conception."

He felt helpless in the face of this marvel, and he did not return her embrace. His arms hung at his sides like useless things. They could not carry her burden. He was only a man, with muscle in his chest, his arms, his back, but nothing to compare with the mysterious power that lay deep in her belly. She had the power to feed this child he had started in her. It would grow, and the world would see that it was there. He had no means to shield her now.

"I was careless, too," he said. "What do you want of me, *waśtelakapi*? What would you have me do?"

She stiffened and drew back. "What do I want?" Her throat went dry. "I thought if you knew, you would be mindful of your safety, just as I must be careful now that I carry a child."

"Since I'm to be a father, I must be silent until MacAllistair comes to repeat the story they won't accept from me."

She stepped back to take a hard look at him and let him see her. "You owe me nothing, Jacob. Do what your pride requires you to do. As for me, I shall care for myself and our child because that's what my instincts require of *me*."

He watched her clap her hand to her breast as she made her claim and saw the tenacity in her gesture. "Do you want to bear this child of mine?"

"Yes!"

"Why?"

"When will you know me, Jacob? I love you. Already I love this child."

He closed the distance between them and enfolded her in his arms. Breathing deeply, he filled his head with the scent of her hair. When he was this close to her, he could lose himself as he had done so many times. He could forget who he was, where he was, how impossible this was, and he could say anything she wanted to hear. He'd told her that they were wrong for each other, yet he'd become her lover. He'd said he had nothing to offer her, yet he'd given her his baby. When he was this close to her, he could not deny the joy of that gift, because it felt so good just to hold her.

"All right, little one. I will be the silent Indian, and maybe they will let me live until MacAllistair gets back. If his word can get me out of this stinking hole, then I will go to you, and we'll talk of our child." He took her face in his hands and managed a sad smile. "I should discipline you for bringing my child to this place."

"His father is here."

"Then promise his father that you will be more cautious. Don't come to town alone. Don't come to me here again." He clasped her shoulders. "There are those like Sanderson who consider an Indian's woman to be fair game. The next man who harms you will die by my hand, Carolina. I swear it."

The keys jangled in the lock, and they jumped apart. "You gotta get outta here now, ma'am," the deputy announced.

Jacob turned toward the window.

"Do you need anything besides a clean—"

"No." His answer was almost inaudible. "Nothing. You are not to bring anything here. Go now, little one."

She reached out to him, touched his arm and then left quickly. The little man led her back to the office. He had large brown stains under his arms and suspenders that hung in two great loops over his hips. He tossed the keys in the desk drawer and looked up at Carolina. His mouth widened slowly in a mirthless grin.

"Most of 'em we lock up swear they never done nothing, but with Injuns, don't make no never mind if they done it or not. This one's prob'ly done enough thieving and whatnot to have it coming to him anyways."

Carolina leveled an icy stare at the man behind the deputy sheriff's badge. "See that he's still alive when Charles MacAllistair arrives, or I will personally pay someone to carve up your liver."

Jim Bates was waiting for her outside. She closed the door behind her, hooked a stray wisp of hair behind her ear, adjusted the starched cuffs at her wrists and marched down the street.

When Charles MacAllistair gave his statement to the sheriff, Jacob was released. Sheriff Pritchard bemoaned the fact that the murderer's trail was cold and his attitude hinted that Jacob was somehow responsible for the existing circumstances. Jacob summoned the full extent of his control as he collected his belongings. He left the sheriff's office without a word and headed for Swenson's, where he bought new clothes and had a bath. He scrubbed his scalp and skin until they felt raw, and he discarded the old clothes. Then he sought the warmth of the sun.

Through the window Carolina could see him riding toward the corral. She recognized him by the way he moved, but not by the way he looked. He rode in a saddle, and he carried a rifle in a scabbard. His clothes looked new. She remembered his brass-buckled belt, but the deep red shirt was a new color for him. And his braids were gone.

He stepped down from the saddle with his customary grace, but with a new sense of impatience. She saw a new hardness in his face. But this was Jacob, and she hurried to the door.

The sight of Carolina put him in touch with the soft part of him that still belonged to her. He carried the rifle, and he wore a harder mask, but the softness yearned for her. They reached for each other, and he pulled her close with his free arm. Her fingers dug into the muscles of his back, kneading his tension away. He felt her breath against his neck.

Her heart hammered in her ears, and she kissed his neck, his jaw and, finally, his mouth. His kiss brought him home to her. She chased his tongue with hers, rubbed his back and welcomed him.

With a groan he tore his lips free and demanded, "Let's go inside." She gave him a look that made his blood surge thick and hot as she stepped over the threshold. He kicked the door shut behind him and set the rifle nearby.

She whispered, "You're really here," as she unbuttoned his shirt and spread her hands over his chest. "This is you. This is Jacob."

He reached for her buttons, which started just under her chin. "I have waited long enough to unwrap this package again."

"You're all right, Jacob?"

"I will be soon." He peeled her dress from her and let it fall to the floor.

"I was so afraid—"

"Shh." He laid a finger over her lips as he unlaced her camisole with his other hand. "I must see you." His words were warm and husky. "I must touch you my way."

She pushed his shirt over his shoulders, echoing, "Touch you . . . touch you." Her trembling fingers fumbled with his belt buckle. "Please let me—"

"Ŏhan!"

"And that means—"

"Hell, yes." He slid his hands over her hips, pushing all the cloth away. She tried to follow his lead, and the buttons on his pants made her groan with frustration. He laughed and flipped them open easily.

She found nothing to laugh about as she leaned her forehead against his chest and tucked her hand inside his pants. She remembered the punishment Jacob had had in mind for Sanderson, and she'd had a nightmare that they'd done just that to Jacob. He answered her sigh of relief with a pleasured groan.

"I could fill your hand, little one," he warned. He slipped his hand between her thighs. "But I would rather fill you here." He tasted her shoulder and tested the way inside her with gently probing fingers. Her quick gasp told him that he'd found his mark. "For you, it starts now."

"Jacob?"

"I'm holding you."

"Jacob—"

"I love you," he whispered. *"Tekicihila."*

"Then be with me, Jacob."

He pulled her down to her knees and moved behind her. She looked back, wary, but he wrapped his arms around her and kissed the side of her neck. "This is my way, *waśtelak-*

api. Trust me." He entered her then, finding his way into the passage he had made ready for his possession, and his hands were free to touch her everywhere and make the most of the need he'd kindled in her. And they soared together.

Later they used the bed. Jacob kissed the place where she cradled his child, and he whispered again, *"Tekicihila."*

"Tell me what that lovely word means."

"Precious." He kissed her again. "You are precious to me."

"Will you always love me, Jacob?"

"Ohinniyan. Always."

She pulled off the strip of buckskin he'd tied around his forehead and plunged her fingers into the thickness of his hair. "I've always wanted to run my hands through your hair."

"Always?"

"Ohinniyan." She tried to imitate the nasal *n* the way he said it. "But you always have it bound."

He moved to nestle his head between her breasts. "The sheriff decided I needed a haircut before I left. When Marissa saw it, she said I needed another one. I let her make it even for me."

She hugged him to her breast. "This is all my fault," she said quietly. "It all goes back to that day at the store."

"I've had short hair before," he assured her. "The first time it happened, I wanted to kill somebody. I felt ashamed, as though I had been stripped in public. Now I know that it grows back. They think to take my pride by tying my hands behind my back and cutting my hair. White men are such fools."

"And white women?"

He nipped at her breast. "I know one who is delicious." He felt her flinch as he drew the edge of his teeth across her nipple. "Tender?" She nodded. He spread his hand over her flat belly and braced himself on his other arm. "Tender and delicious," he whispered. "*Skuya*. Delicious." Tucking his arm beneath her head, he held her close, protecting her belly with his hand. "Does the child bring you other pain?"

"No. I feel fine. I hardly know he's there."

"Do you carry a son, little one?"

"Or your daughter. Whichever we have, it will be a small version of you, with black eyes, lots of beautiful black hair—"

"Then let him be a son. You must have daughters who look like you."

"This baby will be the best of both of us," she promised. She touched his smooth jaw with the backs of her fingers.

"I did not intend for this to happen to you. Lakota women have ways of preventing—"

"I'm sorry, Jacob," she said tightly. "I do not possess that knowledge."

"And I should have realized that. The child is Lakota, Carolina, and he is mine." He touched the smoothness of her shoulder. "I will take you to my home. You will have the child there, and no one will know."

"But . . . I have a commitment to teach school here."

"They will not allow you to teach their children now."

Her whole body had stiffened, and she felt cold. "As you say, we have some time. When it becomes apparent, the parents can decide whether their children are able to learn at the hand of a pregnant woman."

He raised himself on his elbow and looked at her as though she were an untutored child herself. "Have you learned nothing from what has happened? They will spit on you, Carolina. I will not allow that. Teach their children for a while if you must, but when your belly begins to swell, I will take you to my family. The child will be born there."

"And then what, Jacob?"

The muscles in his jaw worked as he studied her for a moment. "And then you will give him to me. I will raise him myself. My mother will help me. You—" His voice softened, despite the fact that he'd steeled himself against it. He felt the pain of losing her even before she was gone. "You, *waśtelakapi*, must return to the East, where no one will know that you once bore the child of a Lakota man."

Carolina fought the swirling nausea that threatened to engulf her. She managed only quick, shallow breaths as she turned stunning paralysis into quick action. Out of his arms and out of the bed, she took herself away, took the baby away. He was too callous to deserve either. She snatched up her clothing piece by piece and put it on. When she turned, he was stuffing his shirttail into his pants.

"When you've had time to think clearly—"

"Think clearly!" she roared. She wrapped her arms around her middle, as though he might take the baby even now. "I am this child's mother!" It took some effort, but she brought her tone down on the next words. "I will be a good mother, and the color of his skin will be just as dear to me as the sound of his voice and the feel of his mouth suckling my breast." He took a step toward her, but she held up her hand to stop him. "I have tried to learn, Jacob. I have put my whole heart into it. But it is *you* who have learned nothing about *me*. I shall never, *never* desert my child."

"Then I will—"

"Don't threaten me with what *you* will do. If it cannot be what *we* will do, then leave yourself out of it. I carry this child in my body. It is mine. If I feel that I need a father for my baby, I know of at least one man who will care for both of us."

Rage flared in Jacob's eyes. "Who? Who else knows about this? Did you tell Bates before you told me?"

"No! No one else knows. Jim Bates has made it quite clear that he would—"

"I am the child's father!" Jacob bellowed.

"Yes, you are. But you will not take this baby from me and send me away. I have a mother's commitment to this child. You have no right to interfere with that, Jacob. No right!"

She trembled on the brink of tears, but she held them back by dint of sheer will. She felt the cold stab of Jacob's sharp glare. "Go to Bates, then," he growled.

"That isn't what I want," she said quietly.

"You seem able to adjust." He walked to the door, retrieved his rifle and stood there, his hand on the latch. She held her breath, praying for him to turn around. "If he changes his mind when you tell him of my child, I will provide for both of you."

It was impossible to turn around now.

Chapter Twelve

Jacob had known from the beginning that the time would come when he would have to let her go. But it had come with a stunning cruelty, and that was something for which he had not prepared himself. The knowledge that she carried his child brought unsparing joy. Some piece of him lived within her. It was cause for celebration, gift giving, spreading the news, but to do more than dream of those things would bring calamity. By loving her, he had put her in a cell, and by making her pregnant, he had shut the door. Somehow he had to leave the door unlocked so that she was free to go, after the child was born.

The days without her were long and tedious, but the nights were a different kind of ordeal. The dull ache that persisted during the day became night's gnawing hunger. He remembered what it was like to be without food and without the prospect of finding any. After a few days a man tightened his belt. After a week he began considering compromises. What would he do for a taste of meat? How important was honor or dignity when a piece of bread was at stake? And now, what would he sacrifice to lie in his woman's arms again?

Bringing his sister to the ranch had been a way to ensure that Carolina would come down from the cabin. As long as she was up there alone, Jacob thought about how easy it would be to ride out to see her. After he brought Ruth, Carolina came frequently to give the promised lessons, and soon she was spending most nights at the ranch. Now she was closer, and absolutely inaccessible to him. At least he could be assured of her safety while she was there. If Bates decided to court her, Jacob would know it. His mind was at war with itself on that point. Letting her go was one thing, but losing his child in the bargain was another. Only in death did a man give his child over to another to raise. He told himself over and over that the child would be better off without him.

In mid-September the younger children started school. The older boys would not come until the harvest was finished, which gave Carolina time to work with the youngest ones. Some were ready to read and do arithmetic, while others needed letters and numbers. The challenge distracted her from herself and from thoughts of Jacob, and the children were eager to learn.

Carolina rode to school with Charlie. On their way home they often encountered Culley, who just happened along and felt that an escort was due. Carolina mentioned the problem to Charles, and the chance encounters ended abruptly.

Nights grew cold in early October. Carolina found the fall foliage in North Dakota to be largely unimpressive. The leaves on the cottonwoods yellowed and withered quickly, and the frequent winds shook them down straightaway. She thought of New England and missed wading through masses of fallen leaves as she followed the curve of the creek bank. She kicked at these small brown leaves in disgust. They didn't even amount to a respectable pile, and they wouldn't whoosh in the air. Instead they made a feeble attempt to scatter. She wondered whether she was homesick, or just terribly lonely for one man.

A horse snorted as it trotted up behind her, and as always she sent up a quick prayer that it might be Jacob. She savored the seconds during which she was permitted that hope.

"Nice day for a walk, Miss Hammond."

Carolina turned and managed to mask her disappointment. "Hello, Mr. Bates. Yes, lovely day."

He dismounted and let the horse follow as he joined her in her walk. "Wanted to tell you I took care of your problems with Culley. I fired him." Carolina looked up quickly. "Hate to do that to a man with winter coming on, but he didn't give me no choice in the matter."

"I didn't expect anything so drastic, Mr. Bates, just another warning, a reprimand or—"

"Well, that was more like what I had in mind, but he heard one of the boys make a remark to me about you—just a little kidding around—and he lit into me like a crazy man. I can't have that."

Carolina nodded and clasped her hands behind her back. "What sort of 'kidding around' was this? Are they still talking about the incident in town?"

"Oh, no, ma'am. They're not talking about that." He glanced across the creek. "They were saying I didn't want Culley going out to ride home with you because I'd rather do that myself."

"As you say, 'just kidding around'."

"I don't know, ma'am." He shoved his hands in the pockets of his wool jacket. "After the way Culley acted, taking a swing at me and telling me you were—well, it might not be a bad idea to go up there and see you home safe. I'm worried about him hanging around the school, waiting to follow you or something."

"That's very thoughtful, but I'm sure it won't be necessary, Mr. Bates."

"What if I offered to send Jake after you every day?" he said quietly. "How would that be?"

"Please don't do that."

"I've got trouble with him, too." The news turned Carolina's head and put a look of concern into her eyes. "We used to get along pretty good, but now he don't talk to me. Nor anybody else, for that matter." Jim thought for a moment. "I'd say he's carrying a torch for somebody."

Carolina stared straight ahead.

"Did you give any thought to the things I said?"

"Yes."

"Made sense, didn't it? He ain't right for you."

"This isn't something I care to discuss, Mr. Bates."

He chose not to hear her. "I don't know what's gotten into Jake, anyhow. Even if you tried to let him down easy—"

"Remember our talk of friendship, Mr. Bates? You seemed to consider yourself a friend to Jacob, as well as to me."

"I've always thought so. I don't think about him being an Indian at all, you know. Man to man, it don't matter. But you being a woman, folks might think—"

"I know all about it, Mr. Bates. It may interest you to know that Jacob decided that I wasn't right for him."

It took Jim a moment to digest that information. "He didn't get uppity or nothing, did he?"

"Uppity?" Caroline chuckled. "No, I don't think that's the right word."

"If it's any help, ma'am, I think he's got feelings for you. I think he's hurting right now. Hard telling with Indians sometimes, but I can see he's not having an easy time of it."

He hastened to add, "It's for the best, though, ma'am. Take my word."

"I'm sure it is," she said absently.

"Maybe it would help if you was to see somebody else kind of social-like."

"I'm not very good at that sort of thing, and I wouldn't be good company."

"Let me be the judge. I'd like to call on you."

She'd known the suggestion was coming. She'd dreaded it, but now it was out. "All right," she said quietly.

The resignation in her voice wasn't encouraging, but the answer itself gave him a place to start. He smiled. "I'll be riding to school with you for a few days, too, just to be on the safe side."

Teaching took on new challenges when the older boys joined the class. Carolina was already determined that any male who insisted on testing her fortitude would not find her wanting. The Friedrick boys, Tom Laughlin and John Rieger had been in class only a few days when they decided to try her mettle. During their noon playtime, while Carolina entertained the younger children with "London Bridge," the boys stuffed the top of the chimney with rags and smoked up the schoolhouse in short order. Rolf Friedrick supposed aloud that school would have to be dismissed for the day.

When Jim Bates arrived to escort Carolina and little Charlie home, he found the class huddled around an outdoor fire. The older boys were reciting math facts. Jim stuck his head inside the building to assess the damages.

"Got a fair amount of soot on them walls, Miss Hammond. Pretty big cleaning job there," Jim announced.

"I have four boys who are more than anxious to make amends, Mr. Bates. Tomorrow being Saturday, they've volunteered to come out here and clean after they get their chores done at home. Right, boys?''

There was a "Yes'm" chorus.

"I don't plan to spend my Saturday overseeing this job, because I know I can rely on these boys to clean the chimney, scrub the walls, the furniture, everything. Isn't that right, boys?" Another chorus. "I've met their fathers, you see. They are men who would not find much humor in this situation. Rolf, see to the fire. And I shall see all of you on Monday."

After the children were gone, Jim allowed himself a chuckle over the boys' trick. "You surely fixed 'em, ma'am. I reckon you could teach a mule to eat with a fork."

Carolina gathered her books. "If I can teach those boys to read and write, I'll be doing well. They've had a rather hit-or-miss education."

"Yeah." It was a description of Jim's own schooling as well. "That's the way of it out here. But we're getting better. Most of these folks are immigrants. They've had a hard life, and they want better for their youngsters."

"We can give them better, can't we, Charlie?" She ruffled the boy's hair, and he smiled up at her. She hoped they wouldn't forget their goals once they learned the teacher was pregnant.

Jim began calling on Carolina in the evenings two or three times a week. Carolina served coffee, and they had the parlor to themselves. Jim took the chair he knew to be Charles's, thinking it would put him in the right perspective. Carolina sat with her back straight and her ankles crossed for exactly one hour at a time because that was precisely how long Jim stayed. Jim found it difficult to think of conversation after Carolina introduced a topic. Consequently they shared long periods of silence. He thought his courtship was progressing well and that it would soon be time to ask for her hand.

Carolina suffered in silence. At first she had planned to tell him about the baby when he proposed marriage. If he accepted the idea of raising a half-breed child, she had thought she would consider the proposal. As the weeks dragged on and the visits became more agonizing, she knew she couldn't marry Jim. She listened to the slurping sound he made when he drank his coffee and studied the center part in his oiled hair. The thought of kissing his mouth, lying next to him at night, allowing him to touch her—all of it gave her heartburn. Those intimacies were for Jacob alone.

As Jim took his leave one night, he dropped the hint that "a fella has to make plans for his future before he gets too old to have one." Carolina closed the door behind him and took the cups and saucers into the kitchen. When she got to her room, she would have to open a window. She felt as though she were suffocating. The thought of stealing away to Jacob's room haunted her as she climbed the steps. She had the same thought every night, and every night she managed to reject it. She had done that once. She had gone to him and told him how she felt, and he had given her a summer of love. During that time, he had also given her a child, and that child had to be her first concern now.

At the top of the stairs, she saw the light shining from her room. She allowed herself to imagine that Jacob was waiting for her in the same way she tortured herself with hope each time she heard a rider approach. But she knew better. She saw him only at mealtime, and then they did nothing but exchange stiff greetings.

She found Ruth sitting at the end of her bed looking strikingly beautiful in the white flannel nightgown Marissa had provided for her, along with other new clothes. Her long braids made black ribbons over her ripening young breasts.

"May we talk, my sister?" Ruth asked quietly.

"Of course, Ruth. I dearly need a sister to talk to tonight." Carolina opened the window before she sat across from Ruth on the bed. "Your English is coming along much better than my Lakota. I need more practice."

"Yes," Ruth told her. "I practice much. I like this house . . . these clothes . . . this bed."

Carolina smiled as she unlaced her shoe. Ruth had mastered the day's lesson on demonstratives. "What do you think of these shoes?"

"My brother says no shoes." She brightened as she leaned toward Carolina. "I practice much English with my brother. He has good English."

"Yes, he does." Carolina's shoe dropped to the floor. "Very good English."

"Why does my sister see this man Jim so much?"

Carolina looked up at Ruth's anxious face. She swallowed hard. "He is a friend."

"You are my brother's woman."

"Yes." She turned her attention to her other shoe.

"Yet my brother does not stay with you."

The second shoe made a loud thud. "No, he doesn't."

"Have you left Black Hawk for this Jim?"

Carolina braced her hands on her knees and gave a heavy sigh. "No. In my heart I am Jacob's woman."

"Has he left you?" Ruth asked quietly.

Turning her head slowly, Carolina considered the innocence in Ruth's dark eyes. "Has Jacob talked to you about me, Ruth?"

"He says nothing of himself. He asks about you."

"What does he say?"

"He say—"

"Says," Carolina supplied.

"He says, 'How is it with my woman? How does she seem? Does she eat well?' He worries. But I do not see him with you." Ruth scooted closer and patted the coverlet. "You must move this bed to that big house where my brother stays." She pointed toward the window. "Put those horses out. No horses in the house."

Carolina laughed for the first time in weeks. "'No horses in the house,'" she repeated. "I think that's a wonderful idea."

"Do it." Ruth's eyes danced with excitement. "I will help you take this pretty bed."

"Oh, Ruth, I would do it in a minute if Jacob would let me." Tears threatened to push the laughter aside, but she tipped her head back and blinked hard. "But he worries about so many things, and he has good cause. A white man tried to hurt me because he saw that I was Jacob's woman."

"Black Hawk will kill this white man." Ruth whacked the edge of her hand against her other palm.

"The man is already dead."

Ruth nodded, smiling with satisfaction.

"Not by Jacob's hand," Carolina added quickly. "Jacob beat him up, but he didn't kill him. You see, Jacob is one man against many in a town like Shields or Bismarck or—"

"He must not go to those towns."

Carolina nodded. Why couldn't it be that simple? "What else does Jacob tell you about us?"

"I am to tell no one you are his woman. I have not. But you must tell this Jim, my sister. He angers my brother."

"Has Jacob said anything about Jim?"

"No, but he sees Jim come here. I see the anger in Black Hawk's face. If he killed Jim, there would be much trouble."

"Why doesn't he tell me? He knows he has only to tell me, and I will not see—"

Ruth touched Carolina's arm. "My brother will not do this. A man does not tell his woman this. She knows."

"You're right." Carolina's covered Ruth's hand with her own. "I can't pretend there might be someone else. There won't be. Tell Jacob I said there won't be."

"We will move this bed?"

Carolina smiled, and a tear slipped down her cheek. "I don't think so. But you've given me a lovely notion to sleep on tonight."

Wintery weather became a reality early in November with light snowfalls and cold temperatures. Soon there would be enough snow cover for a bobsled. Runners would be added to the wagon boxes, and Carolina would drive Charlie to school. She looked forward to that, because she was becoming uneasy about horseback riding.

The baby was a real presence now. She could feel life stirring in the small mound of flesh that was hidden beneath her full skirts. The first time she felt movement, she had wept bitterly because she could not run to Jacob and tell him. The next time she covered her belly with her own hands and wondered at the way it felt.

Jim Bates had taken Carolina's polite rejection of further visits with a grain of salt. He thought she might change her mind if he backed off for a while. During the holidays she would become receptive to his attention again. Everyone got friendlier during the holiday season.

Marissa and Ruth became Carolina's close friends. She needed them, and she needed for them to know about the baby. It had been a secret between her and Jacob, but now she had become lonely with it. She decided to tell Marissa one afternoon as they shared tea, and she chose the simplest words.

"I'm going to have Jacob's baby."

"I know."

Carolina lifted her eyes to Marissa's sympathetic smile. "Did he tell you?"

"Of course not. I wondered if he even knew."

"I told him right away."

Marissa pushed the footstool over with her heel. "Join me. It's important to keep your feet up."

Carolina smiled and scooted over on the settee.

"Spring?" Marissa asked, and received a perfunctory nod. She patted her round ball of a belly. "You're going to look just like this in a couple of months, my dear."

"Yes, I know. I'm sorry, Marissa. I know this may cause some problems with school."

Marissa waved that concern aside. "What are you going to do?"

Carolina set her cup aside. "He suggested I give the baby to him and go back to Boston."

"Very sensible. Of course you refused."

"Of course!" Carolina's face clouded over. "If the man doesn't want me, he certainly isn't getting my baby."

"Be fair, Carolina. His suggestion wasn't meant to be cruel. He's offering you a way out."

"I don't want a way out!" Carolina's hands became small fists in her lap. "I want this baby."

"And you want to be married to the baby's father."

"I am!" She backed away from that claim with an amendment. "I *feel* that I'm married to him. I don't tell myself that our life together would be an easy one. But I love him. What do people do when they're in love, Marissa? They get married."

Marissa drew a deep breath and nodded. "They get married." The breath was expelled. "I notice you're not seeing Jim anymore. Did you tell him about the baby?"

"No. I should never have given Jim any encouragement. That was wrong." She burned with contrition every time she thought of it now. "I told Jacob that Jim would be glad to have me, but I said that out of pride and anger."

"But later, when you were calm enough to consider the real prospect of raising your child alone, did you give it more thought?"

"Yes," she admitted. "I thought about it. I can't marry Jim."

"Then what will you do?"

Carolina folded her hands in her lap. "I shall have my baby. If the school board is willing, I shall continue to teach. This summer I intend to start classes for the Lakota children if Ruth will help me." Her crisp tone took on a harder edge. "And if Jacob doesn't try to take my baby away from me."

"You know he wouldn't do that. Give him time, Carolina."

Carolina covered her belly with her hand. "I want to give him *this* time. I want to share this with him."

"I know." Marissa reached for her friend's hand. "And I know I'm a poor substitute, but share it with me."

The first of December brought a cloudy morning and softly sifting snow. Carolina was in the middle of a history lesson when the wind shifted suddenly. It happened within the space of a breath. The wind turned on itself and brought thick driving snow from the south. The children noticed, too, and they scrambled for a look out the windows. The world had turned white.

"We gotta get home, Miss Hammond!"

"We might get stuck here."

"We might miss supper!"

Carolina opened the door, but a gust of wind and snow pushed her back into the room. With Tom Laughlin's help she got it shut again. She remembered another wind, and she felt an icy tingle of terror. Stay calm, she told herself. You're in charge here.

"We won't be able to find our way home in this. We must wait until the wind dies down before we venture out." She glanced at the small pile of wood beside the stove. The Friedricks were due to donate wood, but the boys had ridden to school on horseback that morning. "Rolf, how much wood is outside?"

"I, uh...I didn't cut any more when you told me, Miss Hammond."

"You've done us all a disservice this time, Rolf. Where is the ax?"

"I think I left it down at the woodpile." He caught a glimpse of Carolina's scowl, and he shrugged. "I went down there to chop wood, but I got kinda sidetracked."

"You won't be able to find it now. Let's make sure we have water. How about the horses?"

"They're downwind on the north side," Tom said. "That's the best we've got for them."

"Well, then, I guess we'll just go on with our lessons." Carolina managed a smile. "By the time this lets up, you might have two days' worth of homework all done."

The gray day gave way to night, and the wind still howled. Carolina's little class huddled near the stove. She had wrapped the smaller children in the blankets from the bobsleds. The supply of firewood was dwindling, and they had eaten everything they had left over in their lunch pails. Eleven children, no food, and no more firewood.

"Maddie?" she said calmly. "Tom? Have you ever had the urge to smash furniture?"

Beyond the ranch house window there was only the wind and the swirling, surging mass of white. It hardly resembled snow. It was a white shroud that had descended upon the house and paralyzed all life. Jacob had tried to ride up to the school, but the force of the wind and the blinding snow made it impossible to struggle much beyond the yard. He'd put the horses up in the barn and found his way to the house purely by instinct. He had kept watch through the night with Charles and Marissa. Daylight was a gray-white glow in the windows, and the wind threatened the sanity of those who kept watch and waited.

"You don't think they started out for home, do you?" It was a question Marissa had voiced in a dozen different ways, and each time she asked it, she received a patronizing response from her husband. This time when she turned to him for reassurance, she found that he had fallen asleep in his chair.

Jacob broke his long silence. "She learned respect for the wind's power last summer. She was ready this time."

The comment brought Marissa's head around. Jacob leaned against the window frame with the curtain tucked behind his shoulder. He could see nothing—not the outbuildings, not the yard fence, not even the willow that grew no more than ten feet from the house.

The animals he and the others had managed to shelter in the barns would soon need food and water. The rest of the hands were probably playing cards in the bunkhouse and grumbling about the lack of a hot meal. Jacob's parents would be holed up in the cabin, and his father would be struggling with his cough. Perhaps this storm would mark the end of his struggle. There would surely be those among his people who would die in this weather. He could be mindful of these things and accept them as they were, but his heart rebelled at the image of Carolina's body lying beneath a snowdrift.

"Do they have weather like this where she comes from?" Marissa asked as she joined him at the window.

"They have plenty of snow, but the wind there is a feeble cousin to this wind of ours. She knows that now." He remembered the way her slight body had trembled in his arms and the way the rain had smelled in her hair. "She stood outside watching that day, waiting to be entertained by a cloudburst. *Ateyapi* brought her a taste of the sky so that she would be ready for this."

His hand went to the top button on his shirt, but he glanced at Marissa and changed his mind.

"I don't mind if you smoke," she told him. "If it helps, I might try it, too."

"Nothing helps," he told her. "It only keeps the hands busy. Mine could be tied behind my back for all the use they are to her now." He reached for the pouch anyway. "The last time they tied my hands, all they took was my hair." He rolled his cigarette without giving it as much attention as he paid to the whirling snow beyond the window. "As soon as I can see, I'll start out on snowshoes. The drifts will slow a horse down too much."

"I know they're alive." she said quietly. "Charlie's alive, and Carolina and the baby are alive."

He lit his cigarette and turned back to the window. "She's told you, then."

"She didn't have to."

He lifted an eyebrow, questioning the possibility. "I've watched for signs. She doesn't look—"

"She will, Jacob. She feels him moving inside her." *Pray God she does even at this moment.* Marissa watched him draw deeply on the cigarette. "She needs your love now."

He blew the smoke above his head. "She needs a husband. Maybe someone like Bates."

"She doesn't love Jim. She loves you."

"I'm no good for her."

"Your child lives inside her, Jacob," she said, deliberately giving each word special emphasis. "If you don't marry her, she's going to raise that baby herself."

"And if I do marry her, we can go to the agency together for our rations each month. And when I am arrested for beating up some white bastard who puts his hands on my wife, she will come to bail me out. She'll hear the insults once too often, and she'll wish she had married Bates or Culley—any man but me."

"There would be talk, yes, but it would become less with time. Don't you think my mother has heard those insults, Jacob? Don't you think my grandmother heard them?"

"I would spare her that," he ground out.

"And you would spare her the rations. You don't use them yourself. You have educated yourself, and you have a job."

"I cannot keep her in a barn."

"No," Marissa whispered. "But you may lose her in a blizzard." The fear in his eyes met with the same in hers. "You may lose her, Jacob. And the baby. For good."

"I will bring her back from this."

"How would it be," she persisted, "to lose her now, today?"

He lost himself in the cold gray shroud outside. "There would be no sun," he murmured.

"And you would die without sun."

He heard the urgency in her words and smiled. She thought she had given him a revelation. "For a Lakota man, giving his life to save his woman is a natural choice, *hankaśi*. It is the choice I make in letting her go."

Ruth startled them both when she appeared from the kitchen. "I have made coffee," she said. "My brother, will you eat before you go? You have eaten nothing. You will be too weak to bring my sister back."

Jacob put his hand behind his sister's head and kissed her brow. "I'll try your coffee."

The wind had blown steadily for nearly two days. As soon as Jacob could see the outline of the barn, he made his way through a range of snowdrifts to get back to his room. There he dressed in the buffalo robe his mother had given him. His winter moccasins, leggings and mittens were lined with warm fur. He carried a supply of matches, *wasna* and dried meat. The schoolhouse was four miles away, and Charles and Jim Bates thought they would do as well with a team of Percherons and a bobsled as Jacob could on snowshoes.

They were wrong. Jacob glided atop the snowdrifts, his snowshoes sinking less than an inch into the heavy snow. He knew that the team would flounder in the drifts, and that Charles and Bates would shovel their way to the schoolhouse.

Panic seized him when he caught his first glimpse of the building. It was nearly buried in snow. The entire south side, including the door and windows, was inundated. There was no smoke rising from the chimney. He snatched a few pieces of wood from a deadfall that had blown clear, and he pushed on toward the schoolhouse. He called out, but there was no answer. Using his snowshoe for a shovel, he dug furiously to free the door. His hands trembled as he reached for the handle.

Inside, there was no warmth and little movement. With the windows and door drifted over, the small room lacked ventilation. The fire in the stove had consumed pieces of furniture and the supply of oxygen as well. Jacob knelt beside Carolina first and put his face close to hers. She was breathing. He shook each child in turn and was rewarded with the sounds of whimpers and groans. The fire had apparently been out for some time, and the stove had allowed some air back into the room. With the front door open, he built another fire before he took Carolina in his arms again and moved her close to the stove.

Her feet burned. Her hands stung. Carolina thought she might be looking through a dark-colored bottle, but she saw Jacob's face. The face of a god or an angel—no matter—it was no surprise that such a celestial being would look like...

"Jacob?"

"Yes, *waśtelakapi*."

He was rubbing needles into her hands. "It hurts."

"Good. There's feeling there."

The feeling was awful. "The children, Jacob."

"Mine comes first."

She pulled an elbow underneath herself to show off her strength. "I'm all right, Jacob. Please see to the children."

Several of them were moving around already. He helped them get closer to the fire and instructed them to rub their hands and feet. The younger ones whined, while the older children complied. Jacob took off his coat, wrapped it around Carolina and cradled her in his arms.

He sucked on her fingers, warming them with his tongue. "I see no sign of frostbite," he told her. He added close to her ear, "But if we were alone I would make a close examination and then warm you very quickly."

"I had to give up the fire." She winced as he took off her shoes and her woolen stockings. "There was no air. I tried to stay awake, but it was so cold. Oh, Jacob, that hurts." She groaned pitiably. "That hurts so bad."

Again he used his mouth, knowing that fingers and toes were the most vulnerable. "You will not wear these foolish shoes anymore, Carolina. Your feet are frozen into a point."

Somewhere deep inside her, laughter bubbled. He looked up quickly, and she saw his fear. He thought she'd lost her mind. But she hadn't. She'd been spared, and the man she loved was sucking on her toes and scolding her about the style of her shoes in the presence of eleven children. It was absurd. It was miraculous. It was life, and she loved every blessed breath of it.

Charles called from outside. "Jacob! Are they...are they in there?"

"Yes!" Jacob shouted. "They're alive." He grinned at the beautiful woman who warmed the room with her laughter. "And this one is as spirited as ever."

The three men worked to restore circulation to the children's limbs. Jacob fed everyone as Rolf berated himself for leaving them short on firewood and Carolina blamed herself for their near-suffocation.

"I didn't realize the snow was blocking the door until it was too late."

"And what would you have done, little one?" Jacob asked her.

"I would have kept it cleared away. I would have—"

"Our greatest fear was that you might have tried to leave the cabin. After a storm like that, bodies are often discovered within a few yards of shelter. You did well. You kept everyone alive."

The horses had stood outside in the shelter of the building and weathered the storm. They fed on the straw Charles had brought in his bobsled. One by one the children's parents made their way to the schoolhouse. Some of the children had suffered minor frostbite, but they were already sharing the story that would be retold for many years to come. The part where they smashed the furniture was everybody's favorite.

The bobsleds went their separate ways over trails that had been broken in dread of what the drivers would find. The rides home would be shorter. Jim Bates drove the Mac-Allistair sled back to the ranch. Wrapped in a cocoon of blankets, little Charlie slept in his father's arms. Jacob and Carolina nested in the straw in the sled box, and he held her against his chest inside his warm robe.

"Jacob," she whispered. He lowered his head to hear her words. "I feel the baby moving. It must be a warm place inside me."

He brushed his lips across her forehead. "It is."

Chapter Thirteen

The front door to the ranch house flew open, and Ruth tottered onto the veranda, shouting in Lakota. Jacob tensed as the sled halted near the front steps. He strained to listen to what his sister was too frantic to relate in English.

"Marissa's baby is coming," he told the others. Then he spoke to Ruth in their native tongue. Jim took Charlie from his father's arms, and Charles vaulted over the side of the sled box and plowed headlong toward the house.

After jumping off the sled, Jacob turned and reached for Carolina. He carried her to the veranda as he continued to pump Ruth for information. His tone became grave and then angry. Jim followed with young Charlie.

"What is it, Jake? What's going on?"

"It sounds like Culley," he said, covering two icy wooden steps at a time. "She says a small, wild man. Says he was hiding in one of the barns—wanted food."

"Damn!" Jim swore. "I shoulda never sent the rest of the boys to shovel out haystacks. Shoulda kept *somebody* here at the place."

Jacob set Carolina on her feet and turned to Ruth. Her lip was cut and swollen, and her eyes were downcast. He lifted her chin in the palm of his hand and gently spoke the name he used for her. *"Tanksi."* Tears escaped Ruth's straight shock of black lashes. *"Tankśi,"* he said again. She lifted her eyes to her brother's face. Pain glistened in them.

Jim opened the door for them and stood there muttering, "Damn! There's things more important than cows." Jacob offered no argument as he took the women into the house.

Charles met them in the parlor. His face was ashen. "Help me, please." His chest heaved on the plea, and his voice cracked. "She's losing—lost the baby. She's bleeding... I don't know how to—"

"Ice." Carolina lunged toward the stairs. "Snow! Fill a tub with snow." She turned as she mounted the first step. "Did this just happen, Ruth?" The girl nodded. Jacob spoke a few words to her, and she followed Carolina.

Charles looked around the room from face to face. His son's confused expression cut through his daze. "Don't let him go up there," he told Jim.

"But what's the matter?" the boy asked.

"Your mother is sick," Charles told him. "Jim's going to take you in the kitchen and get you something to eat, and Miss Hammond's going to—"

"Bring the snow!" she shouted from the landing.

Jacob laid a hand on Charles's arm, and they headed for the back door.

Carolina froze at the foot of Marissa's bed. A tiny body lay there, perfectly formed, perfectly still. Carolina's fingers trembled as she touched her own lips and then leaned toward the bed. But Ruth covered the infant corpse with a shawl and took it up in her arms. At the sound of a small whimper Carolina's hopes were drawn back to the baby for an instant before she realized that the sound came from the bed.

"Marissa? Can you hear me?" The answer was a groan. Marissa's pale face was slick with sweat. Her skirt was hiked up around her hips, and blood, seeping slowly from her womb, spread in an insidious stain on the white sheet beneath her thighs.

Carolina knew what had to be done. She dragged a brocade chair to the side of the bed. "It's going to be all right, Marissa. We're going to get your head down and your hips up."

"Carolina?" Marissa rolled her head toward the sound of the voice. "Help me. I don't want to lose...lose my baby."

"You're going to be fine," Carolina repeated, squeezing Marissa's limp hand. "This will work if we—" She glanced around. "Ruth, I need—" The girl sat on the floor in the far corner of the room, rocking forward and back with the dead baby in her arms. "Ruth?" Carolina said gently. The call went unheard.

Carolina summoned all her strength as she eased Marissa into the chair and tilted it so the back lay against the floor. As she was stuffing pillows beneath her friend's hips, the tub arrived and was set nearby. Carolina flipped Marissa's skirt up above her knees.

"Quickly, put the snow all over her—here—" she plunged her hands into the tub and put the snow on Marissa's abdomen "—and underneath." They got the idea. With Charles's and Jacob's help, Carolina soon had Marissa packed in snow.

"She's lost blood, Charles. We'll need bouillon, liver, anything to strengthen the blood."

Charles touched cold hands to his wife's cool face. "She's talking to me, Carolina! She said my name."

"We're going to pull her through this." Carolina sat back on her heels. "We'll need to make cold packs. Find some oilcloth, Charles, or some kind of canvas. We can't keep her wet like this." She wanted Charles to be busy while she concentrated on stopping this bleeding.

"I'll find something." He stood quickly. "And the bouillon, too. And the liver. We just butchered."

After Charles hurried from the room, Carolina touched Jacob's arm and nodded toward the corner of the room. He uncoiled his body and gradually came to his feet. Speaking in a low, quiet voice, he persuaded Ruth in Lakota to give him her small bundle, but he set it aside when he heard Marissa speak.

"It was Culley," she said. Carolina was mopping water from the floor with a towel, but she stopped when she heard the name. "He wanted food, so... so we let him in... fed him. He wanted to... to know where you were. Said you were going to teach him to read. He went on and on about you—"

"Did he hurt you, Marissa?"

Marissa grabbed Carolina's hand as she rolled her head from side to side. "Ruth. He... Ruth became angry. Told him you were her brother's woman. Culley went wild... slapped her... threw me on the floor when I tried to... He said filthy things, that he was going to show Jacob— called him 'that Injun bastard'—show him what happens when he steals a white woman. He went after Ruth, and I tried... but he struck me down again, and the pain started. Then she tried to help me, but he got her down on the floor. The pain...the pain...oh, God, Carolina, I think he raped her."

Jacob turned to his sister, who had risen to her feet and backed into the corner, her eyes downcast in shame. He spoke softly, but she did not respond. When he spoke again, she nodded slowly. *"Kuwa yo, tankśi,"* he said, and the young girl went to her brother and wept in his arms.

Carolina waited until the two had shared this sorrow before she added hers. She whispered to Ruth, asking about pain, asking about damage to her body. Ruth only shook her head.

"We have to move Marissa," Carolina said. "I'll need to change the sheets."

Ruth lifted her chin. "I will help my sister."

With Ruth's help, Carolina changed Marissa's clothes and the bed linens while Jacob left quietly with the shawl-wrapped corpse. His leaving caught Marissa's eye.

"Carolina?" Carolina knelt beside the chair. "I lost my baby, didn't I?"

She brushed Marissa's hair back from her forehead. "Yes. The baby's gone."

"Was it a girl?"

"Yes."

"I thought so."

Jacob returned and lifted Marissa into her bed. She turned her face to the wall. "I want to see my husband now."

"Of course. I'll get him," Carolina offered.

"Jacob?"

He stepped closer to the bed. "I am here, *hankaśi*."

"Charles must not go after him, Jacob. Culley is mad. He said he killed Sanderson for what he did to Carolina. We must tell Sheriff Pritchard, but you . . . and Charles . . ."

Carolina returned with Charles, who had brought canvas water bottles from the storage shed and made cold packs.

"You're going to be all right, darling," they heard him promise as they left the room.

Jacob sat with his sister in the privacy of her room while Carolina prepared a bath for her. By late evening, Ruth was settled in bed. Without discussion, Carolina took Jacob to her own room. She sat on the bed, and he sat down beside her.

"I would never have thought—" She lifted her fingers to rub her throbbing temple. "Culley seemed like a harmless fool with a schoolboy's crush."

"No fool is harmless."

"I've been a fool, and it is Ruth and Marissa who paid for that."

"Culley was not your responsibility." He put his hand on her thigh. "You survived your own ordeal today. This other trouble did not begin with you, *waśtelakapi.*"

"You're going after him, aren't you?" She spoke with resignation.

"You and my sister are my concern. Culley won't get far before daybreak."

She covered his hand with hers, rubbing her palm back and forth over his knuckles. "If you kill him, they'll hang you. What good will that do Ruth?"

"My sister's name is not Ruth." She looked up, surprised. "The missionaries gave her that name. She is Wakinyela, the mourning dove. Learn who we *are*, Carolina, not who the white man says we are."

"You have only to tell me these things, Jacob."

"I am Canska Sapa—Black Hawk. I have allowed the name Jacob to be used for me, but that is not who I am."

"You didn't tell me."

He smiled for her, assuring her of his patience. "I told you to call me Black Hawk that first day, but you thought I was being too formal."

"You could have explained, Ja—Black Hawk. You've explained so many things. Why did you keep this to yourself?"

"You felt more comfortable with me when you called me Jacob, and I wanted you to be comfortable with me."

"I would have been comfortable with Black Hawk. You said *Mr.* Black Hawk. I assumed it was a surname."

"I live in two worlds, and I have a different name in each. I must be two people or none." He caught a glimpse of himself in the mirror on the wall and saw his short black hair. "We are a defeated people, Carolina. Must we resign ourselves to the white man's uses of us?"

"But I didn't know. If I had—"

He shook his head and chuckled softly. "There is this huge wall of white people," he began, lifting one hand to demonstrate, "and this crumbling pile of rocks called the Lakota. You and I are two small pebbles who have somehow tumbled away from our proper places and met in the middle. Whenever I speak of the wall and the rock pile, you talk of nothing but pebbles."

Her hand went to his cheek. "A pebble by any other name is still a pebble. I don't know what uses white men have for you, but this woman simply wants to call you *husband*."

He captured her hands and held them in his.

"We have the mortar to build our own little wall," she insisted. "How would they use you? What can they—"

"The missionaries collect our souls. The government keeps us as the farmer keeps animals in his pens. They take our children. They want to train us for jobs we still find distasteful." His voice dropped and simmered with his anger. "They use our women. We have surrendered to this. I have not fought back, and because of that, I am ashamed."

"I understand. I can't stop you from going after Culley. But, Jacob, your people need you." He smiled, because she had forgotten already, and she smiled, thinking she would remember next time. "They need *you*," she repeated. "Your father can't help them. Tokala can't help them. You understand the past, but you live in the present. You *can* help them."

He released her hands and braced his own on his knees for a moment. Then he sank back on his elbows and stared at the floor. Carolina touched the back of his head and smoothed his sleek black hair.

"I love you with all my heart, Black Hawk, and I love the child that grows inside me. But it seems I've become an impossible burden. When the child is born, I will abide by your decision. I'll go, if that's what you decide. And the child will stay, because I know you could never send him away."

He sat up, turning slowly, unsure of the words he'd heard her say. She added, "When the time is closer, I want you to take me to your home. I shall have the baby there and nourish him with milk from his mother's breast." Her eyes glittered with tears, but she smiled. "His mother is not a cow. When he no longer needs me, I promise to leave you both if you decide it must be that way." His lips parted to speak. "Please don't decide anything now," she whispered. "Wait. Think."

Awed by the offer, he managed only a nod as he cupped her cheek in his hand. She kissed his palm. "Stay with me tonight," she said. "Hold me. I want to be warm."

"So do I." He pushed his hands into her hair and let them rest at her temples. She closed her eyes. "Your head hurts?"

"A little."

He pressed his hands against her temples and rotated them as he laid her back on the bed. "*Waśtelakapi,*" he whispered, "I would take away all your pain. I would let nothing harm you." Leaning over her, he offered the softest of kisses. "I would carry you on my back, little one, and we would fly above the wall—" he kissed her again "—above the rock pile—" he nibbled her mouth "—above the sun...."

"Black Hawk," she whispered against his chest.

"You adjust quickly, *waśtelakapi*."

"Pronounce it for me again in Lakota."

It came as a hot whisper. "Canska Sapa."

"Canska Sapa," she repeated. "I love the sound."

"It's good to hear you say it." He smiled in the dark and slid his hand over her belly as he had many times during the night. This small protrusion was his own child. He took his woman's nipple between his lips and thought of the milk that would nourish his baby. He would share with the child, he decided. A woman had room for two. "I want to feel him move."

She pressed his hand against her and waited for the familiar flutter. "There. Did you feel that?"

"Yes! My son is restless."

"Or your daughter. You would be happy with a daughter, wouldn't you?"

"A son is the extension of a man's dreams for himself." He slid higher in order to see her face in the soft light of the window. "A daughter is the extension of the life of the people, a gift from *Ateyapi*, who is God, and she is her father's treasure."

"It's moving again! Can you feel it?"

"This is low in your belly. The women say that means a son."

"Marissa's baby was—"

"Shh." He laid a finger over her lips. "Don't talk about it. You must not speak of that one while you carry our child." He gathered her into his arms and held her head against his shoulder. "You will carry this child easily, and my mother will be with you when it's born. She has helped with many births."

"I want you to be with me."

"Lakota men never—"

"Neither do white men. But you are no ordinary man, Black Hawk. You'll bring me your strength."

"Women have great strength, and yours is greater than most. A man boasts of his courage and his willingness to die. It takes greater courage to be a woman and to hold fast to the will to go on living." She felt like such a small thing in his arms, he thought, but this female capacity for endurance was beyond the kind of power that a man understood.

She snuggled against him. "You will be there. I know you will."

"I must be gone for a time, *waśtelakapi*. Care for my sister and my child. Care for my woman, the light of my life."

When Black Hawk prepared to leave shortly before dawn, he found Charles waiting for him in the kitchen. Carolina came down for one more kiss and walked in on a heated discussion.

"Stay with your wife, MacAllistair. You're lucky to have her alive. She needs you now."

"And how willing are you to take your own advice?" Charles slid a glance at Carolina, who stood in the doorway.

"You cannot leave these women unprotected," Black Hawk said flatly.

"I've told Jim to stay at the house. This won't take us long."

"You will only slow me down."

Charles gripped Black Hawk's shoulder. "He killed my daughter, Jacob. He nearly killed my wife. I'm going after him."

"No horse on the place is as strong as mine. When you fall behind, I won't wait for you."

Black Hawk carried a knife, a rifle and a supply of *wasna*. He rode bareback and hung his snowshoes over the horse's back. Charles and his saddled horse were soon traveling some distance behind.

Culley was headed west. By noon Black Hawk came to a line shack where Culley had stopped for the night. To spare his horse, Black Hawk tracked the man on snowshoes for a while, then remounted and picked up the pace. He ate a little. He doubted that Culley had brought food, and he had seen no sign of a kill. As his people knew from bitter experience, being on the run in the dead of winter made a man an easy mark.

A pile of fresh horse droppings told Black Hawk that he was close to his quarry. He circled to the south and found a low bluff. He had left his coat and his rifle with Sagi, downwind of the trail. Now Black Hawk waited and watched.

Culley's horse was winded, but the man pushed him on through hock-high snow. No respect for his mount, Black Hawk observed as he lay flat on his belly and peered over the edge of the bluff. No respect for anything. When the rider reached a point directly below him, Black Hawk squatted on the balls of his feet and sprang, knocking Culley from his horse. Their bodies hit the snow with a loud crunch. Black Hawk rolled to his feet and dragged Culley up by the front of his jacket. The two men glowered at each other, breathing quick white puffs of vapor into the crisp air. Culley's eyes were wild; Black Hawk's were steely and devoid of emotion.

Culley pulled a knife. The big steel blade boosted his confidence, and his wild eyes narrowed to mere slits. "You put your filthy red hands on a white lady, didn't you, Black Hawk! I killed a *white* man for touching her. *You*, you red bastard! I'm gonna cut you up real pretty."

Black Hawk waited like a coiled rattler. The enemy's next move would trigger a strike. Culley's blade sliced the air ineffectually as Black Hawk dodged and caught Culley's arm at the height of its swing. A single-handed, crushing grip on Culley's wrist forced him to drop the knife. Corked rage burst from the depths of Black Hawk's tormented soul with a terrible battle cry. He bashed his fist into Culley's eye. Then he raised his knee and smashed the man's offending groin. Culley's howl brought a rush of satisfaction. The other man's body hit the snow in slow motion—knees, elbows, bloody face—like steaming horse droppings. He clutched at himself in agony.

Strength born of the need to preserve himself brought Culley staggering to his feet. He heard the brittle snap of his own jaw as it connected with Black Hawk's foot. Brandishing his knife, Black Hawk dropped to one knee beside Culley's battered head.

"You aren't much of a man, Culley. Hardly worth my time. Your scalp would bring the stench of you into my camp." He turned the blade in his hand, and it glinted in the sun. "But I've been cheated. I have not counted coups. I have not taken even one scalp." He grabbed a handful of Culley's hair and spoke to him in English even though his warrior's mind thought in Lakota. He wanted Culley to understand every word. "An experienced brave could take a scalp lock without taking too much flesh. Many have lived to tell the tale."

Black Hawk grinned, a terrible pleasure gleaming in his eyes. He laid the edge of the blade next to Culley's hairline. Culley whimpered. "You're my first. I'll hack off everything—" the blade drew blood, and Culley howled "—right down to the skull."

Culley whined. "Noooooo . . ."

It was the sound of a child about to be horsewhipped, but not a Lakota child, Black Hawk thought.

"My sister is fourteen years old, but she didn't beg you for mercy, did she? She would never—" the blade took another bite.

"Noooooo!"

"You killed my cousin's unborn child, Culley."

"Sor-ree—"

"You bet your lily-white skin you're—"

"Aaaaagh!" Blood flowed into Culley's eyes.

"Women, you son of a bitch! Children! Feel their pain!"

The anguished shriek was stilled as the crack of gunfire split the frigid air. Black Hawk froze. From a gaping hole in Culley's chest his life oozed away. Raising his eyes toward the bluff, Black Hawk watched Charles MacAllistair lower the rifle from his shoulder.

Black Hawk gave a final jerk on the knife, then rose to his feet and held the bloody hunk of hair aloft as he trilled his victory tremolo.

"What should we do with him?"

Black Hawk spared a disgusted glance at the bloody, lifeless heap. "Leave him for the coyotes. They need the meat."

"As far as anyone needs to know, we couldn't find him."

"Did you think to give him a quick death?"

"My only thought was to kill him myself," Charles said. Black Hawk nodded, sharing the gut-level satisfaction in being avenged. "Are you going to keep that thing?" Charles gestured toward the scalp dangling in Black Hawk's hand.

"It's rightfully yours. You made the kill." One corner of his mouth lifted sardonically. "But you don't want it, do you?" Charles shook his head. "In the past it would have been a trophy." Black Hawk tossed the hair back to its owner. "I have no use for it now."

Carolina was not surprised when Charles returned alone. It was understood that Culley was dead and that the authorities would not be told, but the details were not discussed, nor was the fact celebrated. Charles told Carolina that Jacob had probably broken every bone in Culley's body, but that he had killed the man himself. Jacob had not discussed his immediate plans except to say, as always, that his family needed meat.

Time became Carolina's enemy. There was more snow, and she knew there was little chance of resuming classes before her baby was born. She helped Marissa get back on her feet, tutored Ruth and Charlie, and watched her belly swell.

Christmas Eve was celebrated quietly, with hot toddies and fruitcake after supper, and gifts for all the hands. Charlie was treated like a king, showered with handmade gifts from the boys and store-bought toys from his parents. When the hands went back to the bunkhouse and Charlie was tucked in bed, a spirit of sadness moved into the parlor. No one talked about it. It was simply there, like a guest for the holidays for whom accommodations had been reserved. Four people who had shared a time of sorrow sat quietly together in the parlor and watched the fire burn itself out.

There was a soft tap at Carolina's bedroom door as she prepared for bed. She dropped the nightgown over her head and hurried to the door, holding her breath. It was Ruth, whom Carolina had come to know as Wakinyela.

"I'm sorry if I disturbed you, my sister."

Carolina reached for the girl's hand and smiled. "I'm sorry if I look disappointed. Whenever there's a knock at the door, I always hope—"

"I know." She tugged on Carolina's hand. "I have something for you. It's in my room."

Lying on the bed was a beaded cradle board with a little hood surrounding the place where the baby's head would be and front laces to hold the soft white buckskin in place over the small body. Carolina sat down and lifted the cradle board, touching the beads and the soft fabric. It was the first thing she'd owned that had been made for her baby.

"It is your husband's sister's duty to make the cradle board. I took great care with this. When my sister Anptaniya gave Tokala his first son, I was young. My mother helped much. This one *I* made."

"This is wonderful, Wakinyela. So beautiful." Carolina looked into the girl's small, heart-shaped face. "How long have you known?"

She smiled, glancing at Carolina's middle. "We should call each other *sćepan*. It means you are my brother's wife, and I am your husband's sister, and we do not keep these things from each other."

"I didn't want to keep it from you, *sćepan*, but I don't talk about it because...because Black Hawk may not come back for me."

"My brother will come for you. You carry his child."

Carolina held the cradle board to her breast. "He will come for the child, but he may not let me... He may send me back East."

"You would let him take the child from you?"

She closed her eyes, clutching the cradle board. "I have said I would." Her voice trembled with the awful reminder of what she had promised. "It's a gamble. I pray to God he'll keep us both."

"I have seen his eyes when he looks at you, *sćepan*." Wakinyela touched Carolina's hand. "I was with him when the storm came, when he was sick with worry for you. You have his heart. He cannot throw you away."

Black Hawk spent weeks alone in the hills. He fasted for days at a time and devoted himself to *hanble ceya*, the crying in search of a vision. At the height of his anguished quest he saw the image of his father. The old man was weak, his chest heaving with the effort of drawing breath into decayed lungs. Reaching for the sky, the withered hand sought the black bird that circled overhead. Not a vulture, but *canska sapa*, the black hawk.

Black Hawk killed two whitetail bucks, gutted them and took them home. He found his father looking very much as he had in the vision. The meat was welcome, and the women set to work on it, leaving Black Hawk alone with his father. They sat on the floor near the stove, and they shared a pipe.

"You look thin," the old man said. "Are you ill, *cinks*?"

"No, Ate, I am well. I have fasted and prayed for direction, for a vision."

"And did you receive one?"

"I saw you. I saw you reach out to *canska sapa*. That is why I came."

"I see that *Ateyapi* answered my prayer by giving you this vision. I did not want to die without seeing my son again. When you came to get your sister, you seemed troubled. How is it with you now?"

"My woman carries my child, Atè. Her time will come early in the spring."

The old man smiled and nodded his approval. "That news could keep me alive a little longer."

"I cannot . . . keep this woman, Atè."

"She has no love for you?"

Black Hawk shook his head. "She has much love for me, but her people will never accept marriage between a white woman and a Lakota man."

"Have they taken her from you?"

"No."

"Has she left you?"

"No." His eyes were downcast, and he spoke in a hushed tone. "She will not leave me unless I send her away."

"And you would do this?"

"I love her, Atè, but I cannot keep a white woman."

"I know nothing of the heart of the white man, but I do know what is between a man and a woman when there is love. Is it different with a white woman?"

"No." Black Hawk drew a deep breath and expelled it slowly. "There is no white or Lakota between us, Atè. It is only all around us."

His father's face was more furrowed with wrinkles than usual as he considered the problem. "I would not have told you to seek this marriage with a white woman. You did this on your own. You took her to your bed, and she became your woman. When you brought her to us, she became one of us. We accept her. She accepts us."

The old man puffed on the pipe, and when he spoke again, it was with the authoritative sound of a father's voice. "Now you have planted your seed in this woman's belly, *cinks*, and she has made it quicken for you. You shame yourself with this talk of sending her away."

"Ate, this life of ours..." He waved his hand at all that surrounded them and shook his head. "There's no promise in it. What can I give her?"

The old man's grip on his son's shoulders was surprisingly strong. "Are you a man, *cinks*? Have I failed to teach you what it is to be a man? Give her your love and your protection. Put food in her kettle and more children in her belly. You can promise to do your best for her. That's all any man can promise. The man who promises an easy life is a liar. Does she want a life with you?"

"She thinks she does."

"Is she a full-grown woman, *cinks*?"

"Yes."

"Then take her at her word," he roared. "Give her that respect."

"She is innocent," Black Hawk countered. "She does not know how it will be."

"Do you? Does anyone know how it will be? Did I know when I married your mother?"

"If you had known what was coming, Ate, would you have married and brought children into the world?"

"Ŏhan! My woman and my children are my life's blood. We have come this far together, and that much is good." A coughing spell interrupted him, and when he spoke again, he had less strength. "I am an old man, and my time is almost over. The buffalo and the old Lakota warriors are dying together. You will live with the changes, *cinks*, but there is this that will not change: your woman and your children will always be your life's blood. Do the best you can for them."

Black Hawk's tears rolled down his lean brown cheeks as he reached to embrace his father.

"It is easy for old ones to give advice, *cinks*. It's too late to worry about having to follow it myself. Bring me my grandchild in the early spring," he croaked, and he patted his son's broad back. "I have decided to live a little longer."

Icicles glistened in the bright January sun as they dripped beneath the eaves of the ranch house. Black Hawk felt good. He had left his parents with a supply of fresh meat, and now he would see his woman. The front door opened, and his sister hurried outside, wrapping herself in a shawl as she bounded down the steps.

Alarm grew in the pit of his stomach as Black Hawk swung down from his horse. He remembered the last time his sister had appeared on the veranda when he came to the house. *"Tanksi!"* he called out. "How is it with my woman?"

"I knew you would be back, *tiblo*. I told her this."

He gripped Wakinyela's shoulder harder than he intended. "Is she well? Is she still—"

"Yes! Yes, she is well, and your child makes her belly fat." She hooked her hands over his forearms. "You will not send her away, will you? I will not allow it, *tiblo*. Do you see the blouse she made for me?"

Black Hawk laughed. "*You* will not allow it, *tanksi*? You are beginning to sound like her. Where is she?"

"If you are quiet, you can surprise her. She sleeps in her room. She grows tired in the afternoons now."

"You're sure she is well?"

Wakinyela took the reins from her brother's hand. "She worries too much. It's good you're here now. I will see to your horse."

He turned the door handle carefully so that it made only a soft click before he pushed the door slowly, savoring the thought that she was there. She lay sleeping just beyond this door, and when he opened it he would see her. Carolina. His woman lay curled on her side, with a soft blue crocheted blanket covering her legs and feet. Her legs seemed to protect the growing curvature of her belly, and her hand rested over it, as well. Already this child of his was cherished by its mother, even in her sleep. She wore a dark blue dress without a waistline, and he noticed a pair of moccasins beside the bed. He smiled. Either her feet were swollen or his woman had come to her senses about footwear.

She stretched out on her back and made a soft sighing sound, but still she slept as he stepped into the room. One blue-stockinged foot peeked out from beneath the coverlet, and she seemed to smile as she nestled her cheek against the embroidered pillowcase. He did not doubt that his dreamself comforted her even now, just as she had sent hers to be with him. His heartbeat intensified like the cadence of the dance drum as the dancers approached their climax. He closed the door softly behind him and walked silently toward her.

Her beauty struck his eyes and filled his head as he lowered one knee to the floor beside the bed. This was not his dream, he reminded himself. This was the woman who bore the flesh of his flesh within her body. Her hair spilled luxuriantly over the pillow, framing the face that dreams had kept before him day and night since the first time he'd seen it. But here was the warm reality, the dream made flesh. The breasts that rose and fell with the rhythm of her breathing looked fuller, and her slim waist was gone. In its place was the small, round promise of his child. Had he the right to touch her? Would she turn from the croaking sound of a coward's voice, or would she smile and open her heart to him?

Closing his eyes and breathing deeply of the smell of her hair, Black Hawk touched his silent plea for forgiveness to her temple with his lips. She stirred toward him, granting his plea even before she awakened.

"You shouldn't invite strange men into your home, Miss Hammond," he whispered. Her eyes flew open, but he pinned her shoulders to the bed with a heavy arm across her chest. "People might get the wrong idea." She turned her head, and he kissed her hungrily, swallowing whatever exclamation she had on the tip of her tongue.

He lifted his head, and she stared. "Jacob!" After all the days and nights of listening for the knock at the door, turning on a prayer toward every sound, suddenly there he was, and the taste of him was on her lips. Instantaneous joy made her head feel light. "Black Hawk," she amended, "how could you sneak up on me like that?"

He grinned, and the light from the window danced in his eyes. "You've heard tales of Lakota stealth."

"Oh, but I've planned so carefully for this moment, and you... oh, you!" She flung her arms around his neck, and he pulled her half off the bed into his embrace. She smelled the crisp winter air in his hair, and his buckskin shirt felt cool under her hands. Her throat became tight and tingly, and she squeezed her eyes against the tears that might scare a man away. "You've ruined everything," she managed hoarsely. "I wanted to be dressed just so, with my hair—"

He plunged his fingers into the soft cloud of sleep-tangled hair and murmured, "It's beautiful."

"I look like a pickle barrel in this dress." She tipped her head back and laughed, her eyes glistening as she swung her legs over the side of the bed. "I look like a pickle barrel in *any* dress."

No dress would have changed the way she looked to him. The brightness in her eyes was a loving welcome, and she received him, as always, just as he was. How could she imagine that a dress could matter to him, when the light in her eyes took his breath away? He laid his head against her belly as he put his arms around her hips. "How is my son?"

"If you wait a moment, he'll probably kick you in the head." She hugged him to the hard mound in her lap and finger-combed his hair.

"Lakota children respect their fathers." A tiny extremity butted the walls of her womb. They both felt it, and they laughed together. "He's right," Black Hawk said. "I had that coming." When the laughter faded, they were still gazing at each other. "Don't leave me, little one," he whispered.

It was a plea from a man who never begged for anything, and it tugged at her heart. She put her hands to his face and pulled it to her breast. "How could I? I've prayed so hard for you to come back and let me be with you. Let me be your wife and mother to your child."

"The child is *ours*," he told her. "My heart aches with the anguish I have caused you. I think of sending you away, and I see the shell of a man that would be left of me."

"I'm not sure I could have kept my word, Canska Sapa. I think you would have had to drive me away with a stick."

"Why would I do such a thing when my heart sings with the sound of your voice?" He pulled her head down to his for a kiss, then sat beside her on the bed. "But you are too honest. For the rest of my life I would have been content to believe you loved me so much that you would have made that sacrifice for me."

"I do love you enough to give you this child." She laid her head on his shoulder. "And several more."

"We'll find somebody in a black robe—a minister or a priest—whatever you need to make you feel married."

She reached for his hand and pressed her thumb against his, recalling the mingling of her life's blood with his. "You have been my husband for some time, Canska Sapa. How long have I been your wife?"

"Since the night you came to me and asked me to make you mine. You became my woman then."

"Would you have let me go to another man?"

He brought her hand to his lips and kissed her thumb. "Like you, I made a promise I could not have kept. I have a new promise. I will fight for the right to keep my woman, my children and my self-respect."

"We can tell the world we're married?"

He rubbed her belly. "The news is past due."

"And I shall be Mrs.... Mrs. what?"

"You will share Black Hawk with me for the benefit of the record. It is a good name."

"It's a wonderful name." She sat up and raised a warning finger. "I won't sleep in this bed another night without my husband. You'll either come to my room, or I'll go to yours."

He laughed as he leaned back against the headboard and drew her to him. "Do you think I'll let you stay with me in the back room of a barn, woman?"

She laid her head on his chest. "When will you understand that it doesn't matter where I am as long as it's with you?"

"You'll be with me, *wasťelakapi*. I will hold you in my arms every night for the rest of your life. We will use the old cabin until winter is over, and this spring I will build you a house."

"It is the woman's job to provide a lodge for her man," she recalled. "But I'm not sure I could build a house."

"I have built this house in my mind already." With a forefinger he traced the line of her jaw. "It is near the campsite where we first made love. The front door and the kitchen face east. It has a cast-iron cookstove. Like Ina, you will boast of this to the other women."

"In the summer you will put the stove outside in the willow house," she mused. "And we will sleep in the cool of our tipi, pitched close by."

"In the winter I will sit before the stone fireplace, which I will build myself. I was a good bricklayer. I think I can manage the stonework, too. And since you will sleep on the ground with me in summer, I will sleep with you in your bed in the winter."

"I will have a school, and the children will not be taken away. I hope you and Wakinyela will work with me."

"Work with you!" He laughed. "You would make me part of your teaching conspiracy? I have better things to do."

"You could still raise horses."

"We don't eat horses, and the beef they send us is short on meat and long on bones. I think we must raise our own."

"But your people are not—"

"We are not farmers, but we are horsemen, and we know these grasslands. I will work for MacAllistair and learn more about beef cattle."

She looked into his eyes and saw hope there. "And we will feed ourselves," she told him.

"And we will teach our children," Black Hawk said. He spread his hand over Carolina's belly and pressed a kiss into her hair. *"Nimitawa ktelo,"* he whispered.

"Ohinniyan."

* * * * *

Lakota Words and Phrases

Note: There are two sounds in Lakota that we represent with the letter *n*. One is similar to the English *n* sound, and the other is a nasal vowel sound made with the tongue near the back of the palate. The diacritical *s* is a *sh* sound, and the *c* represents a *ch* sound. There are many Lakota dialects and few good texts on the language. I have used *Lakota-English Dictionary* by Reverend Eugene Buechel (Red Cloud Indian School Inc., Pine Ridge, SD, 1970). As always, my husband, Clyde Eagle, has been invaluable to me as a source of information, insight and moral support.

Lakota words and phrases used in *Private Treaty*:

anptaniya (ahnp-TAN-EE-yah)—first glimmer of morning

ate (ah-TAY)—my father

Ateyapi (ah-tay-YAH-pi)—God. (Note: The concept of God as father, one great spirit, supreme being and creator is inherent in traditional Lakota religion.)

cahuwayazan (cha-HOO-wah-zahn)—tuberculosis

canska sapa (chan-SKA sah-pah)—black hawk

cinks (CHINKS)—my son

ciye (chee-YAY)—my brother (a man's brother)

cunks (CHOONKS)—my daughter

eyapaha (AY-yah-pah-hah)—crier or herald

hacib (ha-CHEEB)—be quiet!

hanble ceya (hahn-BLAY chay-yah)—crying for a vision (vision quest)

hankaśi (han-KAH-shee)—my cousin (a man's female cousin)

hiya (hee-YAH)—no

Iktomi (ick-TOE-mee)—a trickster spirit, generally evil

ina (ee-NAH)—my mother

kuwa yo (koo-WAH yo)—come here (*yo* is spoken by a man)

lekśi (lek-SHE)—my uncle (my mother's brother)

lila waśte (LEE-lah wash-TAY)—very good

mitawin (mee-TAH-wihn)—my woman (wife)

nihanka (nee-HAN-kah)—your sister-in-law

nimitawa ktelo (nee-mee-TAH-wah KTAY-lo)—you will be mine

ohan (oh-HAHN)—Yes! (emphatic)

ohinniyan (oh-hee-NEE-yahn)—always, forever

okiciyuze (oh-GEE-chee-yu-zay)—to take one another in marriage

Paha Sapa (pah-HAH sah-pah)—the Black Hills

papa (PAH-pah)—jerked meat

śagi (sha-GEE)—auburn color

ścepan (SJAY-pahn)—a woman's sister-in-law

sic'esi (SEECH-ay-see)—my cousin (a woman's male cousin)

siśoka (see-SHO-kah)—robin

skuya (skoo-YAH)—delicious

skuyēla (skoo-YAY-lah)—sweet

ta canta (tah CHAN-tah)—heart (of the buffalo)

taniġa (tah-NEE-gah)—tripe

tanipa (tah-NEE-pah)—meat along the spine (of the buffalo)

tankśi (tahnk-SHEE)—my sister (a man's younger sister)

tatanka (tah-TAHN-kah)—buffalo

tate (tah-TAY)—wind

tate iyumni (tah-TAY ee-YOOM-nee)—tornado

tekicihila (tay-KEE-chee-hee-lah)—precious

tiblo (tee-BLOW)—my brother (a woman's older brother)

tokala (toe-KAH-lah)—gray fox

tonśkapi (tohn-SHKA-pee)—my nephews (a man's nephews)

unciśi (uhn-CHEE-shee)—my mother-in-law

unhcela blaska (uhn-CHAY-lah blah-ska)—prickly pear cactus

wagleza (wahg-LAY-suh)—rattlesnake

waglula (wahg-LOO-luh)—worms

wana (wah-NAH)—now

wanaġi (wah-NAH-chee)—spirits of the departed

wankala (wahn-KAH-lah)—tender, soft

waśicun (wah-SHEE-choohn)—white man

wasna (wahs-NAH)—pemmican made from ground jerky and tallow

waśte (wash-TAY)—good

waśtelakapi (wash-TAY-lah-kah-pee)—beloved

wašte yelo (wash-TAY yay-low)—Good! (emphatic; spoken by a man)

wikośka (wee-KO-shka)—veneral disease

wipazukan (WEE-pah-zoo-kahn)—Juneberry or service berry

Wiwanyank Wacipi (wee-WAHN-yahnk wah-CHEE-pee)—the Sun Dance

wiwašťeka (wee-wash-TAY-kuh)—beautiful woman

winyan (WEE-yahn)—woman, girl

wōjapi (WOE-jah-pee)—a thickened fruit soup

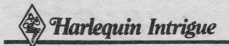

Harlequin Intrigue

Two exciting new stories each month.

Each title mixes a contemporary, sophisticated romance with the surprising twists and turns of a puzzler...romance with "something more."

Because romance can be quite an adventure.

Romance, Suspense and Adventure

**TEMPTATION WILL BE
EVEN HARDER TO RESIST...**

In September, Temptation is presenting a sophisticated new
face to the world. A fresh look that truly brings Harlequin's
most intimate romances into focus.

What's more, all-time favorite authors Barbara Delinsky, Rita
Clay Estrada, Jayne Ann Krentz and Vicki Lewis Thompson
will join forces to help us celebrate. The result? A very special
quartet of Temptations...

- **Four striking covers**
- **Four stellar authors**
- **Four sensual love stories**
- **Four variations on one spellbinding theme**

All in one great month! Give in to Temptation in September.

TDESIGN-1